The Waiting Game

Also by Jessica Thompson

This is a Love Story
Three Little Words
Paper Swans

Jessica Thompson

The Waiting Game

CORONET

First published in Great Britain in 2015 by Coronet
An imprint of Hodder & Stoughton
An Hachette UK company

1

A CIP catalogue record for this title is available from the British Library

ISBN 978 1 444 77655 3
A Format ISBN 978 1 444 77656 0
Ebook ISBN 978 1 444 77657 7

Typeset in Sabon MT by Palimpsest Book Production Limited,
Falkirk, Stirlingshire
Printed and bound by CPI Group (UK) Ltd, Croydon, CR0 4YY

Hodder & Stoughton policy is to use papers that are natural, renewable and recyclable products and made from wood grown in sustainable forests. The logging and manufacturing processes are expected to conform to the environmental regulations of the country of origin.

Hodder & Stoughton Ltd
Carmelite House
50 Victoria Embankment
London EC4Y 0DZ

www.hodder.co.uk

For my family

Prologue

'This is serious stuff'

October 1997

The moon was speckled like a bird's egg. It hung reliably in the blackness above Will Turnbull and Nessa Grier, who sat side by side on a bench as the leaves fell around them, landing softly on the thick, wet grass. Their knees were just touching, hearts pounding hard.

'Oh god, I just don't know what I'm going to do with my life!' Will cried, running both hands down the soft, spotted skin of his cheeks. His right hand caught the frame of his glasses. They creaked audibly before pinging back against the bridge of his nose.

'*Ouch!* That was surprisingly painful,' he muttered angrily, finishing his cigarette and dropping it on the dewy grass beneath him. He crushed it with the thick rubber toe of his trainer.

'Jesus, Will, you don't need to be so dramatic,' Nessa responded, rolling her eyes and nibbling at her bottom lip nervously. She needed to tell him something and he was about to start ranting. She was sure of it. There was a certain tone to his voice. And when Will started ranting, it was very hard to make him stop. When would she find the opportunity to say those words? To utter the sentence that she feared he'd judge her for anyway.

She fiddled with her long mass of dark blonde hair. She always threw it over one shoulder, en masse, draping it across the back of her neck so it hung down the front of her chest like a scarf. It was a nervous habit, but Nessa enjoyed the way it felt to run her fingers through the ends and feel dozens of tiny knots twist and snap between her fingers.

'I know, Ness, I know; I just have such big bloody choices to make, you know? This is serious stuff. It's either staying here and carrying on writing music and going to London all the time to get involved in "the scene" – which is what I want to do because I think that's the best way to get noticed – or going to some dullard university miles away from here to study for a "proper job".' Mocking his mother's posh voice, he spat out the last two words, while sarcastically wobbling his head from side to side.

'And what exactly is wrong with a proper job?' Nessa asked, turning to look at him, her eyes narrowed in suspicion. His handsome profile was illuminated in the luna haze, casting parts of his face in eerie shadows, hiding places for his angst.

Will pulled out another cigarette and lit it urgently, before leaning back on the bench and scratching his head. His thick hair curled around his fingers in great, hazelnut whirls, unravelling slowly when he moved his hand away. A few chocolate-coloured moles were clustered around the base of his neck: a perfect imperfection. These were the things that made him who he was.

'Oh nothing . . . It's just annoying, you know? All Mum

goes on about is personal statement this, and open day that, "Oh you'll love Edinburgh" or "apparently there are a great discoteques in Bath". I mean, *really?!* And I'm not being a snob, Nessa, I promise you . . . It's just, well, you know I've wanted to be a composer for a long time, and it's all I want in my life – to be someone creative and different, someone a bit, well, special, you know?'

Even in the darkness, Nessa could pick up on Will visibly cringing at these words, but she'd always loved him for his honesty. Someone 'special'? So many kids wanted to be like Damon Albarn or Kate Moss, anything but a regular person, an accountant or a secretary. *But we can't all be models and rock stars*, Nessa thought to herself. Although she was sure that if anyone could pull it off, it would be Will . . .

'—And the thought, right, of going off to study business management, politics or some other boring crud would probably destroy me . . . Yes, that's right, it would destroy my actual soul, I'm sure of it. I'd no longer be able to write music,' he concluded triumphantly, crossing his arms. An owl hooted sadly, as if to empathise, and a cool breeze curled through the trees towards them.

Nessa understood where he was coming from, but 17-year-old Will would be fine, and so would 25-year-old Will, 40-year-old Will and so on, and so on, until Will was an old man who religiously ate two boiled eggs for breakfast and always fell asleep in front of *Countdown*. He was the kind of person who would always be fine no matter what he did.

She knew this because:

A) Will had rich parents, and by rich, she was talking a '£3m house in the countryside, five cars on the driveway and a hot tub in the garden' kind of loaded: a kind of wealth that she could never get her head around. Her youthful naivety led her to assume that this would make him essentially immune to serious problems for the rest of his life.

B) He had a magnetic, charismatic quality about him that would always see him rise from whatever gutter of shite he may slip into and come up smelling like a branch of The Body Shop. It was just how he rolled.

C) He was also in possession of boyish, mischievous-but-not-too-obvious good looks, which made everyone simply adore him the moment they saw him.

So, as far as Nessa was concerned, listening to Will having a crisis about his future was hardly igniting her sympathy. If anyone was facing a crisis it was *her.*

A year ago things would have been different. If she still felt now as she had then, Will's talk of going away to university would have left Nessa with a cotton mouth and a distinct feeling of unease. She would have imagined holding on to him while they sat on that bench, trying not to let him go as life began to prise them apart. It would have felt a little like the end of the world.

Before now, the thought of Will moving away and building himself a new life would have resulted in her running home to sob into a pillow while listening to 'Creep' by Radiohead, because, in her own way, Nessa had fallen for Will a considerably long time ago.

She was sure it happened the first time she was asked to sit next to him by her ageing science teacher in Year 8.

Working in partners, the class had been challenged to build a basic circuit using coils of metal and a tiny light bulb. Nessa had liked the way Will smelled a little bit of cinnamon and home cooking, with a hint of Lynx too. And when someone threw their shoe at the back of his head and called him a 'boff job' he turned the reddest she'd ever seen a human go. She knew immediately that she wanted to take him under her wing and make sure he was OK.

As they grew older, and Will had got cooler, and taller and more handsome, with every passing week, Nessa was just waiting for the right moment when she could kiss him. But now she had competition. Even the popular girls who had mocked him callously wore intrusive perfume and provocative lipstick when they were around him these days. They fluttered their eyelashes, showing off in ways that made her shudder quietly behind the door of her locker. She felt invisible. How would she tell him?

Nessa had rehearsed it in her bedroom many a time, with a variety of different approaches ranging from the sudden snog to the breathy confession of love, but something had always got in the way. When Will was 15, it was a girlfriend called Sophia, who was really good at maths, wore expensive-looking leather shoes and pronounced 'pressure' in a way that made it sound like 'prushha'. Trials for the England rugby team meant he was never around at the weekends anymore. And then, when that had gone wrong because of an injury, it was his love for smoking weed, which saw him holed up in his parents' attic for six months, writing music he would never let her hear and acting like the archetypal tortured artist. Nessa had fantasised about going to visit him and discovering one of his songs was about her. It made her blush with embarrassment now just to think of it. It had been so silly! Now he was just, well, *Will* . . .

She had managed to move on eventually, because Will was so horrendously unavailable and Jake had come on the scene. *Gorgeous* Jake. He'd started at her school late, having moved from an arch-rival technology college on the other side of town where the girls pierced each other's ears in the toilets and smoked menthols. His combination of olive skin, dark hair and brown eyes made him impossibly attractive to her. This, coupled with a lovely shyness that was occasionally pulled to one side like a curtain, to reveal a sneak glimpse of who he really was: full of kindness, with a wicked sense of humour. He had finally enabled her to divert her attention elsewhere. She was sure that Jake was perfect. Perhaps she had outgrown Will, she had thought. *Yes, it was just a phase*, she was sure of it . . .

'What are you going to do, Ness? College, or something like that?' Will had asked, before turning towards her and wiping an eyelash from her cheek. He balanced it on the tip of his thumb and studied it. It was only visible because of the moonlight, which lit it up in silver. Moments later, he blew it away, into the autumn night air. Nessa had felt a shiver of something against her skin at his touch, and the hairs on the back of her neck rose on end. She didn't like it when that happened. Not anymore.

'Well, the college thing, that's what I need to discuss with you actually. I—' Nessa started to speak.

'Oh, and that's another thing,' Will interrupted. 'Even if I *do* get to stay at home and follow the song-writing stuff, I genuinely worry that I may go insane because of my parents. They are mad as a box of frogs, they really are. There's really no ideal solution here,' he said, speaking fast and frantically, his hands illuminating his words.

'Listen, Will, I—'

'I know you want to tell me something, Nessa, but actually there is something I urgently need to tell you,' Will insisted, turning towards her and looking really serious now. 'And I'm a bit worried that if I don't tell you right this very moment, I may never gather the balls to say it ever again.' His brow crinkled in concentration as he lit yet another cigarette, cupping it with his free hand to protect the golden flame from the wind.

'You do realise that if you keep smoking at this rate you're going to die, like, tomorrow or something?' Nessa said, aggressively, batting a cloud of smoke away from her face.

'Sorry,' Will responded, moving his cigarette away from Nessa so the smoke poured towards the playground.

'So, what do you want to tell me?' Nessa asked, watching Will stand up and start pacing the grass ahead of the bench frantically, the hot, orange light coming from his cigarette dancing in the air.

'Oh, fuck, here it goes,' he said, as if he were about to jump from a diving board.

'Here what goes?' Nessa asked, starting to feel a little frustrated because she needed to say her big thing too, and he was getting in the way of that and had been all evening with his paranoid melodrama.

'One of the reasons I am freaking out so much Ness, about this big decision to do with going away to uni or staying here, is, is . . . well . . .'

'Oh, Will, come on, please get on with it, I'm starting to feel cold!'

'OK, OK, it's YOU Ness . . .'

'What?' Nessa had asked, totally confused.

'Oh shit-dog, I've said it now!' Will exclaimed, taking a long, deep drag on his cigarette.

'Me what?'

'Right. Here it goes . . .' Will took a deep breath and walked over to the bench. He took one of her slender hands in his own, rather dramatically.

'Ever since we first met we've been close, right?' he asked. Nessa nodded in agreement, a look of concern in her eyes. Surely he wasn't? She would have killed for this before, she really would.

'And you really took care of me at school when everyone wanted to punch me in the face.'

'Well, you know, it would have helped if you hadn't brought quails' eggs and camembert in your lunchbox, but you were too cute to abandon,' she said, smiling warmly at Will and poking him in the arm with her index finger. He instantly shrugged off her teasing, his face becoming serious again.

'But as we got older, Nessa, I started to see you differently. You helped me to be less "camembert-like" and a little more like "cheddary", and I mean that in the nicest possible way. There is absolutely nothing wrong with camembert – in fact it's a highly delectable cheese – but I learnt that sometimes you have to be cheddar-like, just to get along . . .'

Nessa wrinkled her face in confusion. *This cheese analogy is terrible*, she thought.

'OK, the cheese comparison thing isn't working, but what I think I'm trying to say is that you can't get through life at our school being naive and ostentatious in the way I was. Sometimes you have to kind of muck in and settle down, and I think you saved me, you know?'

'That's very sweet, Will, but it was all you. And I love camembert, by the way, you don't have to not have it any—'

'So, anyway, there was that, and then not only were you my best mate, and really funny and all that, but you became very, very beautiful, didn't you?' Will laughed in embarrassment and looked down at the ground as he said this. Nessa had felt her stomach plunge sharply. She didn't know whether it was a bad plunge or a good plunge.

'I mean, look at you now; you are just gorgeous. It's insane. And then that terrible, unspeakable stuff happened to you a couple of years ago, and I realised then how much I care about you, but it wasn't the right time to say cos you were struggling so much, and *oh-my-god-I-think-I-love-you.*' Will said, suddenly grinding to a halt and going quiet.

'You have *got* to be kidding me,' Nessa said slowly, laughing to herself. She gently pulled her hand away from the warmth of Will's, which had become decidedly sweaty.

'Er, no, I'm not,' Will responded, a little doubt in his voice now. He pulled his own hand back, clearly unsure of what to do with it. He twitched around a little until he decided his left pocket would be the best place for it.

'For fuck's sake, Will!' Nessa shouted, frustration teeming through her veins. It boomed out from her chest, the feelings had come from nowhere. They shocked her. The sentence bounded around the playing field, and echoed against the thick row of trees that separated it from the road, coming back to haunt her once again. She wondered why her life felt like a series of missed trains, a merry-go-round of toil and frustration. Drama, drama, drama!

'OK, OK, there's no need to get angry,' Will had responded defensively.

'Listen, I'm pregnant . . .' she said, through gritted teeth. She realised, at that moment, that her hands were balled up into fist, resting at the top of her knees.

'*What?*'

'I'm pregnant, Will. Just three months gone so far, but I—'

'What the fuck? Who's the father?' Will had asked.

'Jake . . . obviously.'

'Jake?? Jake?! I didn't think it was anything serious, Nessa. The guy's got nothing to offer you, he really doesn't . . .'

'I beg your pardon, Will?' Nessa said furiously, starting to feel tears well in her eyes. She knew he would go off on one, she just knew it. That's why she had waited so long to tell him.

'I'm sorry. I just, I knew about you and Jake, but I thought it was just a bit of fun. And now, guess what? You, the love of my *entire life*, are sitting next to me, 17 and pregnant. Oh, and the father of your child is an 18-year-old lad who dropped out of school and works at the local butcher's shop. I mean, what the fuck, Nessa?!'

'I think you need to put your filter on, Will, and consider what you're saying before I slap you across the face,' Nessa growled, crossing her arms angrily and resting them on the top of her ever-swelling stomach. She could only just feel the very beginnings of a 'bump'.

'I'm sorry, Nessa, I'm really sorry. It's just you're so clever, and talented. You have your whole life before you and you're too young to have a baby, surely? You'll miss out on so much; it's a tragedy. And Jake, I mean, *really*? Do you even love him?' Will questioned, incredulously.

'Yes, I love him, of course I do. He's the best thing that has ever happened to me.'

Will sighed loudly, and played with the gravel beneath the bench with his feet, his face angled towards the ground.

'We'll be fine, Will. Yes, it's a little unconventional, and yes, ideally it would have happened later on, but now it *has* happened, it's all I want,' Nessa said, realising she was smiling as she finished her sentence. She placed both her hands on her tummy and rubbed it softly, little bursts of excitement exploding in her heart like fireworks. Will tutted.

The pair sat in silence for a while, still side by side but a little more distance between them. The trees moving gently in the wind and the birds flitting amid the branches sounded strangely soothing, like an orchestra tuning up for a night-time symphony.

Nessa thought about what Will had just told her, news that she had longed for over the course of a few years. Had she known this was coming a long time ago, she would have been the happiest girl alive. Had he told her that he 'loved' her, just a year prior, she would have jumped into his arms. But it was different now, she'd fallen for someone else, and he was wonderful. And even more than that, it hadn't taken Jake four years to realise what she was worth.

After a few minutes of awkward quiet, Will spoke up.

'I might regret saying this, Nessa, but I have to say it anyway because I care about you. I think you should consider it . . .'

'What's that?' Nessa asked.

'I think that, given your history, the fact that you're adopted, and the horrendous things that happened to you a couple of years ago . . . Well, I just think—'

'What do you think?' Nessa hissed, probing him angrily. Swirls of emotion moved around inside her.

'I think you are desperate to be loved, Nessa. You are

desperate for a family of your own, and desperate for something that will make you feel safe and secure . . .' he said, trailing off and looking at her nervously.

'You know what, Will? You don't have a fucking clue what I've been through, and how it feels to be me. You have the most privileged life; in fact it makes me sick. Don't you dare, ever, make judgements about what I've been through from your big, fat, ivory tower. Go fuck yourself,' Nessa growled, her friend flinching as she spoke.

And with that, Nessa walked angrily towards her house.

'Oh, Ness, come on!' Will shouted, as he watched her silhouette bound away from him.

'Nessa! Please come back!'

'Nessa!'

'Nessa?'

And with that he sank back down onto the bench with a great sigh, pulling another cigarette from his pocket and shoving it between his lips.

One

'Do you ever . . . wish it hadn't happened?'

February 10th 2012

'So, do you remember how it felt, at the time? The whole "stardom" thing?' Nessa asked. She sat in the corner of the sofa, which sagged sadly, her legs crossed tightly, her hands cradling a bowl of Chinese takeaway that Will had bought. The house was cold and they couldn't afford to have the heating on much, so she wore a giant, green baggy jumper that seemed to engulf her, keeping the chill away.

Nessa found it strange to look at Will now, aged 30, a 'proper grown-up man'. They still both felt like teenagers sometimes. He had changed so much. Long gone were his sultry, rocker-type days when he dressed from top-to-toe in vintage clothing, dyed his hair jet black and struggled to see through his own fringe. He was still good looking now, but much less pretentious and, in Nessa's view, that was a vast improvement. He had gone quite grey already – that had happened a few years ago, in fact. It suited him, the silvery strands peppering the dark brown shades of his youth. He had a small paunch, which Nessa put down to his love of wine and food and a total reluctance to exercise. His eyes were still very blue, of course, exactly the same. You always straight away knew it was Will when you saw those eyes.

Will fascinated Nessa, and their friendship had somehow endured throughout the years, even though they seemed to come from what felt like different planets. Just a year or two after his declaration of love in the park that October evening in 1999, one of Will's pop songs, 'All I Wanna Do Is Love You (Girl)', was picked up by a dreadful boy band, comprising four skinny-legged young men, who took it triple-platinum in 12 countries. Will's life changed overnight, as Nessa's had too, following the arrival of her little girl Poppy. But, somehow, they'd stayed close.

'I do remember how it felt, definitely,' Will responded. 'It was one of the most incredible moments of my life . . . I guess the problem is, in a way, that it set a benchmark that nothing else could ever live up to. My life changed in the course of five minutes. I was just this 19-year-old kid, you know, with shed loads of money and not a clue about what to do with it: my own money in fact, not my parents' money, for the very first time. And people wanted to hang out with me, I got invited to industry parties and drank champagne like it was water. You get a taste for that life, for that feeling of being the special kid, you know? And then, you know . . . you realise that you aren't special, that you're just like everyone else. You're a fuck up and you make mistakes, and maybe you aren't as talented as everyone said you were, and it's kind of hard to deal with that . . .'

He put his bowl down on the table gently. He'd managed

to clean up its contents within five minutes, hence his nickname 'the Dyson'. Nessa still had most of hers left.

'What happened to the band in the end anyway?' she asked. 'They were going for quite a long time, weren't they? You never hear about them anymore . . .'

'Oh, er, Marco's a raging alcoholic, Isaac managed to shoot himself in the eye with a pellet gun, Aaron is married with three kids and lives a relatively normal life, oh and I believe the last time anyone saw Ben, he was walking around Tesco in a dinosaur onesie, talking to himself and trying to make the Eiffel Tower out of balloons. Bit sad really, isn't it?'

Nessa nodded.

'Do you ever . . . wish it hadn't happened?' Nessa asked, wondering if this was an appropriate question. There was a little quiet as Will thought to himself, studying the rough palms of his own hands in the low light. The sound of Poppy's out-of-tune RnB singing was just audible from the kitchen, a series of screeches and wails that Nessa wished she would grow out of. Her daughter wasn't a very good singer, but you're not supposed to say things like that to kids. Poppy had started listening to hip-hop and soul music when she was 11, and now she was doing everything she could to be able to sing like Jessie J, even if the rest of the house was suffering deeply for her 'art'. She was sure that if the cat had opposable thumbs and a debit card it would have gone to Boots and bought some earplugs a long time ago.

'That's tricky. I guess it's one of my greatest achievements in life, and I'm so glad it happened, but it kind of fucked me up too . . . I feel like I've never really settled since then. I've just been waiting for something as incredible to happen again, for me to feel that way again . . . and so things have turned out a little disappointing. I'm sorry. I know I sound like an arsehole. I know you guys struggle with money and stuff. Jake's away in the army, and Poppy's going through a bit of a difficult time. It might seem like I'm an over-privileged brat with zero *real* problems, but I'm just telling it like it is. I'm just telling the truth . . .' He trailed off, looking out of Nessa's French windows and into the darkness of the garden. He twiddled his thumbs awkwardly. He was still just like he was at 17 really: beautifully, wonderfully truthful.

It would be easy to despise Will, she thought, to write him off as an idiot who needed to grow up. But she understood. People's problems were relative, and she guessed she would probably feel the same way too, had she written a song that had catapulted her into riches in minutes, only to see her flung back down into 'normalville' as quickly as it had all happened. Especially as it happened when everyone else was making decisions about their futures, studying for those boring careers Will had spoken of, buying their first homes and having babies . . . It had somehow derailed him. He seemed a little, lost . . .

While Will hadn't written a note for years, and now seemed to ping from one wacky business idea to the next, trying to invest money in the right places, Nessa had expected herself to have been 'sorted' by now. Midwifery – that was the dream since she was little. The idea popped into her mind the first time she'd cradled a doll across her forearm, pushing an empty plastic bottle towards its waxy lips. Her calling had signalled to her that day, through the glassy, vacant eyes of a Tiny Tears doll.

In her teens she had continued to imagine how life would be when she was a 'grown-up'. And while the planets and stars had been torn from her walls, replaced with posters of Kurt Cobain, her hopes and dreams had remained fiercely and steadily pinned to her heart. While the other girls at school dreamt of being models, actresses or Madonna, all Nessa wanted was something she could work at, something she could grow into. But sadly, all Nessa's dreams had come to a grinding halt just before her sixteenth birthday . . .

Things had been tough. Right now, the only thing Nessa felt that she was good at was washing up and organising books in alphabetical order at work, in her role as the manager of a tiny south London library.

'How's that genius little sister of yours doing?' Will asked, breaking Nessa's chain of thoughts.

'Oh, Kat's amazing, as always. She's coming back from Leeds soon, actually. I can't wait to see her,' Nessa responded, thinking of her 21-year-old sibling, a curious, hardworking creature, who was always having to be reminded to let go and give herself a break. With a desperate need to know that everything would be OK, she had back-up plan after back-up plan, always keen to be able to answer the 'what ifs' of life. Nessa was sure this was a result of their background, and those tragic events of their past . . .

'I take it you're going to tell her soon . . . about what *actually* happened?' Will asked, his face clouding with concern.

'Hmmm . . . sure,' Nessa said. 'Did you know that she's getting outstanding grades already? I really think she's going to make something of—'

'*Ness*,' Will protested, interrupting her mid-sentence, drawing out the vowel in the middle of her name. He didn't look happy. Nessa felt a flutter of panic gather in her chest, as if there was a strange pressure on her ribs.

'Mum. Where are the fucking Sugar Puffs? I can't find them anywhere,' Poppy asked sharply, having appeared at the doorway as if from nowhere. Nessa felt a sense of relief at the interruption. Poppy had way too much black eyeliner on, and her pale skin was positively translucent in comparison to the inky shades daubed around her eyes. Will cleared his throat awkwardly, clearly irritated by the disturbance and unable to mask it.

Poppy was growing to be a beauty, with the same thick, long wavy hair as her mother, but a little darker. She had big, wide brown eyes that sparkled – those had come from her dad. She was going through her gangly phase, where it seemed as if her limbs might never end; her thin arms were punctuated by sharp, pale elbows, and her knobbly knees protruded harshly from the bottom of her grey, pleated school skirt.

'The Sugar Puffs are in the top right cupboard, and don't talk to me like that, Poppy. Why are you eating Sugar Puffs for dinner anyway?' Nessa asked incredulously. 'Will brought plenty of takeaway to go round, just go and help yourself.'

'Because I need to lose weight,' Poppy replied, matter-of-factly, her lips pursed together at the end of her sentence.

'No you don't, that's ridiculous, Poppy, and Sugar Puffs are not the way to go about it,' Nessa responded, sitting up higher on the sofa now.

'Just leave me alone Mum, let me get on with my life. You are just constantly on my back!' Poppy gasped, before walking out of the room and slamming the door behind her.

'I don't know how you cope with that,' Will said, after a moment or two, a serious look on his face.

'Glad you didn't have kids?'

'Yeah. Shit . . . sorry, I shouldn't say that, but yeah, I am . . . I'm far too self-absorbed for kids anyway.'

'It's very difficult, but it's worth it, you know? She will be OK; I know she will. I think she's just messed up because Jake's away . . . She's not taking it well at all, and I think that for some reason she blames me. I don't know why though.'

Jake Bruce.

He was the reason for all of it. At this very moment, Jake was 3,616 miles away in Afghanistan, lying beneath a curtain of stars, trying to picture his wife's beautiful face in the vastness of the galaxy. He was a Senior Non-Commissioned Officer, in charge of a troop of men. He was doing well, had found his groove and was fantastic at his job. It had been the first time in his life that he could say that.

It had all been quite sudden, the whole army thing. One warm Saturday afternoon five years ago, as the family enjoyed a barbecue in the garden, Jake had made the shock announcement that he was signing up. To Nessa, it seemed like the words slipped out of his handsome mouth in slow motion, dropping like lead balloons in the sticky summer air. They left Nessa quietly breathless, like she had fallen down a flight of stairs and all she could do was lie there, staring at the ceiling with tears in her eyes, trying to catch a breath from her spasmodically heaving lungs.

Jake had said he'd wanted to serve in the army 'for some time now'. Silence had descended upon this small family unit, until all that could be heard was the soft popping of meat, cooking on the grill. Poppy had pulled her legs in towards her chest, and rested her chin against the tops of her knees. Nessa would never forget that. The way her daughter looked that day: the sadness, the sense of abandonment. That was where the damage had begun, she was sure of it.

Nessa had felt bad about the situation, like it was her fault, and Poppy's aggressive attitude towards her only served to perpetuate those feelings of guilt. She had feared Jake might be running away from the mediocrity of their lives. She knew Jake wasn't happy at work, and she knew he had very little desire to get one of those city jobs – marketing, accounting, PR . . . Just the thought of him at one of those desk jobs was hysterical. He was a physical kind of man. His strengths lay, and still did, in his practical skills and emotional intelligence, his steely determination and his powerful body. Jake was a problem solver. He could fix anything. He could put anything together. He could hold Nessa in his arms and quell her tears if she was hurting, and no one could scoop Poppy up when she fell over with such love and strength as Jake Bruce.

It was as if Jake wasn't meant to be living the life he did. He was trapped.

He'd been born on September 18th 1981 at Princess Royal University Hospital in Farnborough, to Betsy and Mick Bruce. Since those first rippling cries sounded from his mouth in the delivery suite, he had struggled to fit in anywhere. Jake soon realised that he couldn't stand the shallow popularity hierarchy of the playground, where nasty bully-boys ruled, and any kid with a bit of talent, flair or sparkle would be terrorised until they too despised themselves. And those long, tunnel-like locker rooms at secondary school were his own personal hell – where lads would hock up and spit on his back, or spring out at him and steal his dinner money. The kids had only treated him with anything resembling respect after he'd lost his temper one afternoon in Year 9. He'd broken the nose of a pig-faced boy who had been taunting him with one, fury-powered, punch. It had bust out from his body suddenly, like a flash of lightning from an angry cloud. Jake had felt so bad afterwards that he'd cried in his bedroom that night, but the whole incident had changed him, a turning point in his boyhood, like an indelible stain, never to fade . . .

Even more disappointing to him was the realisation that all this bullshit continued way beyond his playground years. He'd come to learn this in his first office job, fresh from spending a summer working at his uncle's butcher shop in a nice community where people wished him good day and bought him the odd coffee from the bakery next door. He'd watched as people betrayed each other, and bitched about each other in the kitchen. They played spiteful, unnecessary games, when life was already complicated enough.

Jake didn't particularly want to go to university and spend three years getting bladdered and ever-deeper into debt, and yet the alternatives were not too inspiring either. He had no idea what he wanted to do with his life, and felt totally and utterly lost. He was intelligent, handsome, bright and great at communicating, but the world, for him, just felt like a very false place.

He'd left the office job after just two months, and started work as a personal trainer. He'd enjoyed it, but it didn't earn anywhere near enough to support his family. After the recession had hit, people were cancelling their gym memberships and their sessions with him, and he had felt compelled to move into a dull, but reasonably paid job in a local bank, while dreaming of a different outcome . . .

He'd haggled with Nessa about their living choices. Nessa wanted to be closer to central London than Beckenham, the borough they had eventually plumped for. She'd been eyeing up tall, thin town houses to rent in Bethnal Green and Haggerston, that looked as if each floor had been stacked on top of the other by a giant toddler. She loved the buzz of east London, the world food shops and the nail bars on every corner. Jake resolutely refused because he wanted to be closer to the countryside, and so Beckenham was the compromise. It was 20 minutes away from Victoria Station by train, and just a 25-minute drive to Sevenoaks, with its vast, rolling, deer-inhabited playground – Knole Park – where the family spent many a weekend eating soggy jam sandwiches and climbing trees.

Prior to his big announcement, Jake had been in a rut. They both knew it, but it was an unspoken thing. Nessa was now sure that this was why he did what he did, and why he handled it so oddly. Perhaps he was terrified she'd say no, so he just . . . did it. It was the most selfish thing he'd ever done and, in her heart, she knew that she was yet to forgive him. But in many ways she felt responsible for cramping him in a tiny box – a lifestyle he never really wanted but only took on because of his love for her and his little girl . . .

'I have a question actually, though it might be a little weird,' Will said, taking a sip of wine from his large glass and pulling Nessa back into the present moment. 'It's just funny you mentioning that time I talked about wanting to be something special, because, if you remember, that was the night that I . . . rem . . . I . . .'

'Told me you loved me?' Nessa said, smiling and draping an arm across the top of the sofa casually. Two huge dimples appeared at the bottom of her cheeks. Will's face turned crimson.

'Yeah . . . that. Erm, obviously we were just kids then, and it was all very silly, but you, er, you didn't ever tell Jake about that, did you?' Will asked, visibly squirming.

'No, no I didn't, I promise,' Nessa said, starting to giggle now at the memory of it: the teenage Will with his long words, wild curls and his tendency to take everything way too seriously. He was just the same now really, come to think of it.

'Oh, thank god,' he said, smiling now, 'I always wondered about that. And with Jake and me being pretty close nowadays, I was just a bit concerned about—'

'Oh don't worry, Will, even if I had told him it wouldn't matter. He would have found it hilarious too. It happened lifetimes ago. We were completely different people.'

TWO

'Can you tell me what's going on, please? I'm worried'

March 1995

Nessa was at a friend's house that afternoon, lying on a collapsing single bed and watching *Clueless*. She fiddled with a Paddington Bear patterned duvet cover with her toes. The smell of freshly washed linen rose from the sheets.

'I literally want to be her,' Teigen said, chewing gum noisily. They both stared at Alicia Silverstone illuminating the tiny TV and its dusty, convex screen. Alicia's character, Cher, was choosing clothes from her high-tech wardrobe; the girls sighed in unison.

'I wonder how old she's meant to be in the film,' Teigen continued. 'Do you think our age, like 14 or 15 or something? No, maybe a bit older . . . I mean, just *imagine* being that pretty, Nessa, and that rich. Nothing would be an actual problem, y'know? Nothing.' She ran her right hand through her thin, ginger hair.

'Too right,' Nessa replied wistfully, struggling to concentrate on the film. She couldn't stop thinking about what was to come later that night, following the trouble she'd gotten into at school. Her form tutor was sure to have called her parents. They'd almost certainly know by now.

There was a pronounced feeling of dread at the pit of her stomach at the thought of going home. She was used to feeling that way. It was almost permanent, like a cold wedge of something in her tummy – ice perhaps. It was shocking how anxiety could become as routine and as normal as breathing. There was a weight on her chest and a fluttering near her heart: sweaty palms, nausea, always.

'So, I was thinking, in a bit, we could use Mum's new cordless phone and prank call the numbers on the shampoo bottles? That was so funny last time. What do you think?' Teigen asked, an eyebrow raised mischievously, as if she were proposing something seriously wild.

Nessa nodded and smiled to herself, accepting the challenge.

Nessa loved being at her friend's house, watching films and painting their nails. It was the greatest escape. And her little sister Kat could play with Teigen's sister too; they were both only six. It was perfect. Perfect knowing that her baby sister was in the same house and safe, giggling triumphantly from beneath a den made of bed sheets and chairs.

Teigen's mother was called Jan, and she was an 'earth' type. She wore a headscarf pulled across her forehead, which was tied at the back in a little knot. She loved bath milk that wasn't tested on animals, cinnamon and long flowing clothes with funny patterns. During the summer she wore wooden clogs on her chubby feet, and you always knew she was coming towards Teigen's bedroom, to disrupt a chat about boys or periods, because of the 'clack, clack, clack' across the floor.

She had a curious puffiness about her ankles and her throat, which Nessa had never seen before. Jan had to take medicine a lot of the time, and some of the tablets were massive. Nessa couldn't even swallow painkillers because she was afraid she might choke and die, and so she'd stared at the tablets when she found them in the bathroom for the first time, holding them up towards the light between her fingers and turning them around. Nessa didn't know what was wrong with Jan, but she seemed happy enough, so she figured it would go away. In fact, Jan would burst into tears sometimes, saying just how happy she was. She'd squeeze Teigen as if she'd been asked to never let her go. She had more capacity to love than Nessa had ever seen.

'Nessa? Nessa!' the pair were interrupted by the sound of Jan, yelling up the stairs towards the bedroom. Her voice skipped up the steps, rattling in the hallway like a sad song that had lost its way. It didn't have the usual chirpy warmth to it. The call sounded urgent.

Nessa and Teigen looked at each other for a few moments.

'Well, I dunno,' Teigen said, shrugging her shoulders. Nessa hopped up instantly and ran to the door, opening the frame enough that she could see Jan now, halfway up the stairs with the phone in one hand.

'Sweetheart . . .' Jan said warmly, putting the phone into the large front pocket of her stained apron, 'I need you to come downstairs, please.' Nessa noticed that her whole body seemed to be trembling slightly. She looked ghostly pale, frightened even. The whites of her eyes were red. Nessa instantly felt very worried.

'Oh OK, are you alright, Jan? Are you feeling ill or something?' Nessa had asked politely, feeling her stomach tighten. It was distressing to see Jan this way. She was always so positive, so bright and unflappable, and now she looked as if she'd seen something horrendous: like a ghost.

Nessa closed the bedroom door behind her, leaving Teigen to enjoy the film alone. Walking through the cold hallway that smelt of emulsion paint, she felt a sharp plunging feeling at the pit of her gut. Something was wrong. Very wrong. Something dreadful had happened.

'Come on, babe,' Jan said softly as she joined her at the halfway point of the stairs, putting her free arm around Nessa and leading her into the kitchen.

'Can you tell me what's going on, please? I'm worried,' Nessa said, her voice trembling. Jan shut the kitchen door and asked Nessa to sit on one of the old country kitchen style chairs.

'There's something I need to tell you, Nessa. It's terrible news I'm afraid.'

'Has Hammy died?' Nessa asked, feeling tears well in her eyes.

'Who's Hammy?' Jan asked, looking perplexed. Her face had gone from white now to a hot pink.

'You know, Hammy? My hamster, I've told you about him before. We rescued him from the pet shop because no one else wanted him. He's only got one ear. He's old now; Mum said we might have to brace ourselves for this . . .' Nessa had pictured her tiny ball of fluff in its cage, lying on his back with his legs in the air in the early stages of rigor mortis. She instantly felt a sadness so profound it was painful.

'Oh no, no it's not to do with Hammy, darling . . .' Jan had said awkwardly, turning a little red and dismissing it, uncomfortably.

'Something terrible has happened at home, Nessa. I really don't know how to say this to you . . . It's about your mum. Nessa, your mum has passed away. It's so terrible . . .' and as she said this she started to weep, apologising all the while.

'What?' Nessa had asked in disbelief. *Passed away.* She'd heard that phrase before. Adults liked to use it a lot. It seemed easier for them to say, gentler somehow than 'dead'.

'Oh, she was a wonderful, beautiful woman, she really was. I'm so, so sorry sweetheart,' Jan said, pulling Nessa into a tight cuddle and stroking her hair.

She smelt of cinnamon and cloves.

Nessa's world cracked and fell apart.

#23

The photo had arrived in a Bluey. Nessa's heartbeat started to dance as soon as she saw it there on the mat, with its tempting, visible perforations.

The letter sat innocently, snuggled up with a gas bill and a missed delivery slip. She knew those dusty blue envelopes. She *loved* them. They were usually dog-eared and battered by the time they had been flown from Afghanistan to London, thrown from basket to box in great thick sacks. They came every two or three months, without fail. She collected them. She kept them all in a drawer by her bedside. They were precious.

Poppy was at an after-school cookery club, or at least Nessa hoped she was. The house was strangely quiet without her. Nessa bent down to grasp the envelope in her fingers and started tearing at it. It couldn't happen quickly enough. These were the only real moments she had with the love of her life while he was away, and when they arrived she was desperate for them, as if she'd been holding her breath for the whole time until she opened them and she could finally take in some air.

She pulled out the photo: A5; matt finish; photo number 23. She knew this because, scrawled on the white backing of the photo paper, Jake had penned '#23' in thick, black marker. Oily blues, pinks and yellows could be spotted dancing in tight swirls in the ink if she angled it just the right way beneath the hallway light. He always used the same kind of pen, the same gentle handwriting, indicative of him – as if all the wonder of Jake Bruce's beautiful personality had been compacted, silenced and turned into a font.

Whenever she opened these envelopes and stared at the images, it was as if Nessa's world stood still. And even though she knew deep down that reality was continuing without her, in Nessa's mind the clocks were no longer ticking, the traffic in town had ground to a halt and elderly couples waited at the bus stops, frozen still and staring ahead. Even the birds would refrain from throwing themselves into the breeze and tumbling carelessly through the air. These were the stolen moments she could spend with Jake Bruce, while he was thousands of miles away. He and Poppy, they were everything to her.

Nessa flipped the photo round and stared at the image.

New Year's Eve 2001. They were in Bromley, at Will's house party. In the photo, a great, sprawling staircase unfolded in the background. Nessa wore a tight black dress with a flared velvet skirt. She was just 20 and, with the benefit of hindsight, she couldn't believe how slim and vibrant she looked then. Nessa recalled distinctly how self-conscious she had been at the time, constantly obsessing over her weight. But looking at her younger self now, Nessa wished she'd not spent so much time fretting about the way she looked. It was so pointless. She felt like she had wasted some of her youth in a way, worrying needlessly about the shallowest things.

Nessa was cuddling Jake, her mid-length hair tumbling over her shoulders in gentle waves, lighter streaks showing through from the bottom layers making it look like she'd spent a summer on the beach in Australia.

Jake was the most beautiful thing she'd ever seen. He really was breathtaking. He stood sideways on in the photograph, with his arms wrapped around her, dark stubble creeping up the side of his face. Sometimes Nessa looked at him and couldn't believe that he loved her. In all her childhood years of wondering who she'd be with, of obsessing over Will and other guys who were so far from her reach, she never even began to imagine that the reality would be *this* perfect. Jake was smiling cheekily. A metallic blue party hat had slipped off the top of his head, and was hanging at a jaunty angle.

The details of the evening came flooding back now, and it was as if she were there, taken back in time to one of the happiest moments of her life. Poppy was just 20 months old, with curly brown hair and a smile that hung between plump cheeks like bunting. She had been packed off to Jake's parents' bungalow to spend the night. Nessa had kissed her sleeping daughter's soft forehead and crept into the night.

Nessa and Jake had decided to make the most of their rare night off and head to the house party that Will was throwing. Amongst the 'regular' guests – old school friends and distant cousins – were a handful of his 'showbiz' mates, so intense in their mere presence. They were music industry bods who worked in PR and artist representation. They wore colourful tattoos like badges of honour, and smoked slim, roll-up cigarettes that hung from their lips at sad, regretful angles. 2001 was melting into 2002. The year had gone by so slowly, Nessa remembered now, but once it was gone, there would be no getting it back and she missed those times now. Since then, the hours, days and months had continually sped up, until everything seemed to be racing away from her.

The hallway had been cluttered with people. Some were kissing each other hungrily against the walls, exploring each other's bodies with urgent fingers. Others were giggling and chatting, clutching on to glasses and cans of beer. One unfortunate soul was just out of shot, puking into a boat shoe.

It was about to turn midnight, and some of the guests had left already, their vision too blurred by alcohol and class A drugs to see in the new year with any kind of clarity. Apparently some guy from an up-and-coming band had turned up wearing banana-print trousers, a shirt covered in palm trees and a pair of Ray-Ban Wayfarers without lenses. People were excitedly whispering about it, but Nessa and Jake didn't care. It meant nothing to them. They could have been anywhere, really, as long as they were together. They were perfectly tipsy, tottering around in the middle of the hall, dancing in each other's arms to 'Dancing in the Moonlight' by Toploader.

Teigen had arrived with her instant camera, and shouted their names before taking the snap that Nessa now held in her hands. She had a cigarette in one hand and the camera in the other; for a brief moment, the flash cast them in lightning-silver brightness, as a hot red cherry from the top of the cigarette tumbled recklessly to the floor. Afterwards, pretty patterns danced before their eyes in the low light, and they blinked and rubbed at their eyelids with the backs of their hands.

The photo was taken at 11.57 p.m. on Monday, December 31st. Little did Nessa know that at 11.59 that night, as the last seconds of the year slipped through the hourglass, Jake

Bruce would drop down on one knee and ask her to be his wife, clutching a vintage, art deco ring that was the most beautiful thing she'd ever seen. And as what felt like a million party poppers and great blobs of champagne flew through the air, twisting and curling together in drunken, sloppy jubilation, Nessa said yes, leaping into his arms and crying happily into his neck.

She had no idea what she was getting herself into.

Three

'She's so boring, I'm surprised she's even here'

The door edged open, ever so slowly, creaking as it did so. The slight, thin frame of an ageing lady could be seen through the glass, hunched and weary. One eye, surrounded by gentle folds of papery skin, was scarcely visible through the gap between the frosted glass and the white, plastic doorframe. Clocking the identity of the guests standing at the door, the eye lit up as if it belonged to a 17-year-old once more.

'Oh goodness! It's my beautiful little Poppy!' The door was shut hastily again, and a chime that had hung by the front door started clanging frantically. Poppy turned 180 degrees and rolled her eyes at her mother as if to say 'here we go again', her slender arms crossed and her thick, unruly hair tumbling down her shoulders. Nessa noticed her daughter's horrible expression and it instantly made her worry about the visit. Would Poppy be nice or a pain? She really hoped she wouldn't be a pain in the arse. She didn't want

Betsy to know what Poppy was really like these days, how hard things were sometimes . . .

Betsy Bruce could be heard frantically fiddling with three chains that were suspended across the door to protect them from rogue traders, charity representatives and Betterware salesmen. Suddenly the door was freed and thrown open. A wave of fresh air rushed into the stuffy bungalow. Nessa and Poppy's noses were instantly greeted with familiar smells: freshly baked bread, clean linen, furniture polish and cigarette smoke.

'Oh!! Goodness! My little baby girl! Come here, Pops!' Betsy cried, pulling her granddaughter into a tight hug as if she'd not seen her for a decade. The delicate skin of her arms was starting to look like crêpe paper and she was peppered with liver spots.

Nessa loved Jake's parents. The usual stereotype of the nightmare mother-in-law had failed to materialise. They certainly had their quirks, and they were far from perfect, but Mick and Betsy were the pieces of the puzzle she had missed for so many years before she met Jake. It was only right that she and Poppy kept visiting them while their son was away, especially because Nessa felt like their son being away was sort of her fault. She harboured a quiet guilt about his absence, dropping by at least once a week and often running errands for them, fetching items of shopping or replacing light bulbs. Just little things, here and there – whatever she could do to help them.

After Betsy had finally released her granddaughter from her vice-like cuddle, she advanced towards Nessa and lovingly wrapped her arms around her, planting a soft, moist kiss on her cheek. Nessa could smell the familiar odour of cheap perfume rippling from her fluffy, grey hair, which swayed a little in the summer breeze. 'Betsy, you're getting far too thin . . .' Nessa warned, as she pulled away from her.

'Oh I'm fine,' Betsy had said, waving a bony hand through the air as if it were nothing.

Everything about the bungalow on Copers Avenue, Penge, was overpoweringly dense. The carpets had last been replaced in the late seventies, and featured a swirling pattern weaved roughly into the pile. Feet would sink into this carpet-based bog, almost to the ankle, and Nessa sometimes wondered what it held within it. The bedding in the dark pink boudoir was a plethora of tired, sagging layers, totally unnecessary during the summer months but always there, even in 30 degree heat. Powder pink silks, cottons and knitted blankets with pompom details at the edges were draped over the aged single beds, which looked as if they might collapse at any moment.

But despite the dark, stodginess of the place, it was certainly clean . . . Betsy verged on being an obsessive cleaner, constantly polishing things and scrubbing frantically at mirrors until not a single streak of polish was visible.

Sometimes, when Nessa visited this bizarre twilight zone that felt as if it was suspended in time, she felt herself nodding off on the sofa. Her busy life seemed to catch up with her when she was in this dark, overheated abode. She would often wake again, 20 or so minutes later, draped in a layer of sweat and panic.

Mick was sitting in a large chair in the living room by the window, watching the arrow of time surge forwards. A cigarette dangled between the nicotine stained fingers of his right hand, a trail of brown smoke curling into the air.

'He's not so good today,' Betsy whispered, gazing at him lovingly. The three ladies stood at the door frame in the semi-darkness. He liked it that way: dark. It was sad. Nessa silently put her arm around Betsy's bony shoulder and pulled her close. Sometimes, she wished she could click her fingers and make it all OK.

The gentle sound of a ticking clock was strangely intrusive. The atmosphere was electric because you never knew what Mick was about to do next. He watched silently as cars sped by, flashes of yellow, blue and gunmetal grey. The women stared at him from a distance. His bony hands were clasped together in front of his stomach, shard-like knuckles protruded from them, his veins like cables. Even from a few metres away, it was obvious that this was a man lost within his own mind. He looked confused. Betsy gestured silently towards the kitchen and they walked away from the room quietly.

He had been a fine man, Mick Bruce, really one of the very best: a true gentleman with a big heart. Betsy and Mick had met at a mutual friend's twenty-first birthday party in a village hall in Ide Hill, Kent. The possibilities of life had seemed endless then. They had their whole lives ahead of them. But it had gone so fast! Mick had spotted 19-year-old Betsy across the room, holding a glass of flat cola and staring at her pale, sandalled feet. She was wearing a baby blue midi dress, and was the only girl at the party with her ample breasts tucked away and her legs mostly covered. Her hair was shoulder length, and curled up at the edges. A friend had drawn on some eyeliner in the toilets just an hour before. The flicks were almost perfectly executed, if you could ignore the fact that the left one was noticeably higher than the right.

'Who's that?' Mick had asked a friend, unable to stop looking at her. He had torn his glance away momentarily, to brush a few large beads of beer froth from his checked shirt.

'Oh god, that's Betsy. She's a square . . . She's so boring, I'm surprised she's even here,' his friend Padstow had replied, rolling his eyes and passing Mick another beer.

'Ha, yeah, she looks kinda dull,' Mick had said, laughing, but unable to shake his instant obsession towards this slender, blonde stranger, who seemed to be totally detached from the world around her. Why was she even at the party, he wondered. She looked as if it was the last place she wanted to be. Eventually, a red cheeked and smiley friend had prised the object of Mick's affections away from the wall, and eased her towards the dance floor. Mick, locked in fascination, had watched her through the crowds. A soft smile tugged at the corners of his mouth as he took an occasional sip of cold beer and felt something slip and slide within him, to be lost forever. Betsy Taylor was the most awkwardly beautiful thing he'd ever seen.

Later that night they had kissed behind a shed, as a sliver of moon hung above them, streaky clouds turning everything a sentimental grey. She had been so nervous her hands trembled. It was Betsy's first kiss, and Mick's seventh. But he knew he never wanted his lips to touch another mouth, ever again.

Poppy made her way over to a small wooden table and sat at a chair, fiddling with her phone.

'Betsy, I think you need more help,' Nessa said softly, watching her mother-in-law sashay between a steaming kettle and a cake tin, her bony bottom worryingly visible beneath her tracksuit trousers. Nessa leant against a wall; the paint was peeling off and there was a patch of damp starting to show near the window.

'Oh no, it's OK love. We'll be OK; we get by, the two of us. He wouldn't want anyone else looking after him, and he certainly wouldn't want to be anywhere else . . . God, just the thought of him in one of those miserable homes, eating tinned pears and watching second-rate Frank Sinatra tribute acts – No, no that's not for him . . .'

Betsy trailed off sadly, in spite of the smile drawn on her face in pearl-pink lipstick. It was times like these that Nessa felt even more angry and guilty about Jake's absence. How could he miss this? How could he not be there for his family? And then she wondered, what difference would it make anyway? Mick rarely knew who anyone was because Alzheimer's had robbed him so cruelly of his memories. Poppy and Nessa would still be there when Jake came back on leave, loving him more than they did the day he had left. He couldn't really change anything . . . No one could.

'How's my boy doing?' Betsy asked, switching the subject and advancing towards the table with a tray of hot drinks and gargantuan slabs of sticky Victoria sponge. Poppy was momentarily distracted from her phone and the endless lime-green demands of WhatsApp. She had stared at the cake, probably wondering how she could turn it down, no doubt.

Nessa thought back to the last phone call she'd had with her husband. He sounded tired, but well. She could tell from his voice.

'I miss you so much, Ness,' he'd said quietly. Ness had smiled, and something warm in her stomach reassured her that everything was going to be OK.

'I think of you and Poppy all the time. I can't wait to come home soon, and I just, well I want you to know how much I love you . . .' he spoke quietly so he wouldn't be overheard being slushy, and Nessa was so taken by emotion she could barely respond – she just continued to listen to him: 'I love this job too, Nessa, seriously, my life has totally changed, you know? Just to be doing something I'm passionate about, and good at, for the first time ever . . . It's what I was born to do, like this was the missing piece all along. We are strong Nessa, we will get through this . . . I appreciate how much you support me, so, so much . . .' he'd said.

'Yeah, he seems really good,' Poppy said matter-of-factly, eyeing up the cake suspiciously. Eventually, she picked up her phone again and, finding the shot in her photo stream that she was looking for, handed the phone to Betsy.

Her grandmother pushed a pair of glasses down onto her nose, and pulled the phone close to her face, one almost invisible eyebrow arched in nervous curiosity. 'Oh my goodness,' she sighed, like all the words at her command couldn't even begin to form a sentence that summed up her overwhelming love.

Nessa knew the feeling. *It is hard to love somebody that much*.

Missing him was like an insatiable ache. A hunger pain. So difficult that she often felt angry with him. The bed was horribly empty without him, and sometimes she would lie there on Saturday mornings, ruffling up the sheets on his side with her right hand so she could imagine he had only just peeled himself out of it. That he had pulled a grey, cotton t-shirt over his muscular chest, yanked on a pair of jeans and just popped down to the shops to grab a paper and a packet of bacon. Before Poppy had become so hateful towards her, she had made it a little better, sometimes crawling into the bed and wrapping her arms around her mother. But now Nessa felt a new kind of loneliness, akin to physical pain. Sometimes she wondered how long she might be able to take this for.

'How did you get this Poppy?' Betsy asked, astonished by the clarity of the image that shone from the phone. Nessa could remember it by heart, every pixel, every shard of light piercing the background from the hot sun behind him. She didn't need to take another glance at the screen; it was all in her mind. Jake's skin had a slightly dusty sheen to it, his smile, as broad and handsome as his shoulders, a spotless uniform proudly draped over them. Even from thousands of miles away, he melted her heart as easily as if he were standing before her, kissing her face softly.

She was sick of this, sick of feeling this way all the time.

'He emailed it to me and Mum, didn't he Mum? Look, you can zoom in and everything,' Poppy said excitedly, pushing the phone back towards her grandmother, pressing two slender fingers against the glass and spreading them apart softly until Jake's smile was all that could be seen from one edge of the phone to the other.

Betsy pushed her hand against her heart and grinned, like it was the best thing that had happened all week, running a hand over the back of Poppy's head and down her waterfall of fluffy hair. Betsy was almost rough in showing her affections, as if all the years of looking after children and cooking had made her misunderstand the strength in her feeble-looking arms. Poppy grimaced a little, shuffling uncomfortably in her seat as if she were about to wriggle away from this show of affection.

'That's OK, Granny. I'm going to print it out at school next week and bring it to you so you can put it on the fridge or something. Maybe we could get a phone like this for Grandad, so he can take pictures, to help him remember things,' Poppy added. Nessa was surprised, she was being unusually intuitive, a far cry from the rebellious and stroppy teenager she was at home. And while Nessa was glad Poppy was on her best behaviour today, she also wondered why she couldn't be like this more often. What was she doing? Who was the real Poppy?

She'd never imagined that her daughter would grow into such a puzzle. She was just 14, and impossible to understand. Nessa had been a kid too, once, so why couldn't she relate to her own? When Poppy was seven years old or thereabouts, Nessa distinctly remembered brushing her hair as they sat on the sofa together one winter's evening, having read her favourite book, *The Tailor of Gloucester* by Beatrix Potter, for the second time that evening. The snow had been falling softly since she'd been picked up from school, and the window sill had a light frosting on it, like a plump layer of icing on a cake. Poppy had stared out of the window, and said, very quietly, 'You are the best mummy in the whole wide world.' At the time Nessa had naively thought she had cracked it, the parenting thing. She had aced it. Her little girl adored her, despite her flaws. Even though she'd not grown up in a conventional family herself, she was making *this* one work. She genuinely hoped they might stay that way forever.

Now, Nessa felt like the enemy, but all she wanted to do was protect her daughter . . . The things she found in her 'little girl's' bedroom set the hairs on her arms on end. Packets of cigarettes, miniature bottles of spirits, mystery items of clothing from River Island that she knew Poppy couldn't afford. Where had they come from? Nessa didn't even want to confront Poppy because she didn't want to know. She couldn't cope with it all on top of everything else. She needed Jake at times like these.

The sudden appearance of Mick at the doorway tore the three girls away from their moments. Together but separate, three generations of the Bruce family, who had previously been lost in their own clouds of thought and worry, were now looking up at the shadowy figure before them, momentarily united by something.

'Who are they?' Mick asked coldly. Nessa's stomach plunged. To see him now, to hear him speak and to witness the icy glimmer of unfamiliarity in his eyes, it was as if he'd never attended Nessa and Jake's wedding, where he gave the most beautiful and witty speech. It was as if he'd never come to the hospital after Poppy was born. She could almost see him now, wiping a great slop of a tear from his chiselled cheeks as he held his granddaughter's warm, sticky body in his arms for the very first time. It was as if he had never known them at all.

Mick stood with one hand placed on either side of the doorframe to steady himself. He was noticeably slimmer, Nessa noticed, his bony body disguised beneath layers of tweed and cotton in spite of the summer heat. His health was getting worse, and fast. There was no doubt about it. He was slipping between their fingers, and they all felt so helpless.

'Who are they?' he demanded again, staring first at Poppy and then at Nessa, a look of fear-driven fury across his haggard features. 'Tell them we don't want any more sponges or washing up gloves. We have enough. We can't afford it anyway. They have to go. *Bleeding animals!*' Mick's voice jumping up into a shout now, one hand had slipped away from the doorframe and was balled into a fist. Nessa cocked her head to one side and studied his face. Jake had picked up so much from him: that strong, straight nose, the shape of his forehead . . .

'Darling, this is your granddaughter, Poppy . . .' Betsy started, gesturing towards Poppy, who smiled meekly. She waved one hand in the air uncomfortably, as if saying hello to him for the very first time, totally unequipped for the emotional complexities of the situation. Realising how odd this was, and with no warm response or recognition from Mick, she softly dropped her hand into her lap. Her phone started flashing on the table but, for once, she ignored it.

'And this, this is Nessa. Nessa is our son Jake's wife, and Poppy's mum. Nessa is your daughter-in-law, love,' she said calmly. Betsy had been through this many times before. Her voice was soothing. It held no fleck or hint of irritation, or judgement.

'But our son is dead,' Mick said, as if his wife was purposefully lying to him. His face momentarily screwed up in an expression of disgust.

'No, no, he's not,' Betsy said, rising to her feet, and shuffling across the kitchen floor towards her husband, who was still considerably taller than she. Nessa and Poppy stayed at the table, their heads bowed down towards the pink, lacy tablecloth, occasionally glancing at each other reassuringly. Poppy fiddled with one of Betsy's necklaces, her chipped navy blue nail varnish a dark backdrop against the silver chain she was touching.

'Yes he is! He's dead!' shouted Mick, furious flecks of spittle flying from his red lips. He slammed his fist against the door frame and groaned with frustration. Red thread veins flared up in his cheeks, and his breathing began to quicken. A chilling silence descended on the room.

'Mick, our son Jacob Bruce is in the army. He's in Afghanistan. He is still alive, and his lovely wife and daughter have come to visit us. Everything's just fine,' Betsy whispered calmly.

Betsy held her beloved husband's shoulders in her hands, and tried to maintain eye contact with him as he looked at the ground, his bottom lip pushed out. And all of a sudden he was like a child again. Regressing with age. Going backwards. After a minute or so, Mick grew tired.

'I want to go to sleep. I'm tired, I can't, I can't—' he started to sob, great raspy breaths crunching in and out of his chest as he cried. As he did so, he dissolved into his wife's arms and wept. It wasn't the crying of regret, or sadness, but exhaustion and anger. As if he still didn't believe them, but he didn't know what else he could do.

As Poppy and Nessa drove home there was more tension than usual. Nessa turned on the radio to try and swerve the hideous quiet, hoping the 'soothing' tones of the BBC newsreader might calm her. But without asking, Poppy switched the station over to Kiss 100 and turned the volume up. Nessa felt her shoulders tense up with irritation as bassy electronic sounds licked from the speakers.

'Is Grandad going to be OK?' Poppy shouted moodily over the music, finally pulling her attention away from her smartphone. Nessa turned down the radio a little so she could think straight, wondering how she would answer her daughter's very difficult question.

Nessa wondered how honest she should be about Mick. She guessed the years of sugar-coating reality to make Poppy happy were long gone. She took a deep breath as she switched on the left indicator.

Tick.

Tock.

Tick.

Tock.

'No, not really, Poppy,' she said, turning into Mill Avenue, the car eventually able to speed up a little after having sat in traffic for a few minutes. The breeze came soaring through the open windows. It was a relief to them both. Nessa could feel a thin layer of sweat building up on her top lip and her forehead.

'Can he not be treated? You know, can't they make it stop?' Poppy enquired further. There was a condescending tone in what she was saying, as if she could do so much better than the seemingly endless healthcare professionals who had already spent many hours on Mick's case.

'Grandad has Alzheimer's disease . . .' Nessa started.

'Yeah, I know that Mum, for fuck's sake . . .' Poppy shouted, with such aggression.

'Don't interrupt me please, Poppy, and don't be so rude. Grandad's disease can't be cured . . . It's what doctors describe as degenerative, which means it doesn't get better. He might reach a point one day and stay there, and just stay the same, that would probably be the best outcome . . . but often people get a lot worse. It's really very sad. But don't worry—'

'I'm not worried,' Poppy interrupted sharply, her head now twisted round away from Nessa, as if she was studying something carefully through the window frame. But her vocal chords gave her away. The word 'worried' hadn't come out easy. It had been intercepted by a lump in her throat. Nessa had been there before. She'd turned around and pretended to be looking at something through a car window while fighting back a stream of hot tears. Many times before . . .

Nessa turned off the radio entirely, just trying to think straight. How would she make things OK for Poppy? That small part of her that hated Jake for not being here to support her through all this materialised again. As happy and fulfilled as he seemed to be, her resentment towards him was building as much as the ache of missing him.

As soon as they pulled up onto the driveway Poppy scrambled out of the car as if she couldn't get away fast enough. In just a glimpse, Nessa had spotted the tell-tale pallid tones of her skin, streaked with bright red where she'd been crying. Her eyes were pink.

Nessa sighed and got out of the car, pulling her keys out of her bag. 'Poppy, I understand you're upset. Let's get a cup of tea, and we can talk about—'

'Just fuck off, Mum, please, fuck off,' Poppy growled, stamping her left foot on the ground with sheer frustration.

As soon as the door was unlocked, Poppy stamped up the stairs before slamming the door hard behind her.

BANG.

Nessa leant her back against the closed door, and sighed loudly, the keys jangling against each other as she hung them on a nearby hook.

Four

'He must earn, like, loads risking his life everyday like that?'

April 10th 2012

The rebellious tones of Charli XCX leaked from the speakers screwed into every corner of Hotwire's flagship store on Tottenham Court Road. It was the half-term holiday, and the space, designed to look like a warehouse, was packed full of excitable girls wearing frayed jeans. The unspoken code of current fashion had spread quickly, as it always did, in the time it took to fill the ASOS storeroom and for Topshop's PR team to upload a photo of a sulky looking, bow-legged model to Instagram.

Teenage girls wandered around in groups, others dragged reluctant boyfriends, in snapbacks and skinny jeans, by the hand. Hotwire was a den of temptation. Gold, spiked jewellery hung on silver angular display branches. Leggings and slogan tees were uniform, paired with tiny bags suspended from long, gold chains – a subtle nod to the eighties. They were like an army, the young people today . . . Gigs at

Alexandra Palace and the Brixton Academy attracted them in droves. Clones, that's what they were – all wearing identical clothes, nodding their heads in unison to some dull, thick beat, and drinking from the same tall glass bottles.

Poppy whispered the words of the song under her breath, in time to the music, as she walked deeper into the store with her group of friends. Poppy was right at the front, and behind her were her loyal followers: Cara Hewitt, Frances Thomsitt, Rhiannon Smith and Emma McNara.

The girls had arrived at 2.30 p.m. this Tuesday prepared to prematurely spend their half-term allowances on whatever they could get their hands on. This flurry of financial activity would see them front-load their week off school with excitement, leaving themselves with no cash for the rest of the holiday, a decision which would inevitably leave them angry and bored.

As they marched through the shop, heads turned, there was an air of trouble about the group. A thin security guard with curly script tattoos on his neck clocked them and looked them up and down. They were the kind of girls who managed to intimidate ordinarily secure and confident women in their mid-to-late twenties, taking them back to a time when their glasses were taped together and they got hit in the face with a hockey stick in PE.

'How much money did your paarrunts give you?' Frances asked the girls casually, once they had come to a sudden pause by a huge stack of makeup bags with cut-out flock patterns.

'Ya, I got fifty quid,' said Cara, bringing Poppy's meandering focus back to the conversation.

'One hundred smackaroonies,' quipped Emma, at which

the girls all glanced at her enviously and rolled their eyes. Emma's mum was a human rights lawyer.

'Thirty,' smirked Rhiannon, pulling a face of disappointed acceptance, the kind of expression one pulls when taking part in a lucky dip, only to win a set of floral-scented soaps circa 1997. It was Poppy's turn now. They glanced at her expectantly. She felt a prickly heat appear on her arms and legs.

'A tenner . . . for lunch and the bus,' Poppy said, her eyes flicking down towards the floor. Frances cleared her throat and flicked her hair over her shoulder. 'Mum's so tight,' Poppy cut in before anyone had the chance to say anything.

'Doesn't your faaather get you guys money from his waaarrk? He must earn, like, loads risking his life every day like that?' Frances asked, probingly. She fiddled with a rogue strand of hair, a group of bangles clanging around her slender wrist.

'Yeah he pays for things and stuff, but you know, things are still tight, aren't they? He doesn't earn that much, you'd be surprised,' Poppy replied defensively.

Tight. It was a word her mother used a lot, and it was now part of her vocabulary too. It irritated the shit out of her. When Poppy and her mother went to the huge Tesco near home the other weekend and she wanted the new Maccabees album, her mother had shook her head and said, 'Sorry baby, things are too *tight*.' When Poppy wanted to order some decent bras from a catalogue that had been pushed through the letterbox, her mother had blushed a little, and used that word again. *Tight*. When Poppy wanted to get a takeaway pizza after her exams, her mother had tensed up and said it again. *Tight*. 'Why don't we *make* a pizza?' her mother had suggested joyfully, rifling through the cupboards looking for toppings. Everything was fucking tight. Why couldn't they be like other families?

'Ahhh man that sucks . . . I love your mum though, she's well cool,' Emma said with sincerity.

'She's a bitch,' Poppy said, matter-of-factly, before prancing off to the shoe department. Her friends looked at each other quizzically before following.

Half an hour later, the girls were in the changing rooms, having carried bundles of clothes with them past a tired-looking shop assistant who had nodded them through casually. The cubicles were packed and girls could be heard shouting at one another, a buzz of frenzied chatter engulfing the room. Poppy had four outfits to try, but she wasn't sure why she was even bothering. Added up, they came to £335, way more than she could ever dream of spending, but she just wanted to see what it felt like. How it might feel to wear clothes from Hotwire.

Her favourite outfit of the four was a black and white tartan miniskirt in brushed wool with a visible, silver zip, and a black peplum-style vest top. 'This is amazing,' Poppy whispered to herself as she watched herself move slowly in the long mirror, twisting around every few seconds. Carefully angled mirrors enabled her to see the bits that she couldn't spot on her own. *I am starting to look like a woman*, she noticed. The straight-up-and-down, gangly body of her youth was still there alright, but curves were appearing as if from nowhere. A pear-shaped invasion: it was bizarre, as if she were looking at someone else.

Suddenly, all the simmering anger and material longing she could possibly muster overwhelmed her. Her life wasn't fair, she thought. Tears brimming at her eyes, Poppy grabbed her long, dark curls and twisted them round and round. Her mum was a cow, her dad was in the army, and she was poor. *Everything is shit,* she thought to herself, dramatically. Poppy sat on the stool in the changing room and sighed, great big tears spilling from her eyes.

Five

'Where are her friends now?'

Nessa's mobile rang in her pocket. There were only a couple of people ambling around the library. A young, athletic-looking man was picking his nose in the history section, and an older lady was sneaking a look at a surprisingly extensive selection of erotic fiction. She was sure nobody would notice if she picked it up.

'Hello?'

'Hello, is this Mrs Bruce I am speaking with?'

'Yes, it is, how can I help?' Nessa responded, suddenly standing up straighter and taller than she had been beforehand, and taking a few quick steps away from the counter. Something about the cold, official tone of the caller made her feel like this wasn't going to be good.

'My name is Mark, I'm a manager at Hotwire, Tottenham Court Road. I'm here with your daughter, Poppy,' he said.

'Right . . .' Nessa responded, her heart racing. She imagined all the possibilities. Perhaps Poppy had fainted and they had been forced to call an ambulance. She had been having some migraines and dizzy spells recently . . . Or what if she had actually become secretly involved in a gang, and someone had attacked her in a shop? What if a giant piece of advertising board had come loose and landed on her head? There were huge bits of heavy Perspex lettering in there. *JesusfuckingChrist*, she thought to herself, adrenaline rushing through her body as all the possibilities flickered through her mind. She pictured her daughter lying on the ground in agony, impaled by a giant letter 'H'.

'What's going on? Is she OK?' Nessa asked, with urgency.

'Yes, yes, she's fine. Well, she's a little upset, she's here with me in my office . . .'

'Has she been hurt?'

'She's not hurt, but can you come to the store now?'

'You silly, silly girl,' Nessa said, the moment they got off the train at Clock House Station. They trundled up the steps towards the street. Poppy was ahead of her mum. The sun was just starting to set. Sweaty office workers sped past them, clutching bottles of Pinot Grigio and bunches of sagging roses, exhausted from their day in the city.

It had been so hard for Nessa to hold her tongue on the journey home. She was furious at her daughter. Poppy had sat next to the window, glaring out at the suburbs, studying each and every one of the houses she looked upon, as they rushed through Ladywell and Lower Sydenham. The numerous gardens were dotted with old washing lines, broken trampolines and rusty barbecues. Poppy bit her bottom lip, looking as if she was trying desperately not to melt down in front of all these strange, judgmental faces with their sweaty foreheads and piercing gazes. She knew that if too many tears fell, she would cry herself a lake, and she wouldn't be able to stop it happening.

Nessa had wondered about all the things she would say to Poppy when their front door was closed. The approaches she could take as a mother were numerous, and these choices were difficult.

Tough love vs gentle nurturing.

Screaming rage vs stunned silence.

Let's talk about this vs go to your room.

The calm-yet-disappointed approach which was often quite the stinger, she recalled, from her own childhood, when her second foster father, whom she adored, would refrain from yelling and would simply say 'You let me down.' When he uttered those words, it was as if he'd given up on her. That was the scariest thing of all, to be given up on . . . For someone to throw their palms to the sky and decide you were no longer worth the effort.

Nessa considered all the ways a situation like this could be handled, but nothing seemed straightforward anymore. She didn't know the answers. She wanted to call Jake and ask him for help, but she couldn't . . . Nessa hoped everything would have slid into place by now, but she felt like she knew less and less about life with each passing day.

In the end, she'd been unable to wait until they got home, her frenzied judgements spilling from her mouth as soon as they had left the stuffy train carriage. The whole meeting-with-the-manager thing had been utterly humiliating. During the minute or two while she waited, Nessa had stared at the holiday-themed dresses wondering what it was about the clothes in this shop that had prompted such utter madness from her daughter. She picked up a tag and studied it. £45. *Things are expensive now*, she thought, looking at the garment, which had a few threads poking out here and there where they had come loose from the weak grip of a mass-produced seam. Clumsy stitching: blood and tears.

'Mrs Bruce?' a voice interrupted her. She quickly dropped the hem of the dress guiltily as if she herself were up to no good.

'Yes, sorry, yes, I'm Nessa. Nessa Bruce,' she had said, moving away from the rail and extending her right arm to shake his hand. She hoped for a second that if she could come across like the best mother ever, the nicest most well-meaning parent to have ever come to pick up a thieving teenager, she might just sway things in the right direction. Away from any kind of official proceedings, and away from police officer visits and unnecessary court hearings. But there was a coldness in the manager's face that made her feel more concerned than she had been on her way to the store.

He was tall and weedy. His hair was dyed pink, and he had numerous piercings peppering his earlobes. A faded tattoo of a seahorse almost entirely covered his left forearm. A small cow-ring had been punched into the pale skin that straddled the bridge of his nose. He looked tired or perhaps hungover. This was bad, given the circumstances.

'If you'd like to come with me?' he asked, as if she had a choice, before turning around quickly and heading to the back of the shop floor, past a merry-go-round of rails, spotlights and handbags. Nessa followed him breathlessly. His long legs moved much faster than hers.

Nessa followed him through the door, and it shut swiftly behind them, cutting them off from the shiny fashion facade. The corridor behind the shop floor was worlds away from the glamorous showroom she had just been in. The hallway looked a little like an abandoned psych ward.

It was light blue in colour, with the odd pinboard here and there coated in thick, green felt. Rotas and helpline numbers for staff were printed on bits of A4 paper and pinned onto the boards, the notices curled at the edges. 'Are you feeling low?' one poster asked, with the words coming out of a speech bubble suspended from a cartoon worm. The worm went on to offer staff exclusive access to a 24-hour helpline where they could talk about alcoholism, drug abuse, domestic violence and anxiety, amongst a host of other problems. Nessa noticed that one poster right next to it detailed the menu options at the staff Christmas Party, which had taken place months ago: turkey, nut loaf, salmon, tick here.

Great clumps of fluff and bubble wrap had been swept up at some point then left in sporadic dusty piles, waiting to be disposed of. Empty clothes rails on wheels were dotted about, lonely hangers suspended sadly from them, a couple swinging in the cool draft that puffed its way through the corridor, back and forth. And eventually, they reached a white office door with a gold placard on it reading 'MANA GER'. As soon as it was flung open, Nessa was greeted with the sight of her daughter, slumped on a plastic chair, weeping dramatically into a handful of loo roll.

'Here she is,' Mark said flatly, a slight bitchiness to his tone. He flung himself down into a chair opposite his computer screen. A large, greasy McDonald's bag had been left on the surface of the desk to his right. The room smelt of beef and stale gherkins. Nessa padded across the floor and sat next to her daughter, unable to say a word, struggling to even look at her. On a small coffee table before them lay the garments. Nessa studied them sadly. A black top that looked pretty plain, she thought, wondering why Poppy had gone for that. A pair of studded heeled shoes had been laid on their sides either side of a black and white chequered skirt. The skirt was quite nice actually, but that wasn't the point, Nessa reminded herself, mortified by her thoughts.

'Right then,' Mark said, grabbing the brown fast-food bag and scrunching it up into his hands until it was compacted into a small ball, perfect for launching across the room and into a metal wire bin. He managed it in just one shot.

'At approximately 3 p.m. today the alarms at our entrance doors went off. Poppy and a group of friends were immediately approached by one of our security guards. As a matter of routine, he asked to look in their bags . . .' he paused for a moment to mask a quiet burp with the closed fist of his right hand. The stench of stale Big Mac floated across the room a few seconds later. Nessa crinkled her nose.

'The only redeeming thing about the situation is that your daughter cooperated with our guard, and let him search through her bag rather than running away, which is what they usually do.'

Poppy wept loudly.

'Right . . . well, that's a good thing . . . isn't it?' Nessa asked, suddenly realising that it was a bit pointless acting as her daughter's defence lawyer. If that was the only good thing she could highlight in this situation, then she really was clutching at straws.

There was a difficult silence, only broken by Poppy's crying. She was shaking and shuddering. Nessa felt a huge lump of humiliation and disappointment build at the base of her throat. She wished Jake could be there. He'd know how to handle this, he really would. He'd be warm to the guy, but intimidating too, in the way he was with his broad, tall presence and those piercing eyes of his. He'd deal with the situation if he were here, she knew it . . .

'Of course, we asked Poppy if she had stolen the items and she admitted to doing so.'

'Where are her friends now?' Nessa asked, looking around her dramatically, which was ridiculous in retrospect because they very obviously weren't around.

'We let them go,' Mark said quickly.

Typical. Nessa shuddered at the thought of them going home and excitedly telling their parents. What would they think of her? They would assume she was a terrible mother. Fran's mum was a lawyer. Fucking hell. The next parents' association barbecue would be even more awkward than normal.

Nessa reached for Poppy's hand gently, so angry she could have screamed at her little girl, but sad for her too. She was surprised to find that Poppy held it back with her own hand, as hot and sweaty as it was. She'd not done that for a long, long while. *Is this what it took nowadays?*

'On this occasion I won't be calling the police,' the manager said, leaning back in his chair and gazing out of the window for a moment or two.

Nessa felt relief flood her body and she too wanted to cry. She suddenly wanted to hug this weedy man with the expressionless eyes, and tell him how sorry she was for what Poppy did, and how hard things were for her because her dad was in the army and her grandad was ill with Alzheimer's, and everything was difficult, and awkward and uncomfortable, but she would try harder as a mother from now on, and things would be better, and her daughter would never darken his doorstep again, and, and . . . She managed to control herself.

'Thank you,' Nessa said softly, her own voice wobbling now.

'I will have to warn you, though, if your daughter is caught doing this again, I will not hesitate to call the police and I mean that,' he added, turning back to Nessa as he showed them out of the office.

'Why did you do it Pops?' Nessa asked, almost chasing her daughter as she thundered down the road away from the train station. Her daughter careered on, her head tilted down towards the endless grey paving slabs. 'Because my life is shit, Mum,' Poppy replied dramatically.

Nessa tried to reply, almost running now to keep up with daughter: 'Your . . . life . . . is . . . not—' each word was separated by a loud breath, breaking up the sentence.

'Yes it is!' Poppy yelled back.

They turned left off Beckenham Road and clambered down an unmade gravel track. After ten dusty, crunchy steps, they were led into a network of alleyways threading between well-loved suburban allotments. The only thing that separated the cracked, tarmac paths from the cabbages and carrots was a tall, chain-metal fence. Weeds clung to the bottom parts of the fence, growing determinedly day by day, hauling themselves up like athletes. A man in his mid-forties was pushing a rusty garden fork into the dirt with his left foot, beads of sweat glistened on his forehead under the evening sun. Nessa nodded at him to say hi. He smiled back with a knowing look, as if this vision of a speeding teenage girl and her out-of-breath mother was nothing all that new to him.

Once Nessa had chased her daughter back to the house and unlocked the front door, she followed Poppy into the living room. She had thrown herself on the sofa and put the TV on in one heavy swoop. *Hollyoaks* was nearly finished.

'Poppy we need to talk,' Nessa said, grabbing the remote control and putting the sound on mute.

'Hmph,' Poppy scowled.

'Poppy, I don't think you really understand how lucky you were today . . .'

Poppy sighed loudly, and kicked off her trainers.

'*Lucky*? Lucky . . .? Seriously, you've *got* to be fucking kidding,' Poppy responded, glancing at her mother in a loaded way.

'No, really, Poppy . . . That guy could have so easily called the police. I know he was a bit of an idiot, but still . . . he took a chance on you. And you know what? If he had called them, and he would have had every right to, you might have been sent to youth court, and you'd have a criminal record.'

'That's ridiculous,' the young woman chimed.

'No, it's really not, Pops. Even if you *weren't* sent to court, you would have probably had to accept a caution. And yes, they are hidden from your record after a while, which is fine in many ways, but if you want to be a teacher, or work with children, or perhaps for the government, or anything like that, your caution would come up on your record, Poppy. And you would have to tell them at job interviews, for the rest of your life, how you once got in a strop when you were 14 and tried to steal a skirt from Hotwire. It's a bit embarrassing, isn't it?' Nessa said.

'But I don't want to be a teacher. And I don't want to work for the government, so it doesn't matter does it?' Poppy responded.

'That's not the point! By doing things like that, you close doors for yourself, and in life you need as many doors open as possible. You never know how you'll feel, or what you might want in 10, 15, 20 years' time. You are not the sum of who you are right now!' Nessa cried, becoming exasperated.

'Do you think that I wanted to work in a tiny library, Poppy? Do you think that's how I wanted things to go?' Nessa continued, thinking back to her own life-dreams.

'No, but Mum, you never tried. You're a failure, OK? So don't take out the frustrations of your cruddy life on me,' Poppy said suddenly, turning towards her mother and narrowing her eyes. Nessa was momentarily stunned, as if someone had shot a dart directly into her skin, and it was slowing everything down. She didn't know what to say. Poppy could be very rude, but she'd never spoken to her like that before.

'You just never did it. It's your fault, and no one else's,' Poppy said.

They were the cruellest, most cutting words she'd ever heard. Nessa felt as if she'd been winded. She had to defend herself. She couldn't be treated like this by her own daughter.

'Things aren't that simple, Poppy. You just don't understand how hard it's . . . there's a lot you don't know.' Nessa started running one hand through her hair, but Poppy interrupted her.

'Yes I do. I do understand, and I know it's hard, but it's your fault you aren't a midwife, and nobody else's. Not even Dad's,' Poppy said coldly, turning towards the TV.

'I'm sorry to say that,' she continued, turning back to her mother, 'but it's the truth.'

#24

The photo couldn't have come any sooner.

Jake Bruce was due to fly home for leave in eight weeks and two days, and Nessa needed him more than ever. She had decided not to tell him about the shoplifting incident, but he had to have some idea about how bad things were with Poppy . . . She missed his reassuring manner. She needed his advice. She missed her best friend. They were supposed to be in this together.

It had been a long, hard day at work. One member of staff was off sick, and an intern was robbing her of her last shreds of patience, sleeping at the table in the staffroom and calling elderly customers 'dude' and 'homes'.

Poppy was downstairs watching TV. They would have risotto for dinner, Poppy's favourite. It was bubbling away in the pan, and had almost been in there too long. The sound of Sheldon Cooper's voice on *The Big Bang Theory* could be heard from the living room; although slightly muffled, the sporadic outburst of canned laughter distracted Nessa from her thoughts. She had just five minutes to herself. Five minutes until her daughter asked for the umpteenth time when dinner would be ready, until the tomatoes and prawns in the pan would start to wilt, and the rice would fuse itself solidly to the bottom. She grabbed the envelope from the table in the hall by the door and padded up the stairs, shutting herself in her bedroom. She drowned out Poppy, Sheldon and the world for a few, precious moments.

The Bluey ripped open easily. Nessa tipped it upside down and out slid the picture. It landed on the white bedsheet. '#24' was written on the back in black marker pen. Jake's writing. She turned it around.

There she was, with Jake and Poppy, in Knole Park. The picture had been taken about three years ago. Poppy was nine or ten, and still in her pre-monstrous years, when she said nice things and drew pictures of flowers and smiley faces. She was holding her favourite toy, 'Rat Man', in one hand. The family was sitting on a huge fallen tree trunk. Jake was on the right, wearing a pair of loose fitting jeans and a maroon coloured t-shirt. His beard had turned a lighter, sandier brown in the sun. He had his arms wrapped around Nessa. She had worn a black maxi dress that day. Her blonde-brown hair was tied into a messy knot at the top of her head. Her large sunglasses were perched at the end of her nose, as if they might fall off at any moment. Poppy was sitting on her lap, looking away from the camera for a moment, and up towards the blue, cloudless sky. She had on her favourite little dress, covered in embroidered navy anchors. There was a lovely expression on her face of total contentment. Jake was looking at Nessa and Poppy. He looked so happy. They all did. It suddenly slipped into place.

Jake had to come home.

He had to.

His daughter was shoplifting, and goodness knows what else. Life was falling apart . . . This was where Nessa would have to draw the line.

Nessa had spent so much time doing things for others, and moulding her life around other people's plans. And where had this got her? If her daughter's recent speech about Nessa's lack of achievement had any kind of positivity amongst the barb-like pain it had inflicted on her heart, those words *had* made her realise something. Nessa needed to be more selfish. She absolutely had to put her foot down and demand the life she wanted. She'd never stumbled across this realisation before. All she wanted was for Jake to be happy, but she'd sacrificed her own happiness for his, and that was going to have disastrous consequences.

They could handle the job stuff, she thought, her eyes

boring into the shiny photo paper. They hadn't tried hard enough. She'd just accepted what he said about the army because she felt like she was lucky to have him and should do whatever she possibly could to keep him, even if that meant letting him go.

She'd not put up a fight, *and now look at how things are* . . . The situation was a farce, she thought to herself. It was ridiculous.

Jake could come home and open his own business that involved being in the outdoors, or he could become a tree surgeon, or a landscaper . . . or something, she considered. The army was surely not the only route to fulfilment and happiness in his career. They would have to borrow some money while he retrained, perhaps she could persuade him to ask Will for some help. They could make it happen. She felt a flutter of excitement at the thought of him being at home again. She imagined what it would be like to fall asleep next to him, to make love to him at 2 a.m., to kiss the back of his neck . . .

Her attention turned back to the image. She wondered how they had all managed to be in the photo, trying to recall the details of that gorgeous June day three years ago. Because they were a family of three, there were so many pictures of just two of them because one of them always had to hold the camera. On this afternoon, Nessa had asked a passer-by to take the picture, a man who looked to be in his early twenties who was out running. His green vest top was drenched in sweat. Perspiration ran down his arms and legs in tiny rivers. He agreed, breathlessly, to take the picture. He stood a few metres away from them, clutching the camera. It was a Nikon D5000 that Jake had bought on his credit card one weekend on a whim, thinking that perhaps his passions lay in photography and that the simple cure to all his unhappiness could be found behind a wide-angled lens. The camera was now gathering dust in the loft, placed guiltily in its original box and stacked on top of a running machine from the eighties and some tennis rackets with broken strings. The runner's chest had risen up and down as he tried to catch his breath. He blinked in the brilliant sunshine. She was glad she'd asked him now, because they had so few photos like this one.

As she studied the picture, her decision was made. She hadn't even expected to make it. She would ask Jake to quit his job in the army when he next came back from leave. She would tell him face-to-face, when he came back on leave, that he had to come home. Because if he didn't, she knew they wouldn't make it.

Six

'Where's dinner?'

Nessa lay in bed, breathing in the heady scent of cabbage and gravy rising from the kitchen downstairs. Her heart thumped in her ribcage. Her limbs were jelly. An anxious, tingling sensation scuttled across the skin on the back of her neck. She was trying to read Mary Shelley's Frankenstein *but was struggling to concentrate. Nessa's Year 6 English teacher had pulled a surprised face when Nessa told her she was reading* Frankenstein. *Mrs McClusky had said it was 'ambitious', before smiling, shaking her head a little, and continuing to write on the blackboard. Right now it certainly felt ambitious, because as well as not being able to focus, her fingers were trembling so much that it was difficult to turn the pages.*

The owl clock on the bedside table said it was nearly 8 p.m. That was when her foster father would come home: always at 8 p.m., never earlier or later. Luckily, after struggling to settle, Kat was fast asleep in the room next door, so she would go another night without hearing anything. Nessa wondered what her little sister might be dreaming about. Perhaps the value biscuits with the cow imprint on the front that they gave her at nursery, or the sheep she was continuously chattering about, after seeing one in a field off the M25. Nessa had heard their foster mother Sue singing to Kat in soothing tones just half an hour ago, but to Nessa it just sounded ominous as the clock creaked its way to 8 p.m. Sometimes, innocent melodies changed when they met her ears. Soft, sweet nursery rhymes, like the kind Kat fell asleep to, became menacing and dissonant, 'something bad is going to happen' music.

The evening had been nice until then. She, Kat and their mother had been together in the kitchen, making a cake. They had hours to enjoy together, so much time in fact that Nessa could momentarily forget what might lie in store later on. She could lose herself in those moments. It had just been the three of them. It was lovely.

Nessa had noticed the change in her mother when her foster dad Tom wasn't around, she looked different in a way, like something had altered inside her, making her even more beautiful. Because of this, Nessa had grown to love it when it was 'just us three'. Sue would sometimes stop whatever she was doing and bury her face in Nessa's neck and take a deep breath in. She would sigh, and say 'my baby girl, you smell divine', with the happiest look on her face.

As soon as the clock hit 8 p.m., the owl's plastic wings flapped the same number of times to indicate the changing hour. Its eyes would also roll around, powered by crunching, wheel and cog mechanics from the early eighties. She'd loved that clock when it had been given to her years ago and, before she'd understood the concept of time, she'd watched it obsessively, hoping for something new to happen.

Nessa heard the key in the front door. Here we go, she thought . . . In the movies she watched, kids would leap up with joy as soon as their dad returned home. They would fling their arms around him, or chat about how their day at school was, but for 11-year-old Nessa, she just wished he wouldn't return. She felt guilty for thinking that, but it was true . . . Sometimes she just wished more than anything that he would stop coming home.

'Where's dinner?'

That was the first question he asked as soon as he got through the door, his loud, deep voice rattling around the ground floor of their one-up-one-down terrace house in East Grinstead. He didn't say hello, or ask how Mum was; there was never a kiss on the cheek. One of the most frustrating things about these nights, the evenings Nessa lay awake listening to the carnage unfold downstairs, was that she could never make out what her mother was saying. Most of her father's cutting words made their way through the drunken fug and up the stairs to her ears: sentences that haunted her the next day at school like 'you wanted these kids, not me' and 'you forced me into it, I never wanted them'. But her mother's voice was softer, and quieter, and so all she had to work on was a muffled hum. When that hum got a little louder, and a little higher pitched, she knew it was really bad.

The arguing started within two minutes. Something about her dad not liking the way her mum was doing the gravy and that he'd told the 'useless bitch a thousand times before'. Cupboard doors were slammed. With each bang, Nessa felt her body react, all the way upstairs. Twitching, wincing and squirming, Nessa sat up in her bed now and started to cry, wiping the tears away with the back of her hand. Hot, runny snot started to pour from her nose. She could do with going to the bathroom to get some tissue, but she sure as hell wouldn't be doing that.

Nessa wished she had a big brother. She was quite jealous of the kids at school who had one. Ideally, Nessa's older brother would be 17 or 18, and he would go boxing, or play basketball, or something like that. He would be tall, strong and protective, and when he walked past her he would ruffle her hair with one hand. And she hoped that one night he would make it stop. He would come home from football practice and walk in to another row, and he finally would show their dad that there was someone bigger and stronger than him in the family. But there was no brother, and at 11, Nessa was the oldest child, older than her sister by nine years. She had no idea what to do.

The shouting got louder, and she could hear her mother weeping. Nessa wondered what her father would do if she called the police; she even imagined what it would be like to creep up behind him and hit him over the head with a pan. She'd seen that kind of thing in the movies: bold acts of violence against the bad guy. He'd probably lose it even more and hurt her really badly. She was scared of that, of what he might be capable of if he really snapped. She told herself so many times that he wouldn't go that far, to hit her, or Kat, or to really, badly hurt their mum. She hoped that he would never go that far but he was so volatile she could never be sure.

Soon enough there was the sound of hitting. Nessa hated the sound of hitting the most. It happened three or four times a month, when the rows were the worst. Nessa listened to the sickening thud of her dad's fist against her mother's skin, and it felt like he was hitting her too, with his own bare hands. There was that strange silence from her mother that terrified her too. Why wasn't she making a sound? Why wasn't she crying out for help? If she did, maybe the neighbours might hear and rescue her . . . Was she OK? And then, after a few more thuds, she'd hear her mother weep – as if she was no longer able to hold it in – before going silent once more.

Whack, whack, whack. Nessa rolled around in her duvet, trying to cover her ears. It was getting louder. The snot continued to drip out of her nose and her eyes hurt where she'd been crying so much. Where was he hitting her, she wondered? Her arms, her legs, her stomach? Did he avoid her face, so the bruises didn't show? Nessa cried, her breathing quickened in her chest and it felt like she was being strangled. Help me . . . help us . . . please someone . . .

Whack . . .

Whack . . .

Whack . . .

'Mum!!!' Nessa cried quietly with a hoarse voice. She was sitting up in bed and had woken with a start. Where was she? She pulled the duvet over her naked body, the air in the room was cold. Nessa gawped round her in the darkness, feeling her own face to remind herself who she was. She had been crying in her sleep, she noticed, wiping her eyes dry. All the heartbreak had come back, that pounding in her chest and those horrendous feelings. She'd almost forgotten how it had felt until she'd revisited her 11-year-old self in her nightmares.

Nessa's eyes were still blurry. She fumbled around for her glasses, a pair of thick framed, tortoiseshell spectacles that were long due for new lenses. She squinted to read her digital clock, that announced it was 4.02 a.m. in bright blue lettering.

Jesus fucking Christ, Nessa whispered to herself, lying down and trying to slow her breathing.

Seven

'I've been thinking a lot lately about the past . . .'

'God, I find this depressing; this mall really is the pits, isn't it? It's where all hopes and dreams come to die . . . Do you know what she even wants for her birthday?' Kat asked, standing in front of a jumper in River Island with various bits and bobs sewn on to it. They had gone to The Glades in Bromley to try and find a gift for Poppy's impending birthday. With her daughter at school, Nessa had taken the day off work. It was also a great opportunity for Nessa to spend time with her sister. She didn't get to see her very often these days.

'Hmmm . . . let me think . . . She wants tickets for her and a friend to see Taylor Swift at the O2 – they're £70 each; she wants a new iPhone – that's about £350, maybe even £400; she wants a pair of trainers from Nike – which, would you believe it, cost £115; oh yeah, and a silver anchor necklace from ASOS that's £45 . . .'

'Jesus,' sighed Kat. She was stunning at just 21-years-old,

with her porcelain skin and dramatic hair, which she had dyed a gorgeous red. She seemed to be getting more and more beautiful as she grew older. Nessa knew that she would be sure to break some hearts, as soon as she actually realised how many men stared at her longingly from a distance.

'Yeah, it's ridiculous. Kat, we can't even really afford the necklace. I mean, we can, at a push, but the other stuff? No way,' Nessa said, looking down at the linoleum floor and shaking her head to herself. 'And, you know, I'd be angry at Poppy for wanting stuff like that, for even asking for it, but her generation has been kind of conditioned to it with people getting into debt and taking out store cards and stuff. Her friends . . . I mean you should hear the kind of things they get for their birthdays: Mac laptops, big parties, their first pair of Jimmy's. I mean, it's absolutely bloody insane. They just don't have a clue—'

'OK, whoa, Ness, you're getting angry . . . Let's go outside, find a cafe and get a coffee and some lunch,' Kat said, linking her sister's arm with her own and marching her out of the shop.

'So, I've been thinking . . .' Kat said, looking up from her mug and directly into Nessa's eyes. Kat's hands were wrapped protectively around her latte. Her nails were painted a mint green, and she wore several intricate rings on her fingers, which caught the bright light of the fish and chip shop. 'I've been thinking a lot lately about the past . . .' she continued, glancing down at the white, plastic surface of the table.

Nessa looked beyond her sister's shoulder; it had started to rain. 'Oh, right? What do you mean? What about the past?' she asked, feeling a tickling sensation in her stomach.

She glanced around the cafe casually, studying the shiny metals chairs and hoping she wouldn't give anything away with her eyes. Nessa didn't want to talk about the past. It was all about the future now.

'When we lived with our first foster parents . . . Tom and Sue, I was obviously very little, too little really to understand what was going on . . .'

Nessa nodded, feeling a little nauseous at the sound of their names. She closed her eyes for a moment and briefly pictured Sue, walking towards her in the park on a summer's day. She was wearing an orange playsuit made of a soft towelling fabric. Her long, slim legs seemed to go on forever. She had an ice cream in her hand, a 99 Flake: Nessa's favourite. She handed it to Nessa and gave her a cuddle.

'And the thing is, it was all quite sudden when we left, if I remember correctly . . .' Kat piped up again, and the imagery was gone.

'We were fostered by them for ages, and then that was it, we just up and left. Obviously, being six meant I didn't really have a clue what was going on . . . But I've been thinking so much about them recently, and what they did for us, you know? It must have been hard.'

'Yeah, I understand that. You're bound to have questions about it. Because she died so suddenly . . .'

'Heart attack . . .' Kat whispered, squinting as if trying to recall the detail of an old memory.

'Yeah, that's why it all moved on so fast . . . Tom just couldn't cope with the loss of her and having us on top of that . . . It was a little disappointing really,' Nessa responded, tucking a wave of her blonde hair behind her ear and biting her lip.

'What do you want?' The women were interrupted by a

harsh voice, which seemed to boom from a place far above them. The waitress had the classic, school dinner lady look, her dark hair was slightly greasy, and her pale face creased as if she'd only just got out of bed.

'Oh, just chips please,' Kat said. Nessa shook her head politely because she didn't want anything now. This conversation just made her feel nauseous; she didn't fancy eating.

The waitress wrote the order on her notepad, before storming away and shouting orders at a small, hairy man in the kitchen who seemed to be very frightened of her. The smell of vinegar tickled Nessa's nose. It made her feel worse.

'What was Sue like? Can you tell me more about her? Was she, like, a good foster mum to us?' Kat had asked, a gentle smile appearing on her face as she asked the question, as if she were reminiscing on something beautiful that she couldn't quite place.

Nessa felt a stab of guilt because Kat *should* know the truth by now. She should know what had really happened. But Nessa knew she had good reason for keeping it hidden. She wanted to make sure her little sister had a happy life. She didn't want Kat to be haunted in the way that she was. She didn't want her to suffer when there was no need for suffering. *She didn't need to know.*

'Go on, tell me about her . . . please,' Kat prodded further, looking nervous.

'Well, she was very beautiful . . . She had wavy brown hair that was normally about shoulder length, dark eyebrows and very glowy skin . . . I think her mother was Spanish and her father Italian, so she had really stunning features,' Nessa said, starting to feel the emotion build inside her heart, images of her foster mother flickering in her mind.

'She really looked after herself, and us, of course. She liked natural things, so she'd do funny things like mash up avocado and put it in her hair, and make face masks from bananas and oats. She had a tiny tattoo of a crescent moon at the bottom of her spine that she was really embarrassed about. She'd had it done as a teenager when she'd got drunk at some festival. I loved that tattoo though. When I was little, I thought that it was a sign she was capable of magic or something . . .' Nessa had said, trailing off.

'And what else?' Kat pleaded, sitting upright in her seat. There was a look of hope and excitement in her eyes. A huge plate of chips was slammed down on the table seconds later, but the two were so engrossed in their conversation that they didn't even acknowledge them.

'Salt. Vinegar,' the woman said flatly, banging the bottles down on the table and storming off.

'Well, she was really funny about us eating lots of vegetables and fruit every day. I used to cry when she put broccoli on the plate, each and every time, but I love it now, as you know. You used to hide your carrots in the pocket of your school coat; she wasn't very happy about that . . . Mum could sing, or least I thought she could at the time. She had a lovely voice, and she used to sing tunes from the old Disney movies to you when you were just a baby. We found that her slowed-down version of "Everybody Wants to be a Cat" from the *Aristocats* worked pretty well with you; it always got you off to sleep. I did the "rinky tinky tinky" bit . . .' Nessa said, reaching out and squeezing her little sister's hand. Nessa watched as a great big tear brimmed in her sister's left eye, and dropped down the soft, clear skin of her cheek.

'I'm sorry . . . This is embarrassing. I don't know why I feel this way, and why I'm so emotional. I didn't think about it for ages, and now it's like it's all I think about. I've just got so many questions, you know?' Kat said, wiping her face with the back of one of her hands self-consciously. Nessa noticed that the hand she was holding was trembling.

'It's OK,' Nessa said quietly.

'Keep talking to me about her . . . please? What music did she like?'

'Hmm, she liked Joni Mitchell, and Eva Cassidy, and she also loved Madonna . . . Oh and Prince too. Yes, she loved Prince . . . She used to play some of those songs after school in the kitchen when we'd made cupcakes together; we did that quite a lot, it's a wonder we didn't get chubby . . . She was very emotional and warm, always weeping at stuff . . . She cried at Cilla Black's *Surprise Surprise*, and the first time you sang 'Ba Ba Black Sheep'. She loved to cuddle us and stroke our hair . . . Oh, do you remember what she used to do with our eyelashes?' Nessa asked, clasping her hands together with happiness. Kat shook her head, her eyebrows bunched into a position of curiosity.

'If we ever fell asleep on her lap on a Saturday afternoon while watching TV, she'd sort of stroke our eyelashes upwards with her little finger, and then she'd trace her finger over our eyebrows and say how soft they were,' Nessa said, looking out of the window again, 'I loved how that felt. I'll never forget it.'

The rain was pouring now. An elderly woman walked past the window of the cafe, stooped over a tartan, rectangular trolley. Nessa couldn't help but feel a little sorry for her . . . A plastic hat protected her hair from the springtime elements, while miniature streams of rainwater dribbled down the fabric of her mac. Two schoolboys cycled past, their PE bags slung over their shoulders and their bodies angled towards the pavement on one side of the bike. They weaved between the people ambling along the wet pavements, seemingly unfazed by the rain.

'I don't remember anything about Tom really. I struggle to have any memories of him at all. Was he not around very much?' Kat asked, trying to compose herself, and biting down on a chip. Steam rose from Kat's mouth where the piping hot potato had been broken in the middle.

'Tom, he kind of worked a lot. He was one of those guys who worked really long days and then went straight to the pub afterwards, you know? He was a fairly quiet man . . . He kept himself to himself, didn't say much. I guess he wasn't as warm and emotional as Mum was . . . He was loving, of course, but he was, erm, he was, different,' Nessa said, feeling the hairs on her arms stand up on end. She couldn't believe how easily the lies just slipped from her mouth. He was a *fairly quiet* man, he was *loving, of course*. The things she was saying to fictionalise reality.

'Oh, right. I wonder how he's doing now. He must miss her. It must have been very hard on him, losing his wife like that . . . I find it weird that he just moved away and never left contact details for us . . .' Kat said, reaching for another chip. Nessa suddenly felt a flash of concern that perhaps Kat knew more than she'd realised and was calling her bluff . . . But then again, she wasn't the type to play games like that.

'Yeah. It is weird. I think it was very difficult; I guess he just needed to start again and not be reminded of her . . . We must have reminded him of her because she loved us very much,' Nessa said, her heart thumping in her chest at the thought of him. How his breath would smell of ethanol, the banging of his great heavy steps in the hallway while Kat was fast asleep beneath a wooden mobile. The sound of hitting . . .

Whack . . .

Whack . . .

Whack . . .

Eight

'It's a rite of passage. She'll survive . . .'

The annual barn dance had come round again. Nessa, Jake and Poppy had been invited to the 150-year-old tradition on Will Turnbull's tree-lined road every single year.

Jake couldn't always make it, because he was often on tour, but Nessa and Poppy didn't miss it for the world. Each and every year: until this one. Poppy had decided, dramatically, that it was too embarrassing a tradition to be a part of. Poppy had, for the first time ever, shunned the invitation, choosing to stay at a friend's house and watch cult movies from the eighties (Nessa had no idea where this latest trend had come from).

Nessa felt a pang of sadness that this day had finally come, although she had been half expecting it. Last year had been pretty dire. Poppy had reluctantly come along, but spent most of the evening sitting in the darkest corner, scowling and texting her mates. The previous year she'd run off with someone's bottle of Jack Daniel's and managed to glug so much of the stuff, in such a short space of time, she had been taken home projectile vomiting. She almost had to go to hospital. It was absolutely terrifying.

In previous years it had been such a special event for the family. Nessa had had flashbacks of all the times she'd taken Poppy as a little girl. Poppy had been so excited she would chatter about the barn dance on the way home from school for at least a month beforehand. She missed seeing Poppy spinning round and jumping in the air, with a smile on her face revealing her gappy, white teeth. She missed carrying an exhausted, fast asleep Poppy out of the car when they got home and tucking her up in bed.

On the occasions that Jake had come along too, he and Will had gone wild together. It was Jake's one big night of abandon. One year they drank themselves silly before dancing with each other quite violently, and managing to knock someone over like a skittle in the process. They ended up lying on the gravel on their backs, crying with laughter. The stars had glittered above them, shrouded by the smog of the city that blurred Beckenham's sky at the edges like a vignette.

Nessa kind of understood where her daughter was coming from. It was all very cheesy, and it certainly wasn't a night to be taken seriously, but the beauty of getting older was that you no longer suffered the crippling self-consciousness that made smiling, dancing in circles and holding hands with strangers a problem. So this year, it was just Nessa attending the barn dance on her own. It dawned on Nessa that, for the first time in ages, she would be able to let her hair down and have some fun.

Jake was coming home in just three weeks. *Three weeks!*

She felt like she did when she first started to date Jake, like she felt as a teenager: totally, head-over-heels in love and dizzy with excitement. Her stomach tickled at the thought of it all as she got ready to go out. She felt happy for the first time in ages. Tonight would be a good night. The sunlight had cast Beckenham in a golden, romantic glow. Teenage boys walked around in groups, couples in their thirties and forties made their way into town for romantic meals wearing posh blazers and expensive dresses. The air was buzzing with Saturday night promise; excitement rushed through the breeze.

As soon as Nessa turned into Will's road she instantly recognised the decorations that had been used over the years. Handmade bunting was strung from house to house, featuring triangles of clashing fabric in block colours and floral patterns. A couple of them looked a little raggedy now. Nessa remembered that the year before, a pit bull terrier had managed to pull one of the strings of bunting down, before chewing it up gratuitously. Children ran around trying to keep balloons in the air, and dogs chased cats over lawns. The road was closed to cars for the night and had been taken over by tents, marquees and overly complex foldable furniture. Each and every house had its own section where residents and their guests could sit and, if Nessa remembered correctly, competition for space and the best pitch was fierce.

Nessa spotted Will almost straight away, hunched over a bowl of quinoa salad. He was perfecting his dish with such precision he may as well have had a pair of tweezers and a magnifying glass.

'Determined to win the bloody salad competition aren't you?' Nessa said as she walked up next to him and put a bag on the fold-out table. A few candles were scattered around, waiting to be lit. Two bottles of Sauvignon Blanc in Nessa's bag clunked against each other loudly as she set it down. A woman nearby glanced at her judgmentally.

'Oh, Nessa, come here you,' Will said, standing up suddenly and giving her a hug. He smelt of his usual expensive aftershave, some scent from Jo Malone she'd spotted in his bathroom once; ginger, pomegranate and essence of Malaysian flamingo or something.

'Where's your delightful daughter?' Will asked, turning back now to the salad. The quinoa glinted in the early evening sunlight. It was glazed with a thin layer of extra virgin olive oil, and interspersed with thick chunks of avocado and fluffy squares of feta cheese.

'Oh, the spell has broken I'm afraid; she's truly become a teenager . . . She informed me this morning that she cannot come to this year's barn dance because apparently it's "far too uncool",' Nessa said, crossing her arms and raising her eyebrows.

'Well, I suppose it's a bit of a relief really, isn't it, Ness? You don't have to worry about her nicking someone's booze and drinking herself into a stupor, do you? You can just have fun,' he said cheekily, giving her a wink.

'In fact, Nessa, this year you can be the one drinking yourself into a stupor,' he added, reaching towards his bowl of salad and moving it around a bit to work out the best angle.

'Yeah, she'll be back when she's turned 18 and has got over herself. I just bloody hope she's not up to no good somewhere else . . .' Nessa trailed off.

'We all did it Nessa. It's a rite of passage. She'll survive . . . How else do you learn how to handle your booze, when you're not in some field somewhere, with your mates, drinking neat vodka from the cap? Now, do you think I'm going to win the salad contest with this beauty or not?' Will asked, glaring at his offering with immense pride. He wedged a thick wooden spoon into the side of his great salady mountain. It wobbled temptingly in response.

'Well, let's take it over and check out the competition, shall we?' Nessa asked, picking it up gently and making off in the direction of the barbecue. Will walked around her nervously, like he was concerned she might trip on a pot hole and drop it.

They made their way over to the salad bar successfully. It was less of a bar and more of a small ship. A huge fold-out table with metal legs strained visibly beneath the weight of 30 or so huge dishes overflowing with middle-class pride. The centre of the table bowed slightly. Nessa had never realised until this moment how many types of salad there were. Things were no doubt becoming increasingly competitive as the years wore on. The residents of Elm Road had well and truly upped the ante this time. Just five or six barn dances ago, the most daring family were the Jacksons from number 23, and they had only whipped up a potato salad and some anaemic-looking coleslaw. But now things had really changed, she thought, as she scanned the bowls wondering if everyone had gone a little bit bonkers.

Quinoa was the tip of the iceberg lettuce this year and Nessa suddenly feared for Will's chances. There were Moroccan-spiced courgettes nestled sleepily in piles of cracked bulgar wheat. Varying Niçoise offerings tempted the tongue with fragrant pole-and-line-caught tuna lovingly cuddling some plump, boiled eggs. A mixed vegetable salad *a la Grecque* sat proudly between a herring Waldorf and a pile of juicy peaches, wrapped seductively in strips of Parma ham. Butternut squash, pomegranate seeds and sweet potatoes ignited together, in an explosion of culinary colour. There were leaves and pulses and wheats and fruits, and more vegetables than you could shake a silicone spoon at. It was overwhelmingly, ridiculously decadent, and so typical of the people living on Will's road, in their polished, seven-bedroom houses and winding gravel driveways. Nessa was secretly tickled by it all. It was like another universe.

'Oh shit. They've screwed me, they really have. The bastards!' Will exclaimed, staring at the salads. A little boy standing nearby giggled excitedly at Will's swearing, and ran off towards his parents, who were sat under their own tent, guzzling red wine and olives.

'No, Will, come on, yours looks amazing!' Nessa said, with one hand on his shoulder.

'But quinoa is a bit 2010 isn't it?! What was I thinking? Shit, this is almost as bad as the year when I brought couscous,' he exclaimed sadly.

'Come on, let's just put it down and go for a drink, shall we?' Nessa said.

Nessa glanced over at this year's salad competition 'judge' – well, every year's judge – Mr Richard Tomlinson, QC: an elderly man with an eccentric dress sense. Bow ties and coloured cords must have filled his wardrobe in every possible shade. He was a former barrister by profession and the whole road seemed to revolve around him, like he was the mighty sun. People went to this wise old grasshopper for advice about everything from teething tots to broken sheds. At each barn dance, at precisely 7.30 p.m., he would hobble around the table having a taste of each and every salad with a different plastic spoon, so as not to contaminate any of the dishes with his own germs and the flavours of other dishes. It absolutely *had* to be a fair test. God forbid the overpowering flavour of a chunk of mango impair the experience of an Ottolenghi-inspired freekeh pilaff. He even wore white gloves for hygiene reasons. He would write notes on each composition – his weapon, the mighty clipboard. All the residents would watch on quietly as he carried out the tasting, trying to ascertain his innermost thoughts in the occasional twitch of his moustache, the soft rise of a grey, wiry eyebrow.

What did it mean when he grunted? What was he thinking when he shuffled around from one foot to another, masticating like an old camel? The tension was always palpable. Straight after the judging, it would be time to eat. Dozens of people would flock to the barbecue to pick up slabs of sizzling, marinated meat, and sticks driven through chunks of halloumi cheese and green pepper, before diving spoon first into the salad bar, desecrating the artworks in just 15 minutes. Then, at precisely 9.30 p.m., Mr Tomlinson would announce the winner of the salad competition by hobbling up onto the stage and speaking into the microphone. The prize was a medal. Nessa could see him now, preparing to start the judging process. He sat on a chair regally, clutching hold of a walking stick with his wrinkly left hand. His petite wife Barbara adjusted his tie and smiled proudly.

As Nessa and Will went to sit down at their own table, the barn dance band pulled up. Five ageing musicians swaggered out of their minivan, ready for another evening of plucking guitar strings and teaching uncoordinated drunks how to do the 'Reel of Ballymore'. They were grey-haired wilting rock stars, with children and grandchildren and their own holiday caravans on the Cornish coast. They wore shredded denim jackets, vintage leather coats and jeans with holes in the knees, exposing wrinkly, pale skin.

Rogue earrings were shoved through sagging earlobes. They creaked when they walked. The band lugged various bits of equipment out of the vehicle, carrying heavy items, like speakers, in pairs. They staggered across the gravel towards a makeshift stage, avoiding the little children who ran, played and quarrelled at their ankles. Wires and cables were draped over their shoulders.

Nessa and Will watched them set up. 'How's things going with girlfriend number 25 of the year?' Nessa asked casually.

'Oh don't tease, Nessa. It's OK . . . I mean things started off well but—'

'You didn't like the way she ate, or she pulled a funny face when she slept, or she didn't know the difference between fresh ground coffee and instant.'

'Nessa! Crikey, I'm not that bad, am I?' Will asked, as Nessa shook her head and laughed. 'No, it's nothing like that,' he continued. 'It's just, she's a bit high maintenance. And she wants to change me. Not a little bit, but a lot. It's like this kind of encroaching regime. It started off small at first. She started making me drink more water, then she was trying to get me to stop smoking; she nags me about how much wine I drink, and oh, yes, she's bought me an entire wardrobe of new clothes, a subscription to yoga classes at my local gym, and she's started ordering these boxes of nuts and vegetables to be delivered to my door every week. They just started arriving. I mean, what next? I don't even like nuts!'

'Maybe she just cares about you, Will. She probably just wants the best for you,' Nessa said, tilting her head to one side and smiling.

'I get that, but I just want someone who likes me as I am, you know? Messy, smoky, boozy Will who hates the gym and would rather die than spend the afternoon trying on shirts in Harrods. Know what I mean?'

Nessa nodded. She glanced at the floor.

'Are things OK?' Will probed, topping up Nessa's glass with some more white wine. 'How's Jake? Have you heard from him recently?'

'Yeah, well, I mean things are tough but it's fine. I hear from Jake every now and then on the phone, and he sends me stuff through the post. I'm really worried about, Poppy though. She seems to be going absolutely nuts. I'm wondering what I'm doing wrong . . .' Nessa trailed off, taking a sip of her wine and suddenly feeling a little emotional.

Will nodded gently as a chain of fairy lights was switched on, illuminating the friends in a soft glow. Stevie Wonder started pumping out of nearby speakers, a little too loud at first and it made him jump.

'But we are all difficult when we are young aren't we? I mean, god, I smoked enough weed to make Snoop Dogg, or Snoop Lion or whateverthefuck he calls himself now, positively sick. But I turned out alright . . . I think . . .' Will said, shrugging. 'All young people, well at least the ones that grow up to be vaguely interesting adults, get pissed, and take drugs and do silly things. It can't be any worse than that, can it? And she will get over it, she really will . . . She's just testing the limits, learning about herself and the world.'

Nessa took a deep breath and pawed at the tablecloth with her fingertips. She knew he was right but she was terrified.

'She was caught shoplifting in Hotwire the other week. She tried to steal £115 worth of clothes and then later that night, she proceeded to tell me that I was a failure,' Nessa said, looking up at Will and scratching the side of her neck.

'Christ . . .' he said, bunching his eyebrows together in thought and pulling his hands up to his lips as if in prayer. He seemed momentarily lost in thought.

'I don't know whether to tell Jake how bad things are. He hardly ever sees Poppy, but I don't want the rare times he is home to be tainted by this shit, because then he won't spend happy, quality time with her and I think one of the reasons she's so messed up in the first place is because he is away. And yet if I don't get his help then I am keeping secrets from him, and by default I am parenting alone . . . I just want him to come home,' she said, feeling tearful. She wondered if she should tell him what she was planning to ask Jake, but for some strange reason she decided not to. She couldn't cope with that discussion right now.

'And how's Mick?' he asked, leaning forwards now as he spoke to her. His strong, straight nose was angled towards her.

'Oh god, it's just like a perpetual nightmare. He went missing the other day. He had let himself out of the house and he was found four hours later wandering around Beckenham Place Park in his underpants,' Nessa said, shaking her head softly.

Will lifted his foldable chair up a few inches in the air and shuffled over next to Nessa. He put a strong arm around her and pressed his face against the soft skin of her forehead. He smelt good, and his stubble dug gently into her face. Nessa's ashen blonde hair fell across his shirt. While she was trying so desperately hard not to cry, it hit her how good it felt to be cuddled by a man like this, to be touched – for someone to show her affection. She was shocked by how it made her light up inside.

It made her momentarily ashamed.

She wriggled out of Will's grasp and stood up quickly. She thought she spotted him blush a soft pink, before lighting a cigarette and walking over to the bar with her.

Nine
'Erm, there's a TV in the sitting room'

The night had warped into a drunken candlelit blur. All the troubles of Will and Nessa's lives seemed to spin away from them as they danced hand in hand under the moonlight. Violinists played country music and the long-haired MC tried, in vain, to get 150 people to do the right steps, in the right ways, at the same time. Nessa linked arms with everyone: elderly ladies who she had to be gentle with because it felt like they might break; little children who she had to stoop down for; strong, young men who almost pulled her off her feet. She felt carefree, for just a short while. This was what she needed. To not have to think too much. She always thought too much . . .

She was really starting to feel the effects of the alcohol now, and the dancing had made her hot.

'Isn't this just one of the best nights? I know it's cheesy as hell, but I love it!' Will cried, as they dashed through two lines of people, all smiling and clapping as they went.

Nessa didn't know what she would have done without Will all these years. And now Jake would be coming home in a short while and she would have him back in her life again. It was going to be wonderful. The thought of it made her so happy, she became a little overwhelmed. Feeling tearful, and dizzy from the wine and the dancing, Nessa gestured at Will, mimicking the action of lifting a glass to her lips and pointing at his house with her free hand. Will nodded, grabbing the hand of an attractive woman in her mid-forties, and spinning her away in the dust of the unmade road.

The music started to fade behind her as Nessa approached Will's garden gate, which had recently been given a lick of creosote. She could smell the sharp tang of it radiating from the dark brown wood. Soon, the sounds of the band were just off-beat thuds in the near distance. She pushed open the gate and made her way into Will's back garden. It was beautifully landscaped, with lights dotted around the paths and illuminating a water feature. The road Will lived on was unusual in that everyone trusted everyone. He had, naturally, left his back door unlocked during the barn dance, and she just let herself in, something she thought was sheer madness, though the element of trust in the neighbourhood had to be admired.

Nessa took her shoes off at the door, and padded into the kitchen where she could hear chattering. A few of Will's friends and neighbours were gathered there, eating sausages on sticks and helping themselves to more wine. Nessa quietly wished they weren't there – she could have done with a few moments of peace. A couple of them acknowledged her with a gentle nod and she smiled back, hoping to avoid making small talk with them: she couldn't be bothered with it these days.

Will had recently had his kitchen refitted and it was

pretty impressive. Nessa, slightly tipsy from the wine, turned around slowly as she walked through the room, past a couple of people gathered by the fridge. She imagined what it might be like to have a kitchen like that herself: all high gloss surfaces, exposed wood and steel. Rustic-style artefacts accented parts of the room, so it almost resembled a Jamie Oliver restaurant. *Absolutely beautiful*, she thought. Jake and she would never have a life like this. It would always be a struggle, she thought . . .

Nessa made her way over to the sink so she could get a glass of water. She sat down at the breakfast bar for a moment or two to catch her breath, while the mundane conversation around her flowed as easily as the wine. Will had left a small TV on. It was screwed flush against the wall. The sound was off and it was showing *Sky News*. Nessa was barely paying any attention to the scrolling words that ran across the bottom of the screen, struggling to concentrate amid all the different voices. *I should turn the TV off*, she thought, looking around for the control. *No one's watching it*. But as she went to switch it off, Nessa saw the words scrolling across the screen on the news ticker, in thick, white lettering.

4 British soldiers killed in Afghanistan

Nessa felt the booze drain from her blood. She was thrown back into reality, far from the fuzzy joy she'd felt in the previous hours of the evening . . . Nessa turned on the sound and upped the volume. So much so that the people around her stopped what they were doing and stared, disbelief on their faces. A couple of them said things like 'excuse me?' and 'do you mind?', but Nessa ignored them. They sounded terribly far away.

She concentrated on the screen. A woman in a navy blue suit with a brown glossy bob spoke solemnly to the camera.

'Erm, there's a TV in the sitting room,' one of the women said impatiently, walking away from her group of friends now and tapping Nessa urgently on the shoulder, as if trying to wake her from a trance.

'Please, just be quiet, please,' Nessa said, irritably brushing the woman's hand away, desperately trying to listen.

She set her glass down on the table; it clattered against the surface because her hands were shaking uncontrollably.

'And news just in. Four British soldiers have been killed and three seriously injured in Afghanistan in the early hours of this evening. The first reports are saying that the men were hit by a bomb blast in Helmand Province. More as we get it . . .' the anchorwoman said darkly, before shuffling some papers before her.

Helmand Province. That was where Jake was. He was leading patrols . . .

Nessa's stomach flipped. She felt sick. She sat there quietly for a few moments, trying to digest the news. There was a relatively high chance it didn't involve him. But, at the same time, it could. It *might* . . . He was so close to coming home. Nessa felt irrationally, overwhelmingly anxious. She'd had to deal with this before, many times, but at this moment in time she felt completely out of control.

'Are you OK?' the woman asked, walking closer to her. She smelt of an overpowering perfume, the scent bitter and almost offensive. Nessa turned around to look at the lady. Her eyes landed on a string of pearls around her neck and a pink pair of spectacles. The lady looked baffled and almost slightly frightened of her.

'Nessa! I reckon it's time to crack open the champagne!

I'm going to go down to the cellar . . .' Will yelled, having flung himself into the kitchen excitably, seemingly oblivious to the awkwardness unfolding in his kitchen.

'Oh my god, just leave me alone!' Nessa screamed, turning back to the lady, who panicked and took a few steps back into the arms of her husband, who looked outraged. Nessa immediately started to hyperventilate. It felt as if the walls of the kitchen were slanting away from her, as if she were at the top of a tall building, terrified of falling. Fused to the spot with terror, her vision started to blur.

'Nessa, what the hell is going on?' Will asked, finally looking up from his back doormat where he had been wiping his dusty trainers, his voice trembling with concern. The room was silent, and everyone was staring at her.

Nessa pointed up at the screen, her hand was shaking violently. 'I'm just, I'm sorry, I'm having a panic attack . . .' she said, hoping everyone would leave and stop gawping at her.

Will slowly looked up, his face turning to an expression of dismay.

#25

It had rained on their wedding day.

Nessa had been to a few weddings by this point. A dull and distant cousin from her second foster family (with a face as bland as a dinner plate), a pregnant friend from school and a chatty colleague had all invited her to watch them foolishly pay between £15,000 and £30,000 to dedicate their lives to someone else. At the time, the whole point of it had been lost on Nessa. She thought it was bloody stupid. She'd hated the bitchy distant relatives; how horrendously drunk people got; the horrible, mass-produced, gelatine-based desserts that wobbled reliably to the beat of some horrific sixties cover group.

So it had surprised her that she became so wrapped-up in it all when Jake had got down on one knee. The whole tide of wedding-related crap had well and truly swept her away.

On the day of each wedding she had attended, even when the weather had wavered precariously between bright skies and moody showers, the sun had always popped out at a convenient point, as if to say 'only teasing!' It had emerged from behind a grey cloud just before the service and stayed there until the photos had been taken and the lawns had been swept for discarded cigarette butts and plastic champagne flutes. *Lucky bastards*, she always found herself thinking, gazing into the distance while the pomp and circumstance unfolded nearby.

But that hadn't been the case for her and Jake, she thought to herself, looking down at the latest photo to arrive through the letterbox. Jake must have sent it just before the blast, she reflected. She felt a fresh wave of coldness run through her body at the thought that this could have been the last picture he sent to her.

In the photo, she and Jake were standing outside the church, in the rain. Nessa was stood side on, with both hands on Jake's chest. Jake was holding her waist, pulling her close to him and gazing at her face. She was just 24 years old at the time. It was, by her own admission, an absolutely stunning photograph. An act of madness captured in the shutter of a camera. Her friends had said, with honesty, that it was the most beautiful and romantic wedding photo they had ever seen . . . Nessa had remembered that very moment; it all came rushing back. A lump formed in her throat just thinking about it.

They had walked towards the exit of the church

hand-in-hand after saying their vows. They were still protected from the elements thanks to a worn brick entrance that stood tall and imposing, like an overprotective father. Two huge flower arrangements blocked them from the gusts of wind that waited outside like quarrelling siblings, shoving each other about and ruffling their wintry fingers through carefully styled hair. Nessa was still wiping happy tears from her cheeks, her ivory lace dress trailing behind her, swept over the tiles. She couldn't believe she was married. Mrs Bruce. She finally belonged somewhere, and to someone.

Jake had pulled her close and whispered something in her ear.

'Come into the rain with me,' he had said excitably, holding both of Nessa's hands, before looking out at their adoring friends and family members. There were 50 of them gathering outside, impatiently clutching umbrellas and holding onto soggy palmfuls of confetti. Cracked, dry, spray-tanned knees were bent inwards in the cold. Heels clacked against the ground as women shifted from one foot to the other impatiently. Looks of gentle irritation were flashing across made-up features, as guests tried to smile at the same time as being rained on. More members of the congregation were reluctantly filing out of the church and walking towards the car park, their heads ducked towards the ground, readying themselves to cheer the happy couple as they left the church.

Nessa remembered staring into Jake's dark brown eyes as he asked this, and for a moment it was just them. Everything else faded away. He looked like he had as a lad, daring her to do something silly, like jump into a lake or play knock-down ginger on the door of the grumpy old man down the road who smelt of sour milk and TCP.

She couldn't believe he was asking this. It had been *such* a struggle to stay dry on the way to the church. Her second foster dad had tried his best to keep her away from the rain by running beside her with a broken golf brolly on their way to the car. Her bridesmaids had touched-up her makeup and fixed her hair, and reassured her that her wedding would be just fantastic even though the clouds were taking a giant piss on it. There was lots of whispering, and rushing and fussing, and people had done everything they could to stop Nessa thinking that the weather was some kind of bad omen. And now Jake, the man she had tried to look so beautiful for, was asking her to stand in the rain on her wedding day.

'Have you lost your bloody mind?' Nessa whispered, in earshot of the vicar, who cleared his throat and ducked away from them, as if the word had taken the shape of an angry wasp, heading straight for his ear.

'God, sorry,' she said in his direction, before softly hitting her forehead in frustration with the palm of her hand. 'Jesus!' she cried, 'I mean, sorry.' The vicar was, by this point, blushing with anger.

Jake started to snigger at Nessa's social ineptitude. 'Oh come on, Nessa. This is the most wonderful time of our lives, and, as far as I'm aware, we are the only couple we know to be unfortunate enough to have rain on our wedding day, but we are *still* having the best time aren't we . . .? I love you Nessa Bruce and it doesn't matter if it rains,' he added, kissing her forehead.

'Don't you think we'd be happier and have a much nicer time if we stopped fussing over a little bad weather?' he continued.

'Oh, come on you two!' one of Jake's friends yelled from outside. He was smoking a cigarette and trying to cup it with his hand to stop the weather from putting it out.

Mick walked up to them and offered them another umbrella. Betsy stood beside him, grinning expectantly, holding her own small rain guard, her purple, feathered fascinator trembling in the breeze.

'Fucking hurry up!' pleaded another guest, as the rain started to audibly rush down a nearby gutter.

'Nessa, life is full of rain, and if we can stand out there and just get on with it, together, and still make it good, then we will be fine. No matter what happens,' he said, holding her hands up towards his handsome face and softly kissing the knuckles of her left hand. It was very difficult to say no to him.

'Ergh, that was cheesy. Sorry!' Jake said, laughing to himself and looking down at her slender fingers.

Nessa took a deep breath and smiled mischievously. She turned towards Mick.

'No thanks, Mick, we are OK without the umbrella, thank you,' she said, before turning towards the damp day and stepping out into the light with her new husband.

The water came hard and fast. It wasn't the kind of shower that peppered you lightly. These raindrops were thick, heavy blobs of liquid. They ran down her nose, mixing with her dried happy tears and making her lips taste of salt. Nessa's carefully styled hair sprang out in moist, gorgeous tendrils around her face. Jake had said she looked even more beautiful this way. The rain raced down his cheeks. Tiny pieces of confetti were dragged down to the ground by the wind. A few pieces were stuck to Jake's ears.

Hearts.

Horseshoes.

Stars.

It was more wonderful than Nessa could have ever hoped it to be.

The party had been fantastic. Will tripped over the PA system and broke his arm, and Nessa's friend Lilly had started dancing on the tables, making great Aunt Philomena laugh so hard that her false teeth shot out and landed in the wedding cake. It was as chaotic and silly and drunken as a truly joyful wedding day should be.

Now, Nessa was glad it had poured it down on her wedding day, because the smell of wet lawns always reminded her of Jake, and the rain could never really be a bad thing ever again.

Ten

'Oh goodness . . . Is there anything that we can do?'

Officer Christine Wilmer, the Bruce family rep from the Army Welfare Service, had rung Nessa back, after she had called, frantically asking if her husband was OK. Officer Wilmer had reassured them that she was doing everything she could to find out exactly what had happened, but didn't have any specific information at that moment.

Nessa and Poppy had been gathered in Betsy and Mick's kitchen. They were drinking tea from mismatched mugs and staring into space. Nessa was hungover. Her head hurt from the crying too. The cigarette smoke that danced in the air made her feel sick.

She had stayed on Will's sofa, and all night she had grieved for Jake, before she even knew whether or not he was OK. It struck her that perhaps it wasn't the first time she had grieved for him, because the feeling was shockingly familiar . . . She had felt the same way when he left for the army. She had felt the same way when a vague news report eight months ago had mentioned the loss of British soldiers, although they hadn't been relevant to the province he was in. It was nothing new. In a way she felt she had wildly overreacted, but she just couldn't help it . . . The thought that he could be hurt, or dead, was absolutely unbearable. And the wait was like a living hell, each minute trickling like thick, sticky treacle.

Mick was quite well that day, strangely enough. He was organising old books into alphabetic order by author surname, whistling as he did so and listening to The Isley Brothers on his record player. That morning when he had awoken, he had crossed the bedroom to Betsy's single bed and had softly kissed her face and told her that he loved her. A rare moment of tenderness; her husband was back. Betsy had been awake for most of the night as he slept soundly, worrying because she too had heard the news, but she'd not said a word to anyone.

As Nessa's mobile phone had started to ring, Betsy had come in from next door like a shot. She was holding a small pile of freshly washed towels. They were neatly folded and in size order, with the largest at the bottom and a small face towel folded into a perfect square and perched on top. These were the ways that Betsy could have order in a life full of chaos.

Betsy was putting on her default 'brave face', like always.

Nessa's voice had audibly wavered when she answered the phone. Officer Wilmer had a warm, soothing voice, like honey, but she couldn't get the words out fast enough. Nessa almost wanted to scream at her, to beg for information, to know whether or not the love of her life was still alive. There was no time for 'how are you?' and 'fine thanks'. Poppy and Betsy had stared at her, their eyes wide as saucers.

'Hmm,' Nessa said, in response to the vaguely audible voice, squeaking down the line. The clock ticked loudly. The sound of birds chirping outside could be heard through the open kitchen window. Rocco the cat swaggered confidently into the kitchen, his tail curling in the air and forming a giant, fluffy question mark.

'Right . . . yes . . .'

They tried to work out what was going on from her voice and the tone of it. The confusing expressions on her face wavered between one feeling and another in a matter of milliseconds, and it was virtually impossible to guess what was being said.

'I see . . .' Nessa had raised one hand to her face suddenly. There was a sadness in her voice.

Poppy started to cry. Betsy put her arm around her, and squeezed her tight. Poppy tucked herself against her grandmother's chest and wept into her sharp shoulder bone.

'Oh goodness . . . Is there anything that we can do?' Nessa continued, running her hand over her head and turning to face the garden. Betsy and Poppy stared at the back of Nessa, a slender silhouette cast in blackness in contrast to the bright sunshine beyond her.

Nessa had eventually come off the phone after what felt like forever. She sat at the table, looking down at the floor as she did so. Her wooden chair creaked. Nessa's whole body was trembling softly from the adrenaline teaming through her veins.

'Jake's alive,' she said softly. Poppy breathed out hard and almost folded inwards with relief. Betsy raised a hand to her face and wiped a tear away from her wrinkled skin, finally unable to hold in her emotions.

'But. He's not in a good way . . .'

'What's happened?' Betsy asked desperately.

The sound of Mick's record player could be heard faintly from the room next door. He had sung a line, a lovely timbre in his voice. It was astonishing how he could remember the words to songs from decades ago, but conversations had in the past week or so would usually be gone forever.

'It seems to be the case that there was an improvised explosive device that went off when he was leading his men on patrol. He had spotted something that looked vaguely suspicious, but didn't have the time to check it out because something else was demanding his attention . . .' Nessa trailed off, trying to compose herself.

'He walked past it himself first, and led his men on. It went off, killing his men and injuring some civilians nearby, including two children. Jake was blown to the floor from the impact of the blast, and has suffered some minor injuries, but he will be OK, physically . . .'

Nessa watched Betsy and Poppy, taking it all in.

'He is understandably extremely distressed by what has happened. Christine said he is in a very bad way emotionally. Those men, as you know, were not just his colleagues, but his friends,' she said, picking up her cup and trying to drink from it. She was shaking so much she had to put it back down on the table. 'We are really going to have to pull together and support him when he gets home . . .' she continued. Betsy nodded seriously.

'More than ever, OK, Poppy?' she said, looking towards her daughter, who had her face buried in her hands. She emerged from them and nodded too in understanding.

They were interrupted by Mick who stood at the doorway with a wide grin on his face. A slouchy V-neck knitted vest was layered on top of a brown, checked shirt with short sleeves. He wore a pair of sand-coloured summer shorts. Rocco had followed him lovingly, and stood by his slippers, licking at a tiny, soft paw contentedly.

'Betsy, did I ever tell you about the time when I was a young lad and I played the piano in the Royal Albert Hall to hundreds of people?' Mick asked, with one finger in the air, as if he'd had an idea.

'Yes, darling, you did,' she said, smiling now. 'It was wonderful.'

'I want to tell you again. I've got some photos. I want to tell the cleaner lady too,' he said, pointing at Poppy.

Poppy blinked, and smiled softly. There was a moment or two of silence, and Rocco rolled onto his back like a dog, his legs in the air, expecting a tummy rub.

'Will you all please come into the living room, so I can tell you . . .?' he asked, gesturing towards the hallway.

'I've got photos. Come on, hurry up!' he said, excitedly, before charging off in the direction of the room next door.

Eleven

'I just wanted to hear your voice'

The phone rang.

'Jake? Jake . . . Is that you Jake?'

'Yes, yes . . . it's me . . . Oh, Nessa. How are—'

'Oh, Jake, it's so good to—'

'Sorry, Ness . . .'

'No, Jake, you speak first . . .'

'No, I just . . . I haven't got long on the phone. I just wanted to hear your voice.'

'OK, well here I am . . . I love you Jake. *So much* . . .'

'You too, Nessa. How's Pops?'

'She's good, oh she's wonderful. Everything is fine here. She absolutely cannot wait for you to come home. Me too, Jake, we love you so much. It's been so, so—'

'Hey Nessa, don't . . . don't cry . . . It won't be long now.'

'You have no idea how it's making me feel to hear your voice, Jake. It's hard without you, and with what's happened to you recently, I just worry so much. I thought you were . . . I thought you'd been hurt. I love you. We are going to take care of you when you come home . . . I promise . . .'

'Thanks . . .'

'We are going to make lovely food together, and go for walks in Knole Park, and feed the deer carrots, and take your mum and dad to the seaside . . . Everything will be OK, we'll get through this, together, as a family . . . Jake?'

'Jake?'

'I'm sorry . . . sorry, Nessa, I'm just er . . . I don't know what to say. Nessa, it's been awful. I've lost everyone. It was just the worst thing, ever. I don't know how I will . . . Sorry, I'm not making any sense am I?'

'How you will what?'

'How I'm going to be able to . . . no . . . no don't worry.'

'Jake, please, don't say that . . . You are going to be just fine. We will get you some help so you can come to terms with it all. It wasn't your fault . . .'

'Yes it was, Nessa. It was my fault. It was all my fault . . . I lost all of them. It was me. I'm responsible for the boys . . .'

'No, Jake. You made a mistake. That's all . . .'

'This war . . . It's the ugliest fucking thing, Nessa. I keep seeing them . . . How it all looked. I close my eyes and I see them lying there, the smell of blood, torn flesh, bone, muscle, shit like that . . . I can't eat, I can't sleep. It's just – the sounds and smells, around me, like it's happening all the time . . .'

'Jake . . . Is there anyone you can talk to right now, a professional in the army, some kind of support?'

'Oh, Nessa . . . Sorry, hold on a minute . . .'

'Sure . . .'

'Oh shit, I've got to go. Love you, Mrs Bruce . . .'

Nessa wondered how she could make things better. While it was incredible to hear his voice, she had never heard his tone so flat, such desperation in him. Jake would come home in just a week following a period of decompression in Cyprus soon, and she felt like she might have to save him with her love.

She had loved him when she met him because he was fun to be around and made her buzz with happiness, but it wasn't the kind of love that would have withstood this. She had loved him when they 'dated' in their own youthful way (nights in Pizza Express with a student discount code and cheap wine), because as she got to know him, everything about him, from the way he walked to the sound of his laugh, made her melt at the edges. But again, that kind of love wasn't enough . . . Not enough *for this.* And she had loved him when they had Poppy because it would be the three of them vs the world, and they would do this *together.* And even though he had run away from his life and hurt her deeply, she knew she would love him through *everything.* But this? *This was terrifying.* It was going to take so much more . . .

She felt ashamed to think this, but what if he'd altered somehow? What if he came back and his personality had changed? She'd heard horror stories like that before. Women with husbands who looked the same, but just sort of coasted around in a daze. Empty shells. And somehow you had to find a way to love them through it all, even when the man who shared your bed was nothing like the one you married.

Nessa read online about how she could support him, searching for information about emotional and psychological trauma on Google. She knew that she must listen and understand, accept mixed feelings and not push him to talk about his experiences. She knew that he might feel numb and angry, and upset and all feelings in-between. She understood that different people coped with trauma differently, and there was no textbook approach that she could follow to make it all OK again. Most of all, she knew that nothing would be the same ever again.

Officer Wilmer had come over to the house later that afternoon, and had spoken to her about the support she and the army could offer in 'such difficult times'. They had a system Nessa had vaguely heard of before called TRiM which, in army speak, stood for Trauma Risk Management. 'The system' had flagged up that Jake might be at risk following the incident, and so he would need extra support. Jake was likely to be able to take some extended leave to help him cope with what had happened, before returning to full-time work. But Nessa knew he wouldn't be returning to full-time work with the army again. No way. She'd known this even before the accident, she just hadn't told him yet. *God, if only she'd told him earlier.* This would never have happened . . .

Nessa had been given a leaflet about TRiM. She read it slowly once Officer Wilmer had left. A particular line struck her, but something about it made her angry: 'Put simply, PTSD is simply a wound to the mind. If treated properly, it will heal. The sooner those in need are identified, the more effective their treatment is likely to be.'

It all sounded so simple, so easy, like the healing of a wound. Post-operation pain. *Here, just take this pill, it'll feel better in the morning.* Nessa was just desperate to have him back. She didn't want him to ever go back to the army.

'Mum? Are you OK?' Poppy asked, standing in the doorway of the kitchen and turning on the light. Nessa hadn't realised she had practically been sitting in darkness.

'Erm, yes, I think so, Poppy. We will be OK . . .' she responded, looking up at her daughter, who was approaching her twelfth birthday and seemed to be getting taller by an inch each week. She was wearing a pair of grey skinny jeans, and a cropped black t-shirt. Her long, dark hair was flung casually over one of her bony shoulders. Her left hip jutted out like a coat hanger.

'I don't think you look very OK,' Poppy said, shuffling into the kitchen and sitting opposite her mother, looking her directly in the eyes, which was again something she didn't do very often.

'Well, you know, I'm a bit worried about Daddy,' Nessa said.

'Dad,' Poppy corrected her quickly, rolling her eyes.

'Sorry, Dad,' Nessa said, clearing her throat, forgetting that Poppy was almost an adult now. She didn't have a 'Daddy', he was simply 'Dad' now. But Nessa knew that when her daughter got older he would be her 'Daddy' once again. When he was no longer around and she had children of her own, she would miss him more than words could describe, and she would give anything to have him back again . . . These were all the lessons that awaited Poppy, feelings she would experience. Years of pain and joy, and loss, that would come like a bolt in the night and leave you reeling forever.

'I want to tell you something that might make you feel a bit happier,' Poppy said, leaning towards her mother now across the table, and reaching out for one of her hands. Nessa held it back, astonished by this display of affection. Who was this girl sitting before her?

'OK, go ahead,' Nessa said, instantly concerned that her daughter might be about to make some awful announcement, and that the hand holding and the tenderness was just some way of disarming her before the horror would truly begin. What would it be now: a teenage pregnancy, a hidden crack habit, a life-size tattoo of Amy Winehouse's face on her arse?

Poppy looked down towards their hands, her great, black eyelashes catching the light. She took a deep breath, as if what she was about to say might be really difficult.

'So I've been thinking about Dad coming home soon, and what I did that afternoon in Hotwire . . . I feel really bad about it, Mum,' she said, trailing off.

Nessa nodded, but didn't say anything.

'I wanted to do something good, to make it OK, somehow,' Poppy continued.

'What?' Nessa asked.

'Well, I did something really, really bad, so I want to do something positive, you know? Even things out, kinda,' Poppy said.

'Pops, you're not involved in something weird are you?' Nessa asked urgently, worried that she'd turned to an obscure cult and was about to start living in a wooden hut by the sea, eating out-of-date packets of Hula Hoops and knitting her own underwear.

'No, of course not!' Poppy said, her nose wrinkling at the bridge in response to her mother's panicked assumptions. Poppy giggled to herself, before carrying on.

'What I wanted to tell you is that I'm going to be volunteering at the charity shop on the high street,' Poppy said, blushing a little.

'What?' Nessa asked, astonished.

'Yeah . . . is that OK?' Poppy asked.

'Sorry, are you kidding, Poppy? That's not very funny if that's what you are doing . . .' Nessa asked.

Poppy shook her head and giggled to herself once again.

'Which one?' Nessa asked urgently.

'The one that helps people who are ex forces. You know, the one on the corner near the garage? The Something Something Something Irrelevant Fund,' Poppy said.

'The South East Regional RAF *Benevolent* Fund,' Nessa whispered in astonishment, putting an emphasis on the word 'benevolent'. Her daughter nodded excitedly.

'Because I'm only 14 I can't do many hours, and I can't serve customers at the front of the shop, but I will be helping for a few hours on Saturdays in the stock room and taking large deliveries and stuff with the help of another person there. They need help cleaning things, and working out what they can sell. I've got an induction tomorrow night after school from four till half five. I just wanted to tell you about that, and I also wanted to say sorry for saying that you failed at being a midwife, Mum.'

She looked down the table as if she was ashamed of herself. Nessa felt a wave of emotion claw at the bottom of her neck. This was all too much. Tears sprang to her eyes. She desperately tried to hold it all in.

'I'm so sorry, Mum. I never want to make you cry. I didn't mean what I said to you. It just came out funny . . .' she continued, looking up, struggling to see the tears in her mother's eyes.

'No, but you were right, Poppy. That's the whole thing about it, you were right. That's why it hurt so much,' Nessa said.

'No, Mum, I wasn't right at all. You've had to deal with a lot looking after me, and Dad being in the army and stuff. You shouldn't give yourself such a hard time,' she said, before giving her mum a cuddle and padding her way out of the kitchen and into her bedroom, leaving Nessa feeling faintly suspicious.

The following day Nessa Bruce did something she felt slightly ashamed of. She was sure, though, that she was doing it for all the right reasons. Nessa had learned in life that nobody could be 'good', or do the right thing, all the time, and that risks sometimes had to be taken as long as the ends justified the means.

Nessa felt bad even thinking this, but her daughter's speech the day before had been so wonderful, and so moving, and so out of character for her lately, that she had to ensure this wasn't another lie. It wouldn't be entirely set apart from the spectrum of possibility that Poppy could be using this as a reason to be somewhere else without getting caught, and Nessa had to be smart. Her worst fear was that Poppy had a boyfriend. Some smelly, snivelling vile teenage lad who would lead her further down the winding path to trouble. *She had to be sure.*

So, at five minutes past five, Nessa drove to Beckenham High Street. Tired from her day at work, she yawned enthusiastically while parking behind a branch of Waitrose. Her jaw clicked. Jake would be home in a matter of days now, and she wanted to be on top form.

Nessa scuttled down an alley between a ballet outfitter that had been there for about 20 years and a Greek restaurant. The thick, tempting scent of souvlaki waltzed in the air. She found her way to the back of the charity shop. Her heart was beating hard and fast in her chest.

The car park had become a kind of informal loading bay or dumping ground. There were crates and boxes piled up everywhere. Nessa scanned the dark space behind the shop. Two large rubbish bins were overflowing with refuse. A beer can had been left by the foot of one of them. She looked up towards the windows at the back of the shop. They were protected by large metal bars and hadn't been cleaned for a very long time. A thick layer of grime had formed over the windows and spiders were making happy family homes in the corners of the frame without any risk of disturbance. Nessa could just about see two teddy bears through the grey, filthy glass: one was a rabbit, the other a frog. Their great beady eyes, held to these curious faces by thick, cotton stitches, surveyed her as she sinned.

Nessa walked quietly and slowly towards the double doors at the back of the shop. She had it all planned out. If she was seen by her daughter, she would act casually, like she was just coming to pick her up and it was nothing. If she wasn't, then she would watch and listen, and then disappear, never mentioning what she had done to anyone.

Nessa pushed her palms against the doors very gently and slowly. She bit her lip as she did so, deeply nervous about what she may or may not discover. The doors were unlocked and Nessa was easily able to push her way into the back of the shop ever so slowly. Her eyes surveyed the dim hallway before her. It was clearly in a poor state of repair. The paint on the walls was peeling and the place needed a good dust. Nessa shut the doors behind her as quickly and quietly as she could. All of a sudden she was cast in terrifying blackness. For a moment she wondered if she'd gone crazy, doing something like this. She was just sick of not being in control anymore. She had to take control.

Nessa could hear voices. She felt her way along the walls and followed the sound. She kept going slowly, until her left foot hit a step. It hurt. She struggled not to gasp out in pain. The voices were muffled. She couldn't tell if they belonged to a man or a woman. Trembling with nerves, Nessa made her way up the steps, feeling her way around before she took each one by the foot.

One.

Two.

Three.

And as she turned a corner, there was finally a tiny bit of light, leaking from the edges of a door that was slightly open. Nessa could make out one of the voices now. It sounded like an older woman. Soft and high pitched. It was still tricky to make out what she was saying, so she tiptoed ever so slowly towards the door, and holding her breath she pushed her face up to the gap, the blood rushing through her veins.

'We have to make sure that people are safe, don't we? So if someone brings in an electric whisk, or perhaps a hairdryer, what would you say to them?' she heard a lady ask.

Nessa could just about see the woman through the gap separating the door and its frame. She must have been in her late seventies. She wore a soft, thick green cardigan and a pair of loose chinos. Nessa could just about make out that she was wearing a pair of thick padded shoes, with big Velcro straps on the top of them. She smiled to herself softly.

Nessa pushed the door open a little more and surveyed the room. It was packed full of unwanted things that were once loved. The remnants of divorce and death, Nessa thought, the musty smell of the sorting room making her want to sneeze.

She couldn't sneeze. That would be terrible.

Nessa pushed her fingers against her face tightly.

The tickling was unbearable.

And then she saw her daughter step softly towards the old woman. She was holding a rag doll with black stitched-on triangles for eyes. She was still wearing her school uniform.

'We would say . . .' she heard Poppy speak in response to the question, pausing to think a little first. 'We would say that we are terribly sorry, but we don't take electrical items, but please do feel free to take them to the British Heart Foundation shop where they can take them to sell on. Thank you very much for supporting the South Regional RAF Benevolent Fund, and have a lovely day . . .' Poppy looked up towards the ceiling as she spoke, trying to remember what she had to relay.

'Brilliant!' the old lady said, clapping her hands together with glee. 'Oh and what else?' she asked, putting a gnarly, trembling finger up towards her own head, as if she was prompting Poppy to think.

'Oh yeah, and here's an RAF Benevolent Fund sticker for you to wear because we are glad you thought of us,' Poppy said, smiling with glee because she'd finally got it all out.

'That's wonderful, Poppy. Well, you've done incredibly well today, dear. We are so grateful to have you helping us. And the ladies and I can't wait to have a lovely, young face around here!' the woman exclaimed.

'Say, you can take that home, Poppy, as a way of us saying thanks to you for volunteering with us,' she added, pointing towards the rag doll that hung sadly from Poppy's hand by one arm.

Nessa squirmed a little inside. She wondered how Poppy would handle this. Poppy was *not* the kind of girl who would want a rag doll. In fact, lately, she had been the kind of girl who would singe its eyes with a molten cigarette, tear it apart in fury and throw it out of her bedroom window to be repeatedly run over by passing traffic. She would normally be too self-conscious to take it, and to carry it home, worried that someone from school might see her.

'Oh really? Thank you!' Poppy exclaimed, giving the old lady a hug. It was genuine, and kind. Nessa felt her heart melt. She had managed to be real about her feelings, to seem genuinely grateful for this thing she knew she would hate, deep down.

Nessa had to go. She'd seen everything she needed to see. She suddenly felt ashamed of herself, to have doubted Poppy over this. She took two, gentle steps backwards before turning and fleeing the shop.

When Nessa got back to the car she was breathless. The

rain was starting to fall on the windscreen, and she wept with relief and happiness. It dawned on her that everything was going to be OK . . . It was going to be hard, but it was going to be OK.

Twelve

'I just wish we were a normal family'

It was *finally* time to see him again. After months, weeks and hours of waiting – chunks of time that all eventually felt the same in their torturous, unending length – the day had arrived. It was a moody Saturday afternoon. The sky flickered with soft, 4 p.m. sunshine in between coltish rain clouds that swept across the horizon. Today, they would meet Jake Bruce at the army base after six agonising months without him.

In just over an hour, the Bruce family would be together again, Nessa told herself, smoothing her thick hair with a trembling hand. She thought about how she'd greet him. Would she encourage Poppy to run up to him first? Would she cry? Or would she feel suddenly shy at the return of this man who sometimes felt like a stranger, somebody she used to know. A silhouette of the person she was so deeply in love with, a man who sometimes, nowadays, felt like a figment of her imagination.

They waited in a long queue of family members, mainly women and children. They were all clutching passports and various reference codes so they could get through security. It was standard army stuff, but it felt like it took an eternity. There was so much red tape, so much admin. Happy chatter and laughter emanated from the other families. Nessa overheard a woman say how excited she was to see her husband again. She talked loudly about how they were due to go on holiday to Paphos the following weekend, and that they had their own pool. She heard two ladies before her giggle wickedly about something sex-related, throwing their heads back and making gossipy 'o' shapes with their mouths. Nessa rolled her eyes behind her sunglasses. *How simple other people's lives were*, she thought. While she desperately missed that side of her relationship with her husband, she had other, more pressing things on her mind . . .

Nessa would finally be able to ask Jake this weekend, no *beg him*, to leave the army. The thought of it filled her heart with excitement and fear. She didn't know how he'd react, but she also knew that she couldn't continue the way things were. If he said 'yes', she would be happy, she just knew it. Life would be OK again.

Poppy and Nessa were both nervous about what they might be about to face, even though they didn't say it aloud. There was a quiet understanding between them now. Poppy had refrained from playing loud music during the car journey there, which was unusual. She bit her fingernails and yawned unnecessarily, a trait she displayed when she was tense. The nerves had made Nessa feel nauseous. As she drove she became increasingly tetchy, as if every motorist ahead of her was needlessly in the way, conspiring to make things more difficult for her on purpose.

'What are we doing tonight?' Poppy asked eventually, breaking through the quiet. Raindrops started to fall on the windscreen; the sky was suddenly grey and imposing.

'I was thinking we could take Dad for dinner. What do you reckon?' Nessa asked, looking at her daughter, who seemed surprised. She tried to put on her most enterprising smile.

'Where?'

'Pizza World.'

'At the cineplex?'

'Yep. I have some money off vouchers,' Nessa said. 'I was thinking we could tell him all about the work you are doing at the charity shop and celebrate. Maybe you can have a little glass of bubbly wine? He will be so proud of you Pops,' she continued, feeding the wheel with her hands as they turned a corner.

'Yeah, whatever. Cineplex, for god's sake . . . You're so basic,' Poppy growled, sinking further back into her seat and putting her feet on the dashboard.

'Put your feet down Poppy.'

'Oh why?'

'Just do it . . .'

'No, tell me why. My shoes are clean!'

'Because Poppy, if we have a crash, the airbag will come out from where your feet are, your legs will fling back in your face, really hard, and that will probably break your spine and YOU WILL PROBABLY DIE, alright??!!' Nessa yelled, rather melodramatically.

'FINE,' Poppy hissed furiously. There wasn't much she could say to that.

After a few moments of peace, Poppy piped up again: 'Don't you think Dad might not be in the mood to go out pretending to be all happy tonight? Don't you think he's probably been through too much to be sitting in a skanky cinema complex with us, eating pepperoni and cheese twists and drinking cheap beer? Do you *ever* think, Mum?' Poppy asked incredulously.

Nessa took a deep breath. The old Poppy was here. A surge of disappointment raced through her body. But this time it was tinged with rage. Nessa wanted to cry with anger; her feelings were overwhelming her.

Her little monster was back.

But she knew why . . . Poppy behaved like this when she was frightened and nervous. She took it out on her mother; that was how this always went. Nessa knew she had to try hard not to internalise it. Even she was nervous about seeing her own husband again.

The windscreen wipers scraped loudly against the glass.

'It's quite possible that Dad won't be in the mood. Yes, you're right, Poppy, but it doesn't matter does it? I think we should suggest it to get him out of the house and give him that option, and if he really doesn't want to then we can make pizza at home together. We don't have to go do we? What do you think?' Nessa said, trying to be as positive as possible.

Nessa remembered the last time they tried to make pizza at home. Poppy was ten, and had dropped the mixture on the carpet. The dough was too sloppy, and they had spent the following eight months trying to scrape it out of the floor with a stiff toothbrush.

'Whatever,' Poppy said, pulling out her phone.

'Oh come on, Poppy, you're always moaning that we don't go out for meals . . . I thought you'd be pleased?'

'Pizza World is a shit hole. It's actually an insult to Dad. You just don't get it,' her daughter responded with such hopelessness Nessa wanted to laugh for a moment, at this ridiculous teenage girl who thought she knew better than anyone else. Yes, of course Pizza World was a bit of a dive, *but this was all she could do*. And Poppy used to love Pizza World anyway, because they had a self-service pudding section where she would pump endless ribbons of instant ice cream into a bowl and cover it with chocolate sprinkles and stars made entirely from e-numbers. That was a few years ago, though, to be fair.

'I don't get what?' Nessa asked, feeling defensive.

'How to treat people . . . Don't worry about it. I just wish we were a normal family,' Poppy said, trailing off and staring out of the window. There went the sting again. The words that hurt, like salt on a wound.

Nessa started to think about 'normal' families, and what that even meant, and why her own daughter made her feel like such a worthless, dysfunctional individual. They'd driven past these illusive groups of 'normal' people on the way to the hangar, going about their business. They looked happy, well most of them did. They had emerged from beneath shop frontages, bus shelters and restaurant receptions when the showers had retreated. They embarked on walks together: wellington boots, umbrellas and scruffy dogs in tow. Laughing, smiling faces; in-jokes. *Do you remember that time when?*

She'd seen these 'regular families' gathered in petrol station forecourts, arguing about which ice creams they should buy for their journey and whose turn it was to drive. They had waited outside the supermarkets Nessa and Poppy glided past, carrying heavy shopping bags in one hand, with contented sleeping babies slung across loving shoulders. They were the mums dropping their kids off at a party, wearing yoga gear and drinking lemon water. Who were these people and how were they managing their lives so well?

'How was the shop this morning?' Nessa asked changing the subject. She wanted to focus on something good.

'Yeah, alright,' Poppy said. The rain disappeared for a short while once again. Nessa was glad to turn off the wipers; they were making a horrible noise.

'How's the elderly lady you work with?' Nessa asked.

There were a few moments of quiet.

'What lady? How do you know I work with an elderly lady?' Poppy asked aggressively.

Nessa's stomach felt cold. *Think fast . . . Think fast . . .*

'Oh no, it was just a guess Pops. You know how it is: retired people, particularly ladies, like to work in charity shops don't they? They have more time, don't they?' Nessa said, her voice shaking a little. Her daughter tutted, and she instantly felt like a cretin.

'Yeah it's fine, although someone tried to bring in a taxidermy fox earlier. It looked like Tony Blair. We said no, of course, because we don't take stuffed animals,' Poppy said flatly, turning away from her mother and staring out at the streets again, her big, beautiful eyes scanning the wet, glistening pavements.

When Nessa and Poppy had finally made their way to the front of the line, their documents were checked thoroughly by a lady who had all the softness of a drying rack. Her hair was scraped back against her head, her face long, thin and lacking in warmth.

'The company will be arriving through there shortly. Next!' she yelled, as Nessa and Poppy made their way past her. She had pointed towards a large hangar, where they would wait with the other families for their soldiers to return.

The place was heaving with emotion. A low buzz of chatter reverberated from wall to wall. It sounded like the hum of insects on a muggy summer's evening. Benches were laid out for people to sit on. Tearful mothers perched with their tired, restless children. The excitement and nerves in the room were so overwhelming they could almost be touched . . . The energy buzzed, and it was starting to get hot.

'God, I'm so excited,' a lady with a soft Irish accent said out of the blue. Nessa and the lady locked eyes for a moment. There was so much understanding in that glance, as if hours of drunken chatter about loneliness, worry and longing had passed between them in a second or two. She understood.

'Me too! Well, both of us are, aren't we Poppy?' Nessa asked, looking at her daughter proudly. Poppy grunted and kept staring ahead, refusing to even look at the lady who was speaking to them.

'Sorry, she's a bit tired,' Nessa whispered to the strange lady, embarrassed by her daughter's rudeness. Her cheeks flushed a searing magenta.

'Oh, it's OK. I know it's very hard. Days like today, they are so exciting aren't they, but it can be surprisingly difficult too,' the woman said, in a warm, honey tone.

'Yes, it really is,' Nessa responded, smiling at the woman and her child.

'There's so many different emotions flying around and it's like—' All of a sudden the entrance to the hangar swung open, and the first soldiers came through. 'Oh my god, Mark!!! Maaarrrrkkk!!!' she yelled, standing up suddenly. The woman's eyes instantly filled with tears, both her hands were raised to her mouth.

Her daughter giggled, and jumped up and down, looking from her mother to her father. 'Daddy!' she cried.

'I'm sorry. It was lovely talking to you,' the woman said urgently, grinning widely before bending down, grabbing her daughter's hand and running towards her partner. Nessa watched them. She smiled. Everything seemed to go silent for a moment, and it played out as if in slow motion. The woman flung her arms around him; he was so handsome in his uniform. The raw emotion was so clear on their faces. He picked up his little girl and they just stood there, the three of them, united again. Sunshine poured through the entrance, framing them in a golden light . . .

Nessa started searching the crowd for a sign of Jake. All she needed was a flash of his hair, that gorgeous sandy brown colour, those big brown eyes, strong, distinguished stature, those tanned muscular arms, and his hands – his beautiful strong hands. Lots of soldiers were filing into the hangar now; more women and their children running towards them. Little boys in t-shirts and shorts were lifted up in the air by the strong arms of their fathers and uncles. People wept, and laughed, and choked up with tears. A tsunami of emotion swept through the room.

Nessa and Poppy were standing up now, raised up on to their tiptoes every now and then, trying to see Jake. Only about half of the soldiers had come in, and the army officials were trying to usher reunited families to another area so there would be plenty of room in the hangar.

'Ergh, like where the fuck is he? It's so hot in here and there are loads of annoying kids around,' Poppy said irritably.

'I don't know honey, I'm sure he will come round that corner any second now. We just have to be patient,' Nessa said, putting her arm on Poppy's shoulder to soothe her, trying to forget about the things she'd said in the car earlier.

Poppy wriggled away from her touch self-consciously. More men filed in. Some of them looked exhausted, but they were finally home. But where was Jake?

Nessa started to feel a little panicked. There were only a couple of soldiers walking in now . . . The majority of families and couples had now shuffled along to the next hangar. Things were suddenly quietening down.

After five minutes or so, there were only four families left in the tent.

An eerie calm had arrived. They could only hear two or three conversations in the hanger about fish and chips for tea, and what films were on later, who had won the *X-Factor* final, and the distant buzzing from the space next door. An older lady, who had clearly come to meet her son, looked over to them with concern and smiled a kind of sympathetic half-smirk before walking away, with her head turned in the other direction, like people do when there's a car crash and they can't bear to look anymore. Nessa felt her chest tighten. Panic started to grip at her throat.

Now come on . . . There has to be a simple explanation for this, she thought to herself. There was no way that Jake wasn't close by. Someone would have come to see them by now if there had been any kind of problem. In fact they would have heard well before now. He would only be a moment or two . . . Just a moment or two . . .

The moments slipped by until there were no more families in the hangar. Everyone had left, floating away in their own swirls of love.

Nessa sat back down on the bench slowly. There was no need to stand any more, she could see perfectly well. She felt like she might have a panic attack again, so she closed her eyes and rocked softly back and forth, stroking her left forearm with her right hand.

'What are you doing, Mum? You look like a nutter. This isn't helping! God you're so embarrassing!' Poppy cried.

'Just give me some space Poppy . . . please . . .' Nessa said, feeling tears well beneath her eyelids. Her top lip twitched in that way it always did when she tried desperately hard not to cry, as if someone had attached a little invisible thread to it and kept pulling every now and again. It was a humiliating sensation for her, to be on the verge of crying.

'*Fuck this*, I'm going to ask someone what's going on,' Poppy said, storming away.

Nessa kept trying to breathe deeply through her nostrils. Betsy had given her a book about mindfulness a month or two ago. She'd ordered it from a shopping channel because they were doing a special promotion in their 'New You Weekend'. They were giving away free pomegranate-scented mood candles with each copy, and naturally Betsy had been unable to resist. In reality, the candles smelt more like the cheap deodorant sprays she used to use as a girl. But rather than putting it in the cupboard under the stairs to join the other strange gifts her mother-in-law gave her, Nessa had quite enjoyed the book.

She had tried to listen to the audio meditations at night when she couldn't sleep. And now she tried desperately to reach out for this mindset so she wouldn't have a meltdown in the middle of this empty aircraft hangar. She attempted to focus on the way her toes felt against her gold, leather sandals. She thought about the way her bottom felt against the cold, hard bench, and considered the way her breath filled her stomach before swooshing out again. She focused on her fingertips, and traced them against the fabric of her jeans. She did whatever she could to—

'Mrs Bruce?' a voice asked.

Nessa opened her eyes suddenly. Her vision was blurry from the tears. 'Yes. Sorry . . . I can't find my . . . my husband, he hasn't . . . well, you know, he's not . . . hmm, clearly he's . . . There's a problem,' Nessa said, trying to get the words out, though the sentences didn't seem to come.

'Sorry, Jake Bruce, is it? This is strange,' the lady said, surveying her register. She pursed her lips together tightly and her forehead seemed to stretch away from her tight hair-do.

'Perhaps he's been held back for some reason. I will go and have a look. I'll speak to the sergeant, and Officer Wilmer, to find out where he is. I'm sure he will be with you in no time; there must be a reasonable explanation,' the woman said, with a soothing smile.

'Sure,' Nessa said. The woman turned away sharply, her boots squeaked as she paced across the hangar and out through the door.

'See? Everything's fine Pops, he will be here in just a moment,' Nessa said, drumming her fingers against her knees.

The seconds passed to make way for minutes, minutes that hung and drooped away from each other, getting longer and longer. *The Persistence of Memory*. Tick. Tock. Nessa had looked at her watch. Twenty minutes had passed, then thirty, then fifty . . . *What on earth was going on?*

Eventually, a uniformed man softly opened the door to the hangar. He was at least 30 metres away, so it was hard to make him out . . . Was that him? Nessa's heart felt like it might burst into flames. She stood up suddenly and grabbed Poppy's hand, steeling herself to run towards him. To wrap her arms around him, and tell him that she loved him more than anything in the whole world. To tell him that he was half of her and, without him, life was grey and sad. That being without him was intolerable, and not at all OK, and that she needed him back with her so they could all be happy again.

Thirteen

'How is that even . . .? How could that happen?'

But as the man approached it started to become clear it wasn't Jake. His walk wasn't the same. His stature was different. He was shorter, perhaps stockier. Officer Wilmer was walking a few steps behind him. Nessa felt Poppy squeeze her hand harder. It was sweaty, but cold.

The man walked up to them until he was just half a metre or so away; his face was expressionless. He took off his beret and held it to his chest with his right hand. The man looked down towards the floor before clearing his throat and speaking. Nessa's world ground to a halt. She could hear the blood rushing past her ears, the thudding of her heart. It felt like the air had stopped coming into her lungs. Her head started to tingle and ripples of nausea tickled at the base of her throat. Nessa heard from what sounded like somewhere in the far distance, the sound of Poppy weeping. She put her arm around her daughter's waist and pulled her close, still looking ahead at this stranger who looked so solemn.

'Mrs Bruce, my name is Sergeant Daniel Troy. I'm sorry to say that your husband Jake is nowhere to be seen at this moment in time . . .'

'What?' Nessa whispered. She had felt her eyes narrowing in disbelief and anger. Officer Wilmer looked down at the ground sadly.

'He was counted coming off the plane, so we know he got onto the aircraft from his period of decompression in Cyprus to come back to the UK. He was also counted coming off the bus that took them from the landing bay to the site here. So, somehow, he's disappeared between getting off the bus and coming into this hangar,' the man said seriously.

'*What?*'

Nessa studied his features, her eyes flickering across his face, trying to take everything in. She tried to work out what was real because this felt like a bad dream, something she was merely imagining. He looked to be in his mid-forties. He was tanned, and his hair was already a soft silver. He had kind blue eyes; he looked honest.

'How is that even . . .? How could that happen?' Nessa asked, feeling her daughter's body rise and fall with emotion.

'It's never happened before Mrs Bruce, I can assure you. It's just not something we are usually prepared for. We've looked everywhere and we have sent people out to search the land here on site, but there's no report of him yet . . . Listen, please sit down, Nessa is it, and Poppy?' he asked. The ladies sank down slowly, still holding on to each other. The man looked decidedly embarrassed. Officer Wilmer sat down beside Nessa, and put an arm around her.

'I was out on tour with Jake . . . I know him quite well.

As you know, he went through a massive ordeal just three weeks ago . . . The loss of his men – Thomas, Michael, Liam and Gabriel – hit him very hard. We tried our best to support him as much as we could.'

'Why are you speaking in the past tense?!' Nessa cried, her voice echoing along the hangar. The sentence bounced around the space, and came back to haunt them. Nessa could hear crying: her own. Officer Wilmer was rubbing her back now, making the kind of shushing noises used to pacify small children.

'Nessa, if you could please try and remain calm,' the man asked, sinking down to his knees and facing Nessa as she wept.

'Why! Where is he? What's happened?! Why are you talking about him like he's gone!' she screamed, pushing her hands towards the man's knees, which were coated in camouflage uniform. Nessa dug her nails into his legs, shaking him as she cried. He was a strong man, built like a boulder, so he only moved a little bit as she pushed him, able to absorb her anger and the weight of her fury.

'Help us, please. I can't take this,' she begged, looking around her as if she too might run away.

'What I want to say Mrs Bruce is that your husband was suffering serious emotional trauma after the tragic loss of his men. We were, and still are, doing our very best to offer him the highest level of support . . . Now it could be that he finds the idea of seeing you again extremely difficult.'

'But why? I love him. We love him,' Nessa whispered, looking at Poppy and then back again.

'It's not because he doesn't love you or miss you. Honestly, Nessa, you are all he ever speaks about. It may be because he is feeling extremely guilty about what happened . . . You are the people he loves and looks up to most in the world, and he feels ashamed of himself right now. He might not be able to face you.'

Nessa's crying slowed now, and she listened. Her breathing started to calm down.

Officer Wilmer started to speak, 'There's every possibility that he has fled the site to get some space and have some time alone. We just didn't expect it, to be totally honest. We will be looking for him, and we will let you know as soon as we hear anything. I must warn you though, Nessa, he is at a higher level of risk at the moment . . .'

'Risk of what?' Nessa asked.

'Of . . . of harm . . . He has been showing signs that have caused concern ever since the incident. He was extremely withdrawn in Cyprus. He's been suffering night sweats, bursts of anger, some aggression . . . I do have reservations about his welfare, and I have to be open and honest with you about these concerns. Regardless of his disappearance today, we were going to sit down and talk to you as a family about what might happen next in terms of rehabilitating Jake and supporting his transition back home.'

Nessa nodded in silent understanding.

Sergeant Troy said calmly, 'All we can do now is search for him. We will do everything we can Nessa. I hope sincerely that he just needs a little time alone, and that he will be back very soon, ready to be with you again.'

Nessa wept.

'I'm so sorry . . .' he repeated, 'I'm so, so sorry . . .'

Fourteen

'Look, I know this sounds selfish, but it just feels cruel . . .'

'So, basically, Jake has run away,' Will said flatly, blowing a jet of breath towards his coffee to cool it. He cradled the mug in his hands, biting his bottom lip.

'Er, yes; I guess so. Well, we hope that's what's happened . . . If you can ever *hope* for that kind of thing,' Nessa said.

She was exhausted. She'd not slept a wink for the past two days, since they had waited at the hangar for Jake to turn up.

He had been missing for more than 48 hours now. That was quite a long time in missing person terms. The police had said the first 24 hours were crucial, and they'd just trickled by. There had been no revelatory phone call, no gentle knock at the door. There had been no activity on his bank account, no withdrawals or debit transactions. His phone was still dead. There was no data trail.

'I'm really hurt, Will, actually.'

'What do you mean?' he asked, his eyes narrowing a little.

'We've not seen him for so long, and he knew how much we missed him. If he supposedly loves me, if he trusts me, then why is doing this? How could he?' she said, noticing how shocked Will looked. 'Look, I know this sounds selfish, but it just feels cruel . . . I feel bad, but I'm angry at him. I'm sorry, I just am.' Nessa started to cry. Will reached out and held one of her hands. He didn't say anything.

'I've tried so hard to step into his shoes . . . to understand what he might be going through. I just lie awake in the early hours of the morning, trying to understand how it might feel to lose your friends, to feel entirely responsible for that. I'm doing my best to understand, but how could he not want to be with us? How could he not lean on me to get him through all of this? It feels like he's rejecting me.'

Will nodded gently. 'Of course he loves you and Poppy, more than anything in the world . . . Don't you ever doubt that. He's probably experiencing trauma and shock, and neither of us will ever understand how that can make a person behave. I promise you, it won't be personal.'

Nessa nodded at his words. She worried about Jake every second, but particularly overwhelming was the way she worried about him at night. In those lonely, dark hours everything felt hopeless. Summer was ending, the warm tendrils of sunshine that had slowly baked the soil for the past few months were retreating, making way for the arrival of a front of colder, wetter weather. They provided room for the inevitable. The leaves had turned and were starting to tumble to the ground like romantic ballerinas, twisting and turning through the air. Street sweepers tried to clear the roadsides while wellington boot-clad children undid their hard work, kicking the debris of old leaves into the air, giggling with glee.

The thick, black duvet of the night-time wrapped around the curve of the earth earlier and earlier each evening now, and even the birds sang a different song, preparing themselves for a very cold and drab few months ahead. It wouldn't be so simple or comfortable for him to be sleeping rough now. By two in the morning the temperatures were dropping to just two or three degrees. The grass would be covered in crystals of damp in the early hours. Was he even still alive?

'Suicide risk.' Christine Wilmer had said those words when she came round on Sunday night to see how they were doing. The thought of him lying somewhere, all alone and bereft of life, kept flashing in her mind. Horrific images of his silhouette, visible in the branches of a tree, wouldn't leave her. She'd had flashes of imagery that made her feel ashamed. She and Poppy at Jake's funeral; the police finding him somewhere – in the woods, perhaps – staring at his lifeless body and writing things in their notepads. The waste of it all. It hurt the bottom of her stomach. It filled her with an urgent desperation she simply couldn't live with, so it was best to try not to think about it. Nessa had to do everything she could to just imagine him sleeping quietly beneath the stars in some soggy field off the M5, simply waiting it out until he felt ready to come home. That was the best outcome here.

'How are Betsy and Mick holding up?' Will asked.

'Oh, she's naturally beside herself. She's hiding it from Mick for now. I feel bad when we have to lie to him like this, but sometimes it's easier, and kinder too. To try and explain all this to Mick could push him over the edge. He needs calm, with his dementia. He needs things to be simple and predictable, and expected.'

'I totally understand,' he said, scooping another spoonful of sugar from a pot on the table and stirring it into his coffee. 'Listen Nessa. You need to leave work right now, and you need to tell them that you won't be back for a little while until all of this has calmed down a bit. I can assure you that they will be absolutely fine about it; they have to be Nessa.'

As Will spoke, Nessa shook her head in protest.

'Nessa, seriously. Your husband has disappeared; you have no idea where he is or if he's even alive. You have a 14-year-old daughter who is in some serious distress. Please, just get real. Go home and take care of what you need to take care of to be able to cope with all this.' Nessa felt the warmth of Will's hand now wrapped around hers. She wanted to cry, but a numbness had made that impossible.

'I'm going to take Poppy out tonight, Nessa. I'm going to Westfield with my sister and my niece, Fran, and I thought she could come along too.'

Nessa nodded.

'So, I will come and pick Poppy up after school, and we will go out to the shops, go for dinner and ice cream or something, and you can stay at home, have a nice bath, contact some friends. How about Teigen, maybe she can come round or something? Nessa, you need to look after yourself, you really do. Without you, the whole thing collapses. I will do whatever I can, anything, to make this easier for you.'

Will leaned across the table and planted a shaky kiss on her forehead, holding the back of her head tightly, as if to say 'I've got you'. Nessa noticed that his eyes were a little teary when he sat back down again. His hands were trembling. Sometimes she forgot just how much he cared about her.

Poppy came home laden with shopping bags, which Will and Fran helped her carry into the house. Nita's daughter Fran was just as glaringly teenage as Poppy, though in a different way. More like a long-limbed animal struggling to learn how to walk, she was less aggressively self-assured, but growing into herself clumsily, and with great difficulty all the same.

'Mum! Oh my god, oh my god, oh my god. I've literally had the BEST night ever. Look what Will got for me!' Poppy cried as she ran into the kitchen. Two huge Forever 21 bags were swinging from her hands.

Nessa had been drinking a cup of herbal tea and attempting to write a log of action to ensure they had thought of everything. She had considered asking Teigen to come round, like Will had suggested, but in the end she just wanted to be alone, unable to cope with her friend's high energy presence and all the wine and perfume that went with it. She had to think about all the places Jake could be, all his friends: who had been contacted, who hadn't. There was so much to do, but Poppy and Will's arrival was like a gust of fresh air. Hours had slipped by.

'Oh my goodness. Will, seriously . . . you didn't need to. I mean this is just . . .' Nessa stood up, her stomach rumbling loudly. She'd forgotten to eat. Poppy's bags clashed against each other, the sound of tissue paper and plastic rustling with every movement. Will turned red with embarrassment.

Nessa felt bad. She could never keep up with Will and the way he could spend, just like that. Expensive meals out, bottles of wine that cost as much as her weekly shop. It was nothing to him. Spending £500, £600 or even £700 on Poppy that evening was the equivalent of Nessa finding a spare 80p to get a sausage roll from the bakery on the way home from work. She was so grateful, but there was a sting too. It embarrassed her sometimes.

'It's really nothing. She needed a few bits and bobs, didn't you Pops? It's no big thing. It was nice to treat you – take your mind off things,' Will said, brushing it off, but turning a deeper shade of plum.

Nessa felt a flutter of paranoia. Had Will and his sister Nita looked at Poppy and thought that perhaps she wasn't dressed appropriately? Did she look like she was being neglected in some way? Perhaps this was a gentle hint, that she needed to take care of things better . . . She'd been so busy lately that perhaps she hadn't noticed her daughter's clothes were looking a little tired. Feeling humiliated, she tried to tell herself not to overthink it, to just be grateful for their help.

All of a sudden, Nessa's train of thought was broken by a loud thud, as a small box fell out of Will's inside coat pocket, or perhaps the pocket of his jeans, and landed on the floor. Nessa looked down at the box and saw the name 'Alex Monroe' etched into the top of it. Will blushed a deeper crimson and frantically scrabbled to pick up the box and put it back into his pocket as quickly as he could, it seemed.

Nessa felt a chill run over her body. She *loved* Alex Monroe jewellery. Not one to normally covet expensive things, she had cared enough to drag Will to a sample sale one afternoon in the Hoxton Hotel as part of a day out with Poppy, just to look at them in real life. Nessa had sighed at the pieces as they glittered in boxes – intricate feathers made of gold, and tiny bumble bees dangling from impossibly delicate chains – lamenting that she couldn't even afford them at cut price. Will had stood in the corner of the room, distracted as usual, making intense phone calls and pacing the thick, expensive carpet.

'What was that, Will?' Nessa had questioned, a look of suspicion on her face.

'Oh, literally nothing. It's for my . . . for my girlfriend,' he said, unconvincingly she thought.

'Oh, nice. That's nice. Where's Nita?' Nessa asked, still baffled, but keen to change the subject as she seemed to be reading way too much into everything at the moment.

'She's in the car. Headache. Sends her love,' Will responded flippantly, the colour starting to drain away from his cheeks until he began to resemble his usual self.

'Oh cool, send her mine please . . . Did you drag this poor man around the shops, Poppy? Or was it Nita who had to come in with you?' Nessa asked, wanting to laugh at the thought of it. She knew Will, and she knew he didn't really 'get' shopping, unless it was a booze cruise.

'Oh no. He just hung around outside, and then came in and paid, didn't you, Will? Nita helped me pick things,' Poppy exclaimed, delightedly looking down at the haul. Will smiled to himself, crossing his arms over his stomach. Nessa felt a stab of something . . . another uncomfortable, arguably neurotic feeling. *Nita helped*. She imagined it, another woman helping her daughter pick out her first proper wardrobe of 'grown-up' clothes. Nessa would have loved to be the one to do that, but it had already happened. The moment was gone.

'So you've got something new on the go, business-wise, have you Will?' Nessa asked, glancing at her friend.

'Yeah, new idea. It's taking up rather a lot of my time . . . I'm thinking of buying into some vineyard thing. I only just found out about it actually,' Will said, trailing off. 'I'll explain another day.'

Nessa smiled and nodded. She scanned the bags with her eyes. There were ten of them altogether. She could make out all sorts of fabrics and shoeboxes.

'Did you get anything, Fran?' Ness asked. Fran was very sweet, standing shyly in the corner of the kitchen. She was the kind of girl you wanted to just scoop up in your arms, to warn her about how shitty the world was but reassure her that everything would be OK. Tell her that she could really do with plucking her eyebrows now because those bad boys had become one, to eat more fruit and spend time in the outdoors every now and again.

'Yeah, I don't really like clothes and stuff like that, but I got some more science books. Oh and a telescope,' Fran said, her voice so quiet it was barely audible. Nessa glanced at Poppy, who was trying desperately hard to not pull a face.

'I've never had a telescope before,' she added, enthusiastically. 'I've wanted one for ages. This is just a starter one – the Skywatcher Explorer 200P – but I should be able to see some basic planets, moons, nebulae, star clusters . . .' A sprig of frizzy hair pinged out from the side of her head and stood on end, like a little indicator. It wobbled as she spoke. Nessa noticed a small piece of lettuce was stuck in her brace.

'Wow, Fran, that's amazing. What lucky girls you are . . .' Nessa said warmly.

'I'm sorry about Jake,' Fran said, suddenly, her face turning a patchy pink. She raised her left hand towards her mouth and looked embarrassed by herself. The sleeve of her jumper had been violently chewed; strands of thread were coming away from it.

'Oh . . . thanks, Fran. That's nice of you . . . We are just hoping he comes home soon,' Nessa said, suddenly reminded of the horrible truth, that cold feeling returning to her stomach. Poppy's posture dropped and she looked guilty, as if for an hour or two she had forgotten about it all: forgotten that her father was missing, and may not even be around at all anymore. That was how weird things were these days.

Fran nodded.

There was an awkward quiet.

'Well, thank you, Will, you're so, you're just so kind . . . I don't know what we would do without you,' Nessa said, walking up to him as he scratched his head and gazed out of the window. She gave him a hug.

'That's OK, Nessa . . . Right, it's time to get this little astronomer and her mother back home to bed. School tomorrow!' Will exclaimed, glancing at the clock. It was 10.20 p.m.

'Thanks again Will,' Poppy said, beaming.

'Anytime Pops. Listen, Ness,' he said, just before he left, 'if you hear anything about Jake, let me know, yeah? If you need anything, even just to talk, in the middle of the night, I don't even care. You know where I am.'

Nessa smiled and nodded. She couldn't say anything. She felt her eyes well with tears.

As soon as they had left, Poppy become solemn once more. Usually she would be parading around the house in her new things, staring at her bum in the mirror and repeatedly taking selfies from the same angle. But she just took her bags upstairs to her room as if she were a little ashamed of them and came back down to watch some TV on the sofa with a cup of tea. Quiet, and reflective, she was lost in her thoughts as the bright light of the television flickered, lighting up her face.

Later that night, Nessa was struggling with insomnia. Sleep was escaping her yet again, another night in a row. She didn't know how much longer she could function with so little sleep, and the more stressed she felt about it, the harder it became to drift off when she did have the chance. She sighed angrily and pulled her pillow over her head, enjoying the peace it brought, before remembering that she wouldn't be able to hear the phone if Jake just happened to call . . .

Nessa heard a little knock at her bedroom door.

'Mum?'

'Yes Pops?' Nessa said, sitting up in bed, the moonlight filtering through a tiny gap in the curtains.

'Can I come in?' Poppy whispered.

'Sure. What's up? Are you hungry? Have you had a nightmare?' Nessa asked, pulling her pyjama top down, because somehow it was all crinkled up around her middle from the tossing and turning.

'No, I've not been hungry for days. I just can't sleep,' Poppy said quietly, before padding over to the bed and sitting on the edge of it.

Nessa could just about make out her daughter's pyjamas. A t-shirt and some bottoms with clouds and little bolts of pink lightning printed all over them.

'New jams?' she asked, trying to change the subject.

'Yeah, I picked them out tonight . . .'

'They are lovely, Pops. What a lucky girl you are . . . That was very kind of Will wasn't it? You've practically got all new clothes—'

'Yep. Move up then, Mum,' she demanded.

'Oh, right, OK,' Nessa said, confused. She wriggled across the sheet to Jake's side. It was much cooler there. And with that, Poppy climbed into the bed, crawling beneath the duvet like a puppy. She'd not done this since she was little. She put her arm around her mother, and rested her head on her shoulder.

'Do you think Dad's OK?'

'I hope so, I really do. I'm praying for him . . .'

'But you're not religious, are you Mum?' Poppy asked gently, laughing a little to herself. Nessa couldn't believe how grown-up she sounded sometimes. There was a kind of knowing in Poppy's voice that emerged occasionally, and every time it surprised her.

'No, no I'm not usually . . . but I think, I think we need a bit of extra help right now.'

Nessa could feel Poppy nod her head in agreement.

'Do you reckon that if there is a God, that he's cool with that kind of thing? Like not believing in him, and then suddenly believing in him when things are bad?'

'Hmm . . . well . . . it's not ideal, is it? We'll just have to see if he'll give us a chance, won't we?' Nessa said, giving her daughter a squeeze, and smiling to herself in the dark.

'Have the army been in touch today, or the police?' Poppy asked.

'Yes. I speak to them all the time. Honestly, Poppy, I'm on it and I would tell you if anything happened.'

'And?'

'Nothing right now. I'm sorry, honey.'

'I love you, Mum,' Poppy whispered.

After a minute or two of quiet, she piped up again. 'Mum, I find the whole idea of suicide really upsetting. Like, people are saying that Dad might be dead because of that, and I can't stop thinking about it . . . I feel bad for thinking about it, because I know we are meant to be positive, but I can't get it off my mind.'

'Me too baby. Me too.'

The images came back to Nessa's mind and all the hairs on the back of her neck stood on end. Her eyes started to sting with tears, and she summoned every last shred of energy to not break down.

'I mean why do people kill themselves? How do they manage to actually do it?' Poppy asked. 'I've felt sad before, but never that sad. I just can't imagine how someone like Dad, who was always so funny and happy and stuff, could do something like that to himself.'

Nessa took a deep breath in and tried to breathe out gently. Her heart was pounding in her chest, and a wave of nausea clawed at the bottom of her throat. How do you talk to a child about suicide? How do you discuss something so complex?

'It's sad, Poppy, and very difficult to think about. I'm glad you are telling me how you feel, and you shouldn't be ashamed of your thoughts, OK?'

Nessa could feel Poppy nodding in the inky blackness. Her shoulder started to get wet from her daughter's tears.

'Some people go through things that are so bad that they get very low . . . And there's a level of low that they reach where they can't see their life ever getting better, you know? They lose hope, hope that things will ever get better, and it's difficult to live without hope . . . I guess at the time, they feel like there's no other option for them, but of course there is; there always is.'

Nessa stroked her daughter's thick unruly hair, a huge lump in her throat. She was scared. About what might happen if Jake never came home. If Poppy had to grow up without her father, if she had to carry on without her husband . . . As time went on, it all felt more and more hopeless. Her previous fury at Jake's absence had melted away, only to be replaced by complete panic and desperation to just know whether or not he was OK.

'I love you, Pops,' Nessa said. 'I will take care of you, no matter what happens'.

'Will loves you too, you know,' Poppy said sleepily, after a moment or two.

'Oh yeah?'

'Yeah, he said it earlier . . .' she added, yawning.

'Oh, right . . .'

'We were in Nando's right, and basically, right, Nita had gone to order the food and Fran was in the toilet, and he said it then. He said, "I love your mum you know. I really do love your mum . . .", and I wondered for a moment if perhaps he had wanted to say it for a long time.'

Nessa felt a little stunned. What was she talking about? Was she insinuating something?

'Oh, well, that's nice. That's sweet. I think he sees us as being his family,' Nessa said eventually.

'Yeah, he feels like he is anyway. Sometimes, he feels, well, he feels like my dad . . .' Poppy added, matter-of-factly, before hugging her mother tighter and falling asleep, her soft snores joining the hum of the night.

#26

'Poppy . . . Poppy? Where did you find this?' Nessa cried, running into the kitchen, holding an army blue envelope in her left hand. It had been sat innocently on the hallway table, beneath two poorly spelled takeaway menus that boasted of culinary delights ranging from 'sweat and sour chicken' to 'beef dumpings'. Nessa had only uncovered it because she couldn't find her car keys.

Poppy was sitting at the kitchen table, licking a thick layer of pink yoghurt from a silver lid. Her skin looked bright and youthful in the Saturday morning sunshine. A couple of red spots had appeared on her chin and she'd tried to cover them up with a concealer that was slightly too yellow for her skin tone. Her hair was scraped up into an eye-wateringly high, messy bun. There was a tiny blob of yoghurt on her nose.

'Oh, I found it under the doormat when you asked me to shake it out . . . I told you about it; do you not remember?' Poppy asked with concern, getting up and opening the kitchen bin with her elbow.

'No, I don't remember. For fuck's sake, Poppy! When? When? When did you find it?' Nessa asked desperately, tears in her eyes. As she spoke she shook the envelope, and it wobbled in the air pathetically.

'Jesus, calm down, Mum. I don't know . . . the other day, a week or so ago. I can't remember now. I told you about it!' Poppy replied, starting to cry, and throwing the plastic pot in the bin. Nessa noticed how tired she looked, as if she'd been crying in the night.

'Recycling Poppy,' Nessa said sternly.

'Oh it's too late now. I'm not getting it out; there's loads of crap in there now and it stinks,' Poppy said, looking into the bin with disgust, her voice wobbling with anger and hurt.

'Christ,' Nessa said angrily, before running upstairs with a furious thud so characteristic of her daughter. For a moment it was as if their roles were reversed. Nessa ran into her bedroom and slammed the door behind her. She paced the carpet a few times before slumping down on the bed, fanning herself with the envelope. She felt sick with nerves, nauseous with anticipation and instantly guilty for being so angry at Poppy about this. Nessa had no memory of Poppy telling her about it, but yet she'd had so much on her mind . . . It wasn't exactly Poppy's fault anyway, even if she *hadn't* told her. It wasn't her fault they were in this mess in the first place. She was just a kid, it really wasn't fair on her . . .

Nessa's heart was pounding in her chest. All she could do was hold the envelope in her trembling hands, turning it round, over and over again, to double check it hadn't already been opened, that it wasn't an old one that had been misplaced. That would be so disappointing. But it was unlikely; she always kept them in her drawer . . .

Nessa studied the envelope. It was almost just like all the others, but *something* was different. Something was missing. And why had it been left beneath the doormat anyway? That made no sense at all. Nessa frantically opened the drawer by her bed and found the others. She laid a couple out on the bed and studied them. The rest had an airmail stamp on them. That was the difference; this one didn't . . .

So what did that mean? And why would a postman put

the letter under the mat? Perhaps there was an Amazon parcel stuck in the letterbox . . . That happened sometimes. She couldn't believe she'd missed it. It broke her heart to think that it was just lying there unopened for god-knows-how-long.

Nessa tore open the envelope and tipped it upside down. A photograph slid out and landed on the white cotton sheets. She didn't recognise it at first, her eyes blurred with fresh tears. She turned the image upside down and blinked. It was the strangest thing: a photo of Jake – just Jake.

It was a recent one. He looked like he was lying down on a dust sheet or something, and he was wearing his uniform. The sunlight and the dusty haze of it gave her the impression it had been taken in Camp Bastion, although it could have been taken in any number of places. He had the strangest look on his face. His eyes were red and tired, as if he had been upset, or he hadn't slept for a long time. There was a look of desperate sadness on his face. And yet somehow, despite this, there was so much love in his eyes. It was the strangest thing. Nessa simply couldn't work out if it was the most heartbreaking, or the most hopeful thing she'd ever seen.

Despite his tiredness, he looked even more beautiful than she remembered him. The pictures he'd sent over the years were always pre-existing images. Photos they had treasured for years, even. This was new and he wasn't the type to take photos of himself . . . What did this mean?

Nessa turned it over gently, expecting it to just have the usual photo number scrawled on the back and nothing else, but there was more. Words:

I'll be watching over you . . . always . . . I'm so sorry I had to leave . . .

Oh god, Nessa thought, raising a hand to her mouth. *He's gone . . .*

He's gone . . .

Fifteen

'But what are we meant to do?'

'Nessa, I appreciate that things are very hard for you right now. While everything points towards the fact that Jake has taken his own life, it's likely that we cannot take this case forward for some time yet. I'm sorry,' the policeman said, stroking his thick brown beard with his right hand.

Asil Bakkal was a 23-year-old Turkish policeman, with eyes as black as olives and the smoothest, silkiest skin she'd ever seen. He was a man of awkward mannerisms. Nessa had spotted him a few times recently, during meetings discussing the details of Jake's disappearance, as he stood uncomfortably by the window, looking out at the rain as it coated the streets of Beckenham in a charcoal gloss. Asil glanced at his hands uncomfortably, studying them for a moment as if there might be some relief in the soft skin coating his bones from the difficulties of the conversation.

'But what are we meant to do? I know you're trying to

help us, but my daughter and I, we've just been living in limbo these past few weeks, you know? It's so bad for both of us. We've been waiting for Jake to come back, waiting for him to reappear, and now waiting to know for sure, to be able to hold the funeral he deserves . . .' She trailed off, struggling to hold back her emotions. Asil nodded understandingly.

'Poppy's in bits; it's so messed up. This is such an important time for her, but she can't focus on anything. I need some closure for her the most. We just want to remember him in the right way, together. I mean are we going to have to wait seven years until the government will officially acknowledge that he is no longer with us? And despite the fact that he sent me what was practically a bloody suicide note?' Nessa said, great tears spilling over her cheeks. She noticed that her hands were trembling. A general feeling of discord ran through her body. Everything ached and hurt. She was breaking from the inside out. She was exhausted, unable to sleep at night because whenever she started to drift off she would imagine herself drowning, or falling from a building, over and over again, the vertigo of her anxiety so overwhelming that she would have to sit up in bed and rest her feet on the scratchy carpet until she felt grounded once more.

'I understand, Mrs Bruce. While we are in no doubt Mr Bruce he is deceased – we always have to follow procedure. We will keep looking for him, we might find his, erm . . . his body, and then you'll be able to have a funeral. For now, we just have to sit tight,' Asil said, looking her directly in the eyes. 'I'm sorry, this is a really tough situation for you and your family. I can't even imagine what you must be going through,' he finished, clearing his throat and rubbing his beard again.

Nessa felt a sudden rage bubble away inside her. This was horrendous. She couldn't take it anymore, but she wasn't even sure what she was angry about. It was as if she'd reached the end of her fuse and she might just explode. Ness had been waiting for Jake for what felt like years now and, even now he had died, she was *still* waiting for him. She couldn't cope with a second more of it. She wanted closure more than anything in the world.

'Listen, I've got to go. I've got to get Poppy from school. I just really wish you guys were trying harder, you know, to find him. It can't be that hard,' she said furiously, standing up quickly, trying to stop herself from screaming in frustration at this poor man, who had done nothing wrong but find himself an inevitable part of the system. Another officer muffled by paperwork, blinded by procedure and bound by red tape.

'Nessa, I can assure you that we are doing our very best. We'll let you know if we hear anything, OK? Just look after yourself. You can get in touch anytime,' he said softly, understandingly, and standing up now too. He smelt of cologne and cigarettes. The expression on his face said it all. She was the hysterical, irrational woman. He, the voice of reason. *Just keep her calm. She'll settle down.* Nessa struggled to get her hand in the left arm of her coat and frantically flapped it around, stabbing away in the right direction in the hope she might locate the hole sometime soon. An empty fabric arm flapped around in the air violently. Nessa was becoming increasingly frustrated, a kind of hot anger rose within until her hand finally slipped through, appearing at the bottom of the sleeve.

Just look after yourself. People kept saying that. But what did it even mean? Nessa thought. She could barely look after Poppy, let alone herself, these days. Poppy had pretty much stopped eating altogether, and had taken to scratching herself with a compass in her room to let out the pain. It had taken Nessa's breath away, the thought of her beloved daughter scratching at her own flesh just to release the feelings she was battling, because seemingly there was no other way to deal with them. She wished she could talk to her, but Poppy was impossible to reach – so distant and quiet.

Everything was spiralling out of control. She wanted to make sure her daughter was OK but she couldn't even pick Poppy up from school in her own car, as it had broken down a fortnight ago and was still sitting on the roadside near the old cinema, collecting leaves, and globules of spit from the odd passer-by. Will had offered to pay for the repairs, but she didn't have the energy, or even the time, apparently, to do anything about it right now. The council could tow it away for all she cared. Instead, Will was going to meet her at home in half an hour, so they could go together.

She pushed open the heavy police station door with the palms of her hands, feeling the cool glass in contrast to the hot rage rushing around her body. Her legs were shaking and her stomach felt so empty it was painful, like her organs were dry and glued together. It terrified Nessa, feeling like this. She was so used to being in control. But just when she thought she was stronger than she had ever been – capable of handling anything – this had happened. In many ways, she was just as fragile now as she had been as a teenager, just as angry and prone to fly into a rage, just as tearful, just as insecure.

Just keep calm. Just keep going, she whispered to herself, as she made her way down the high street, dodging the people going about their business. But when she got home there was a deafening silence. She stood in the hallway, took one look at the photos of her once-happy family on the wall and tore them down. That felt good – alarmingly so. She stamped on the glass frames as they landed on the carpet, feeling the crunch of materials shattering beneath her boots: wood, glass, dried glue. A strength she didn't know she possessed trembled through her limbs. She wanted to destroy everything in sight.

This is so unfair. Jake is gone and I love him; this is so unfair. She tore the phone out of the wall socket and bashed it against a shelf corner until the plastic cracked and split satisfyingly. Walking into the kitchen, she opened cupboards and swept the glasses and the plates with her hands so they spilled out and broke into smithereens on the linoleum floor. She wrenched the cutlery tray from the drawer, and launched it across the room. Metal clattered against worktops loudly. *I loved him, he was my family.* Nessa stormed into the living room next and kicked the coffee table, turning it upside down with a bang. *Why can't someone just give us a break?* A pile of magazines hit the floor, their pages splaying out and tearing near the spine. A small vase of flowers landed on the carpet, remarkably unscathed.

The world is so cruel. I can't cope. I can't go on. This is the end of my life. I will never recover from this. She picked up a mug of cold coffee and flung it across the room. A great lick of brown liquid curled through the air. She reached down to grab a plate that Poppy had left on the floor, decorated with rock-solid swirls of stale ketchup.

'Nessa!'

It was Will. He was standing in the doorway. Nessa turned around, completely out of breath. She could barely focus on him. Her whole body was shaking.

'What the *hell* are you doing? What's going on?' he

asked, shock written across his face. His chest was rising up and down; he was breathing fast.

It hit Nessa that he seemed almost angry, or perhaps horrified by her. She felt a hot red sting on her cheeks – the flush of humiliation – and the chill of cold sweat. 'I just . . . I . . .' Her mouth felt dry as cotton. She dropped the plate softly to the ground where it broke in two with a dull thud.

Will walked quickly across the room towards her, broken things crunching beneath his feet, and as he did so, Nessa sank to the floor. 'I think I'm having a breakdown, Will. I can't carry on anymore. Please, please help me . . .' she said, sobbing into his chest as he stroked her hair away from her face.

He gripped on to her so tightly. It was as if he was holding her together. 'Oh Nessa, I'm going to help you get through this OK? I'm going to take care of you, I always will,' he said, as she wept.

Will looked around him at the carnage, stroking her forehead softly. The siren of a police car could be heard pulling up outside. He felt a shiver across the back of his neck. Everything was destroyed.

Sixteen

'Sorry . . . This is difficult'

Thursday, September 20th 2012

Nessa's living room was packed with mourners wearing suits and dresses in varying shades of black and grey. A brightly coloured tie or the flash of a crisp white handkerchief occasionally broke the dimness. Triangular sandwiches with the crusts cut off, sausage rolls and carrot sticks were crammed on every available surface.

It seemed like people were everywhere. They were bunched close together on the sofa, perched on chairs and leaning against walls and shelves. Young children sat at their parents' feet, their legs crossed on the thick carpet.

'One of the hardest things about having lost Jake, in the way we have, is that none of us had the chance to say goodbye. He sort of slipped away from us,' Nessa said, taking a pause and clearing her throat. She looked up at Teigen, who smiled at her nervously and tucked a swathe of hair behind her right ear.

An image of Jake was projected onto the only free wall space, which had been kept clear by Kat as people filed in, muttering to each other about how sad they were. He was wearing his uniform. A ribbon on his hat was blowing in the breeze. He looked happy.

Perhaps this is a mistake, Nessa thought, studying the picture of Jake and wondering if she'd turned into a mad widow. Were people talking about her in the neighbourhood, discussing how she was holding some bizarre memorial for her dead husband who no one had found? Did they stand in queues for the butchers and the newsagent, gossiping about how fucked up she'd become, how tired she looked? Were there rumours swirling? That a friend of a neighbour's aunt might have seen her drinking wine as they walked past her kitchen window one Monday morning?

'Sorry . . . This is difficult,' Nessa said, glancing away from the wall for a moment to take in the sea of faces before her. She wiped her eyes with a tissue before being able to continue. Her legs were trembling, as if they might just give out at any moment. *I have to be strong*.

'Because circumstances have meant we've not been able to have a proper funeral service yet, and might not be able to for some time, Poppy and I wanted to hold something special in Jake's memory, here at home. I'm so glad you have come to celebrate his life with us . . . Thank you.' Nessa looked down at Poppy who was staring up at her with blood red eyes. A vacant horror lay behind them, as she wildly tried to process this monumental loss, one that would undoubtedly touch her forever.

Everyone was here. Old school friends of Jake's, former colleagues, neighbours and his small family were all under the same roof. Nessa wondered why it took someone's death for this to happen.

The quiet sound of Betsy's weeping could be heard from somewhere near the sofa. Mick grumbled quietly to himself and fiddled with a flower that he'd plucked from an arrangement in the hallway, plucking out its petals absentmindedly, one by one. It was getting cold out and Nessa had turned on the heating so people would be comfortable. The tapping and gurgling of radiators could be heard every now and again, momentarily breaking the quietness.

Will stood by the door, looking smart in his suit. He watched Nessa compose herself, smoothing her hands down a grey, woollen dress, tied with a thin black belt around her waist. When Nessa turned to look at him for reassurance, she noticed that he looked quite upset, moved perhaps. He nodded softly and smiled at her, with an expression that urged her to continue. His tie was bright green – Jake's favourite colour.

'As I look around my living room right now, I see a group of people who Jake wholeheartedly loved. Betsy and Mick, for example. I know he wasn't always the most expressive, sentimental kind of man, but Jake always said to me that he couldn't have asked for better parents. You loved him unendingly and your kindness made him the wonderful man he grew up to be, with a huge capacity to love. I'm so grateful to you for bringing up a man like Jake.' As Nessa said this, Betsy wept into her tissue, nodding softly. Mick squeezed her wrinkled hand, looking confused.

'And Will, our wonderful and most treasured friend. Despite some animosity in your teenage years, Jake considered you to be one of his best friends in adulthood. He adored you, and I'm sure he missed the barn dance nights very much when he was on tour,' Nessa managed a little wink here and a titter of sentimental laughter spread across the room. A tear spilt from Will's eye and ran down his cheek.

'Nick. You always served Jake in the pub when he came home and he said you were the funniest guy he'd ever met. He went through a lot with work – as you can probably imagine – but your small gestures of kindness helped him through those difficult times. The odd free beer, the jokes, just having a man to talk to about the things he'd seen. I'm really grateful to you for that; I'm not sure you know how much you helped.' Nessa extended her right arm in a gesture of friendship towards the barman, who was wearing a black shirt and grey trousers. He had tattoos on his knuckles, which where white from where he was struggling to hold it together. Trembling, he nodded and smiled at Nessa.

'And, Robert, you were Jake's very best friend from school. You two were like conjoined twins for years, and for a moment I feared I might be marrying the both of you! But on a serious note, I know he missed you deeply when he was away.' Rob was standing near the edge of the room, looking at the floor. His lips were pursed tightly and his jaw was set hard, as he desperately held back his emotions.

'I could stand here and talk about all of you and the impact you had on Jake's life, but I hope you all know that you were adored by him . . . It would have meant an awful lot to him, too, to see how much he was loved. I only wish he'd truly known sooner . . .' Nessa whispered, struggling to get the last part of the sentence out into the open. A few people smiled wistfully, and made soft sounds to signify their agreement. A clock ticked loudly in the momentary silence.

'We might not know where Jake is right now, or exactly

what became of the wonderful man we knew. Our answer might never come, but that doesn't mean we can't remember him with the fondness and love he deserves, because he made us all so happy. He changed each and every one of our lives just by being who he was: a warm, special man with an incredible sense of adventure . . .'

Nessa continued, 'I know it could be easy for this afternoon to be sad, for us all to weep for Jake until we can't cry anymore. I sure know that's what I feel like doing. But I think we should be celebrating the fact that we were lucky enough to know and love him.'

Poppy pressed a key on the laptop, and the image of Jake in his army uniform was replaced with a picture of him as a schoolchild. He was holding what looked like a lunchbox, and a small brown satchel almost the same size as him was slung over his bony shoulder. He had a harsh, thick fringe, which looked as if it had been cut by Betsy in the kitchen with a blunt pair of scissors one rainy Sunday afternoon. There was a look of excitement on his face, a look of pride. He was standing up straight, his bright-red school jumper almost glowing in contrast with the terracotta brick wall behind him. Could he perhaps have sensed, even then, all that lay ahead of him?

'Some of you may know that Jake used to send me photos from the army, and I would send him letters in return. I've been lying awake at night recently, thinking about what I would say to Jake if he could hear me, or perhaps if I could write to him now. Sadly I can't tell him these things, but I want to share with you all today, the words I would say if I could,' Nessa said, reaching for a piece of thick white paper that was being passed to her by Kat.

Nessa cleared her throat and wiped her eyes with a tissue

before starting. Towards the back of the room a baby started to cry, only to be whisked into the kitchen with the door shutting softly behind them. The distant sound of a cooing mother swept through walls. Nessa felt the hairs stand up on the back of her neck.

'Jake, I'm proud of you. I'm proud of you for going out to the army to follow your dreams, even though it was hard for me to swallow when I first found out that was what you wanted to do. I know I wasn't always totally supportive, and I'm sorry for that. I'm proud of you for saving so many lives while you were on tour. I'm proud of you for everything you've done throughout your life. I love how you've always just done your own thing, listened to your heart and followed what you've known is right, despite the judgement of others. Not many people can do that. You were inspiring and unshakeable, and I loved you for that . . .'

Nessa paused for a moment, as Poppy pulled her chair closer and wrapped her arms around her waist, crying into her dress. Holding the paper with one hand, she stroked Poppy's hair with the other.

'Thank you, Jake, for helping me bring up our beautiful daughter, Poppy, who you loved to the ends of the earth. Thank you for the endless happiness you gave us during your short life; because it was too short. I looked forward to growing old with you Jake. I imagined us at Poppy's graduation, our twenty-fifth wedding anniversary and beyond. I even imagined us at 85, as crazy as it sounds, holding hands as we slept. You stopped me dreading growing old, it became something to look forward to. I never thought I'd feel that way about it . . .'

People had been nodding their heads in agreement. Tears spilled down cheeks and men cleared their throats, uncomfortable with the swell of their emotions. Out of the blue, Mick cried out, as if he'd had a realisation about the truth of what had happened.

'Our son . . . Our little boy!' he cried, holding on to Betsy, who was nodding sadly, as he spoke and trying to calm him down.

The room fell quiet. People didn't want to look. It was too difficult, like a drunken loon shouting nonsense on a train. You couldn't stare. It was too sad . . . Tears that had thus far been successfully suppressed, spilled urgently over cheeks. Emotion swelled like the sea.

'Our beautiful little boy has gone . . .'

A couple of representatives from the army, Jake's seniors, stood in pristine uniform with their hats pressed against their hearts. Grade 2 shaved heads were angled towards the ground.

'You may have made a mistake, Jake, but we are *still* proud of you. My darling husband, you were human. We all are. We all miss things. It breaks my heart that the one thing you missed caused us to lose one of the most beautiful people we have ever had the luck to have in our lives. You would have always been forgiven, Jake, because we love you and that's what happens when you love someone.'

Poppy was sobbing, pressing a large tissue against her face. A lady sitting nearby reached out and squeezed her shoulder. Poppy's mascara started to run from her eyes and down her cheeks. Shakily, she pressed a button on the laptop keyboard and the image projected on the wall changed to a picture of Jake on their wedding day. He was kissing the side of Nessa's head in the rain, his arms wrapped around her waist.

'But now, Jake, somehow, we are going to have to learn how to live without you . . . and I'm going to be totally honest here, I'm really not sure how we can,' Nessa said. Will crossed the room, almost tiptoeing, and sat down next to Poppy, gathering her in his arms as she cried into his chest.

'How will we live without you, Jake? I don't know at this stage exactly how we'll ever be able to move forward, but I have to have faith that we will and that we will keep you close to us forever. I promise you that I will take the very best care of our gorgeous Poppy. She's amazing, Jake, and she's like you in so many ways, so I know I've not lost you altogether. When she laughs, I hear you; when she daydreams, I see your expressions in her face. I'm so lucky to have Poppy. Your memory will stay with us forever. I love you Jake, we both love you and we always will . . . *Thank you* for making our lives so wonderful,' Nessa said.

'I think it was beautiful, Ness. You should really stop doing that and go to bed, you must be absolutely beside yourself with exhaustion . . .' Kat said, bringing the last plate into the kitchen. Nessa was bent over the kitchen sink, finally getting to the end of what had felt like an endless pile of washing up. Poppy was upstairs in bed, sleeping, and Will and Teigen had left just half an hour ago, having helped around the house. The last guests had filed out, the smell of alcohol that had tinged their breath lingered in the empty sitting room, mixed with the odour of stale peanuts and crisps.

'Thank you Kat . . . but don't worry, it's better for me to be distracted, it really is. I'll only start crying again and I'm sick and tired of crying,' Nessa said, grabbing the plate and throwing the few stale sandwiches left over into the kitchen bin. They'd only been out for two or three hours, but the thick, white bread had started to curl at the edges.

'How do you feel?' Kat asked, switching on the kettle.

'Exhausted, and I'm genuinely not sure I've ever had a headache this bad. Feel like I'm going to pass out. I'm really glad we did it. I think we needed to, do you know what I mean? It felt like the right thing to do by him,' Nessa responded, peeling off her washing up gloves and resting them on the side.

'It was really brave of you,' Kat said, pouring out two cups of coffee.

'God, I didn't feel brave. I felt like I was going to collapse.'

'Well you were amazing. Nessa, please go to bed. It's half past ten and you look green with tiredness. Please. I've never seen you like this before; you look really ill,' Kat said, tilting her head to one side, her painted eyebrows wrinkled in the middle. Her flame red hair was piled into a bun on the top of her head, and a few strands had fallen away from the hair band, surrounding her face in a halo of rose-coloured fluff.

'Wow, thanks,' Nessa said, rolling her eyes and managing to force a smile.

'Oh come on, you know what I mean. Just let me finish things off round here. I will clear everything up, and then when you come downstairs tomorrow morning your house will be spotless. How does that sound?'

'Yeah, well now I think of it, I'm not sure I can really argue with that,' Nessa said, raising her right hand to the back of her neck and massaging her skin with her fingers. A look of pain shot across her face.

'Come on, up you go,' Kat said, walking over behind her sister and pushing her in the direction of the stairs.

'Ohhh, Kat, are you sure?' Nessa asked, walking heavily like a child, her feet banging against the floor as she reached the foot of the stairs.

'Yes. I love you. Now go to bed,' Kat said, pulling her in for a cuddle and softly kissing her on the cheek.

Kat had finally finished the clearing up. It was 1 a.m., and the moon was shining a brilliant white in the sky. The pale light poured through the glass doors that separated the living room from the garden. She stood alone in the room having just turned off the lights, absorbing the atmosphere, noticing the way the moonshine illuminated every surface, revealing the depths of the darkest corners that were usually shrouded in gloom at this time. It was as if silver fingers had touched everything, turning innocuous items like vacuum cleaner handles and coats into amazing shapes: the gargoyles of Notre Dame, the backs of tall, broad strangers. *Creepy*, she whispered to herself, noticing the cold and rubbing her upper arms with the palms of her hands.

She could feel the craving tickling away at the back of her mind, in her tummy, jangling at the tips of her fingers. It had been there all day, but didn't seem to be going away. She was meant to have given up ages ago. She'd tried so hard, so many times, but she always folded and found herself puffing away regretfully in some rundown pub garden, or the driveway of a friend's parents' house. Nessa would be furious if she knew what she was about to do, but it had been a long, tough day. *Who cares,* she whispered to herself, heading back into the kitchen and rifling urgently through her bag. She pulled out a packet of cigarettes. The packaging, once pristine and perfectly rectangular, had been battered and weathered by the jagged environs of her backpack, scratched by keys, moistened by the condensation of water bottles and jostled roughly against imposing library books. Kat opened the packet to find a solitary, slightly worse-for-wear Marlborough Light looking back at her.

She couldn't risk going to the back garden because, if Nessa or Poppy had their bedroom windows open, the curls of smoke would rise up and fill the house. Plus, the next-door neighbour's very simple dog was likely to start throwing himself at the fence like a misfired rocket at the slightest sound. She was going to have to go out of the front door. It was the only way.

She grabbed the cigarette and a lighter and crept back through the darkness of the hallway until she reached the front door. She gently opened it, doing everything as softly as she possibly could so as not to make any noise . . . When she opened the door the brisk, cold air hit her face instantly. Her breath gathered before her in clouds of thick condensation. Looking down as she closed the door softly behind her, she spotted a white envelope, sitting on the mat.

She bent down to pick it up. It wasn't addressed to anyone, and the back of the envelope hadn't been sealed. It just flapped open, temptingly. She hungrily pulled back the flap of the envelope and pulled out a piece of A4 paper, which had been folded neatly into four. Kat placed the envelope between her teeth, and opened the sheet. There was a poem, printed on one side, in Times New Roman. Kat turned the paper over twice and checked inside the envelope once again. There was no name on it. No clue as to who might have done such a lovely thing. Then, Kat recalled that she'd seen something white and envelope-like poking out of the pocket of Will's suit jacket. It had caught her attention because she had thought it was a pocket square at first, which she had thought was a nice touch, but wasn't sure, and had been studying it absentmindedly, trying to work out what it was. Perhaps it belonged to him and it had fallen out as he left. Lighting her cigarette and wiping her tired eyes, she started to read:

Do Not Stand At My Grave And Weep

Do not stand at my grave and weep;
I am not there. I do not sleep.
I am a thousand winds that blow.
I am the diamond glint on snow.
I am the sunlight on ripened grain.
I am the gentle autumn rain.
When you wake in the morning hush,
I am the swift, uplifting rush
Of quiet birds in circling flight.
I am the soft starlight at night.
Do not stand at my grave and cry;
I am not there. I did not die.

Mary Elizabeth Frye

Seventeen

'I wish you'd asked first'

Tuesday, December 11th 2012

'Right then, if anyone fancies bloody-well helping me, that'd be great, because to be brutally honest I've got pine needles in places I never imagined pine needles could go,' Will said, standing halfway through the front door with a huge Christmas tree under his arm.

'Oh god, Wiiill . . .' Nessa protested, appearing in the hallway after hearing all the commotion. She wore a black woolly jumper, a pair of skinny grey jeans and a blanket wrapped around her shoulders, and she still felt chilly. Great gusts of cold air were filling the house as the door was kept open. Nessa wasn't expecting any visitors. Her hair had been piled into a thick, messy bun, and she was wearing her glasses. Poppy stood by the door still in her school uniform, clapping her hands together with glee like she was 11 again.

'Oh god, Will what?' he asked innocently, giving the tree another tug and whipping himself in the face with a branch.

'Fuck,' he said.

'I don't want a tree, Will. It's very kind of you, but we aren't doing Christmas this year, it just doesn't feel right . . . I wish you'd asked first,' Nessa said, looking down at the hallway carpet and shaking her head. She pawed at the ground with the toes of her right foot. Enforced, manufactured happiness. This was the last thing she needed.

'Oh, so you've made the executive decision, Nessa, to cancel Christmas have you? How do you think Kat will feel when she comes back from uni in a couple of days to spend Crapmas, sorry, Christmas, with you? And also, what does Poppy think about this?' Will asked, holding an invisible microphone to Poppy's mouth and raising an eyebrow quizzically. This was something he used to do when Poppy was little that always made her laugh hysterically. The effect wasn't quite the same now; she was nowhere near as impressed.

'I dunno . . .' Poppy said, the smile falling from her face. She looked down at the ground, a sudden expression of guilt replacing her previous excitement.

'Come on, Pops, give me a hand – I've bought it now and I doubt the guy who sells them near the corner shop welcomes returns, so you're having it, and that's that,' Will said defiantly, heaving the dead plant into the hallway. The sound of branches swishing against the white wallpaper made Nessa cringe, especially after everything had been carefully fixed up by Will after her outburst . . . Poppy hopped over the tree, and bent down to lift the rear end, helping him bring it into the sitting room. She kicked the door shut behind her with her left foot, starting to smile again.

'And heave!' Will cried dramatically as they managed to push and pull it into the corner of the room, swiping magazines and books off various surfaces and causing picture-frames to clatter and fall like dominoes. Detached roots and clods of mud speckled the carpet where they had been, leaving a trail of yuletide destruction. Nessa ran into the kitchen to get a dustpan and brush and started to clear it up, feeling quietly irritated. She loved Will, but the last thing she needed was one of those annoying twats in her life who felt it necessary to tell her to smile when she was sad. The kind of tool she occasionally encountered on the street, yelling phrases like 'Cheer up love, it might never happen'. But it *had happened*. Her husband was dead.

But he's just doing something nice. Be kind, Nessa thought to herself, as she swept the last little bits into the pan. It was too late now anyway. Nessa stood up and saw Will standing there proudly, wiping his hands together in satisfaction and staring at the tree. He was still wearing his black woollen coat, in which he looked terribly handsome. He'd recently cut his hair, and his grey stubble had been tidied up. His cheeks were a healthy pink from all the effort.

'It's a bit tall, isn't it?' Poppy said, starting to giggle. The top of the tree – a good 15 inches – was haphazardly squashed against the ceiling so that it resembled a tall commuter rammed into an over-packed tube train.

'Yeah . . . bit of an oversight wasn't it? Oh well!' Will said, laughing to himself, 'it's a beauty though.'

'You forget sometimes, Will, that we don't live in a palace like you do,' Nessa said, warming again and poking him in the stomach.

'Ouch. I don't live in a bloody palace!' Will protested, rubbing his side. 'The decorations are in the car. Back in a moment!' And, with that, he disappeared again to fetch them, the door slamming behind him. Good job he's got a key, Nessa thought.

'I love Will,' Poppy said, a huge smile across her face.

'I know you do darling. Hey, I didn't realise you wanted a tree so much,' Nessa said, walking over to her daughter and pulling her close for a cuddle, which was met a little reluctantly. It was like trying to embrace a coat stand.

A month or so ago, Nessa and Poppy had talked about Christmas and how they would handle it, so soon after Jake's death. It had been a difficult conversation, for Poppy was not only grieving for her father, but also going through her cynical teenage years. They had decided to keep it very low key this time around. The whole Santa Claus myth had been categorically destroyed by Jake years ago, when he had got drunk and tripped over Poppy's stocking while 'tiptoeing' into her room, squashed the mince pies she'd left out for Rudolf and knocked out one of his front teeth. But seeing her reaction now, it made Nessa feel guilty . . . Clearly something had changed since they spoke.

'Well I didn't want to bother with any of it back then, but I was a bit sad in the end that we weren't going to have one. I didn't want to say anything to you, though, because you've been so depressed lately . . .'

'Oh, Poppy,' Nessa murmured, kissing the top of her daughter's head.

'Ta da!' Will said, suddenly reappearing in the hallway with a huge box of decorations.

'Where the hell did you get those from?' Nessa asked, as the box approached closer. But she couldn't help but start rooting through the collection.

She usually hated Christmas decorations. She found them so brash and so cheesy. Garish red tinsel always reminded her of her first foster father and the horrible Christmases where he had got pissed and started shouting and smashing things up because there was a lump in his gravy. But the decorations that Will had brought were all in a winter countryside theme. Gorgeous ceramic berries and crab apples dangled from golden thread. There were tiny squirrels and foxes, fashioned by talented fingers, and four old-school miniature Santas, lightly dusted with fake snow. Bunches of cinnamon sticks had been pulled together with string, and real candy canes glistened in the light. There was no tinsel, but instead a few rolls of soft gold ribbon with sumptuous bows to punctuate them. They were the most beautiful decorations she'd ever seen.

'Will, this is just amazing. This is so kind of you,' Nessa sighed, gently digging through the box and uncovering even more beautiful things. Will blushed a little and shrugged his shoulders. Poppy smiled widely.

'There's one more thing,' Will said, setting the box down on the sofa and digging around a little. The decorations jangled against each other and he bit his bottom lip as he rooted around.

'Careful . . .' Nessa said protectively, suddenly worried he might break something.

'Ah, here it is,' he said with a smile, pulling out a small wooden box. 'Poppy, you can open this with your mum,' he said, handing her the container.

Poppy pulled back the lid, which creaked gently as she did so. The first thing they saw was a bunch of tissue paper. Poppy held the box in one hand and started to move the paper away, revealing the top of a small, glass dome, which looked as if it had pretend snow settled at the bottom.

'What is it?' Nessa asked, as Poppy started to pull it out.

'Be careful, Pops, it's very delicate,' Will said thrusting his hands into the air as she uncovered it fully, as if preparing to catch it.

All they could see was an empty snow dome with a white

background. A beautiful snow dome all the same. It looked like a valuable antique. It was clearly old, very well made and amazingly light. But it didn't really make sense. It had some weird clips coming out of it too, as if it were meant to go on the tree. Poppy looked up at Will, confused.

'So, just give it a gentle shake and turn it around,' Will said, crossing his arms and smiling nervously.

Poppy followed his instructions, flipping it around in her hands. And there it was. A picture of Jake – young, holding baby Poppy, and looking up at the camera with that missing thing sparkling in his eyes: hope. It had been taken a few days after Poppy was born and they'd just brought her home for the first time. It was the most terrifying and exciting experience of their lives. Jake looked sublimely happy, like he'd been given the most special gift.

Tiny snowflakes fell through the water and past his limpid eyes.

'And there's the angel for the top, well, nearly the top of your tree,' Will said, as Nessa burst into tears and wrapped her arms around him.

Eighteen

'These must have cost a small fortune'

'Oh, Nessa, your house is looking lovely and festive. Your neighbours must be incredibly jealous!' Betsy said, as she shut the front door behind her and peeled off her scarf. 'I'm so glad you are both celebrating Christmas now,' she added, smiling brightly. 'It was sad when you said you wouldn't. Jake wouldn't have liked that; he loved Christmas.'

Betsy gasped as she walked through the hall and closer to the tree, examining the beautiful decorations.

'Oh goodness me, that's incredible. These must have cost a small fortune . . . Oh and look, there's Jake – how wonderful,' Betsy said, pointing towards the glass decoration with his picture inside.

'It's amazing isn't it? We have Will to thank for all this, don't we Poppy?' Nessa said, putting her arm around her daughter as her mother-in-law studied the tree, touching the decorations with her slender fingers and smelling the cinnamon sticks by pulling them closer to her face.

'*Will?* He did all this? Really now . . .' Betsy said emotionally, having studied the globe for a few moments. There was a strange inflection in her voice and Nessa wasn't quite sure how to take it. Betsy had never been the kind of woman to be bitchy or jealous or presumptuous. She wasn't the kind to make statements with the tone of her voice, rather than just saying how she felt . . .

Nessa tried to fathom Betsy's intention as she watched the elderly woman study the tree. Maybe she was shocked and overwhelmed by Will's kindness, which would be understandable given that the tree was rather grand. Or perhaps she was unhappy about it for some reason. She really hoped it wasn't the latter. Nessa swallowed hard and tried to ignore the anxiety that was building inside her chest.

'Tea? Coffee?' Nessa asked.

'Oh a tea would be lovely, thank you,' Betsy said, tearing her gaze away from the tree, and turning around to sink down onto the sofa. She looked a little pale, Nessa noticed.

'Pops, you wouldn't mind would you?' Nessa asked, turning to her daughter with a pleading expression on her face. Poppy rolled her eyes and stormed off into the kitchen, switching the kettle on. Had Betsy not been there, Nessa was pretty sure she would have been sworn at.

'It's lovely to see you, Betsy. We've missed you. How's Mick, where is he tonight?' Nessa asked. She felt bad for lying. She hadn't missed Betsy at all. She loved her – in fact, adored her – but she'd been so wrapped up in her own vacuum of sadness lately she hadn't even realised that it had been two weeks since she'd last visited.

'Oh, he's alright. He's having a much better day today, and our neighbour Samantha is keeping an eye on him for a little while this evening. I thought it would be the perfect opportunity to get out of the house, come and see you and my lovely granddaughter,' Betsy said, smiling widely and back to her 'old self' again. Nessa berated herself for being sensitive earlier; she was clearly imagining things, still feeling a little out of sorts.

'How are you coping, Nessa?' Betsy asked, her voice full of concern.

'Erm, I don't know really . . . I feel a little flat, to be honest. After Jake died I would cry a lot, and I felt very angry, and a whole load of other really quite strong emotions, but lately, I don't know, I'm starting to feel as though I'm not feeling very much at all. Do you know what I mean? It's like I'm a little dead inside, and there's something worse about that in a way,' Nessa said, suddenly stopping the conversation as Poppy appeared with two steaming mugs.

'Thanks Pops,' Betsy said, smiling at Poppy, who gave her a kiss on the cheek before waltzing back out of the room and dashing up stairs.

'I do understand, Nessa. It's a horrendous thing, to lose your husband. Naturally, you are going to feel all sorts of things. You'll have times when you feel completely numb, you'll have downs of course and, weirdly enough, you'll have ups too. Grief is a very strange thing, never simple, never simple . . .' Betsy said, taking a sip from her tea and looking at Nessa with her kind, understanding eyes.

'I know. But how about you, Bets? I mean, you've lost your son,' Nessa asked, staring at a tiny fox decoration, dangling from one of the branches. It spun round slowly, a porcelain tail catching the light.

'I'm finding it hard, well horrendous, to be quite honest, Nessa, but you know us Bruces; we aren't so good at talking about feelings. I'm trying to be better at that lately though.

To be honest, I always had the thought of Jake coming home as something to look forward to, you know? What with everything that goes on there, with his father, the prospect of seeing him again always kept me going,' Betsy said, looking down at her tea and almost drifting away for a moment or two.

'I know,' Nessa said, reaching out and putting her hand on the back of Betsy's. It was soft to the touch, despite how bony it was.

'Poppy and I are always here for you; you know that, right? We're family and always will be. Nothing changes in that respect, OK?' Nessa added.

'Oh don't, you'll make me cry,' Betsy said, sliding her hand gently away from beneath Nessa's and waving it in the air near her face to cool herself down. She smiled as tears came to her eyes.

'I have some great news about Mick,' Betsy said, changing the subject. 'Well, obviously Mick won't ever get better as such. Or at least, certainly he won't go back to the way he was. You know as well as I do that it doesn't really work like that. But he hasn't exactly been getting worse either; he's even having a few good days as well, like today,' Betsy said, with a hopeful smile on her face. 'That's why I felt confident enough to leave him with Sammi. It's not often I can do that.'

'Well, that's fantastic. Why do you think it is? Have you changed anything in his routine? Have they altered his medication or something?' Nessa asked.

'I genuinely don't know. No change in meds lately, but he's got some new care worker who takes him on trips from the day centre he goes to. They never really had that before, they just kept them kind of cooped up in a big room playing card games and listening to music. But it seems they've put this bloke in the post recently. Very good at his job too . . . Mick gets along so well with him, and he's been a lot brighter ever since . . . But then again, I can't imagine something as trivial as that would have such an effect, would you?'

'No, not really, although you never know . . . It's interesting. I'm glad to hear that the support he's getting has improved though; it's been like banging your bloody head against the wall with the council, hasn't it? It must really help you as well, to know he is safe and happy and able to go out with someone who knows how to cope with things that might trigger him,' Nessa said, taking a sip of her tea.

'Yes, it's a big relief. I'm just going to enjoy things as they are for now, because I never know what the future holds when it comes to Mick,' Betsy said with a resigned smile and a shrug of her shoulders.

'Oh well, I better head off now, Nessa,' Betsy said rather suddenly, as if catching herself from a daydream. She set her mug down softly.

'So soon? You can stay for longer, I can make you some food or something?' Nessa asked, desperate for her to stay. She could have spoken to Betsy for hours now she was here, and suddenly the thought of being practically alone on a Friday night, a week before Christmas, filled her with dread . . . She would ask Will to come round, but she knew he was with his girlfriend. All her friends would just want to go out to the pub or something, and she couldn't bear the thought of that, jostling at the bar for a drink and the headache that would inevitably follow the next day.

'Oh no, I must dash. I shouldn't leave Sam for too long with Mick, just in case!' she said, rising to her feet now and walking slowly towards the corridor.

Nessa hugged Betsy tightly before she opened the front door.

'Night night, Poppy,' Betsy yelled up the stairs.

After a short pause, Poppy's bedroom door could be heard swinging open, and she materialised at the top of the landing. 'Oh, night Granny!' Poppy said.

'I love you both,' Betsy said, blowing her granddaughter some kisses, before walking through the front door.

Nessa stepped forward and watched her leave. The cold air felt nice against her cheeks. She leant her body against the doorframe and sighed.

'Goodness me,' Betsy said, turning around once more as she was just a few steps away from the house. Her face was bright, an almost golden light across her skin as if it was being lit up by candles.

'What?' Nessa asked.

'Just the lights – they are stunning. It's lovely seeing them now it's even darker than it was before, when I arrived,' Betsy said, shrugging happily before turning around and walking away. Nessa stood fixed to the spot, stunned.

'Bye, Nessa,' she called out before getting into her car and starting her engine. Nessa waved limply in Betsy's direction.

'What lights?' Nessa asked herself, stepping out into the cold air as Betsy's car pulled away from the curb.

And that was when she saw them. Two strips of twinkling Christmas lights, strung hurriedly across the front of her house: small, simple, but beautiful.

Nessa poured a large glass of wine and texted Will.

Thank you Will. Not just for the tree, which looks lovely, but for the lights too. How on earth did you manage to put them up without us knowing?! Absolutely incredible. You may have made our Christmas . . . Thank you xxx

Two hours later Nessa woke up, having fallen asleep on the sofa. A trail of her drool was running down her face, and had formed a small pool on the cushion she had rested on. *Ergh*, she said quietly, wiping her mouth with her sleeve. The house was silent. The distant sound of Poppy's TV had stopped. She must be sleeping now, Nessa thought.

She picked up her phone; there was a message from Will, sent an hour ago.

What lights?

Nineteen

'Well, on that note . . . I'd like to propose a toast'

Christmas Eve 2012

The lights on the tree twinkled softly in the candlelight. The scent of mulled wine was curling out of the kitchen and filling the house with spicy sweetness. Some old china figurines of reindeers and lambs were organised on the surfaces between picture frames and scented candles. Nessa had bought them in the charity shop Poppy worked in for £5: a bag of sad-looking, unwanted decorations, which she found beautiful, even if their previous owner no longer did. Nessa had also persuaded a reluctant Poppy to help her hand-craft some decorations, making pomander balls by pushing cloves into oranges in neat rows, before wrapping the fruit in shiny red ribbons. These were dotted about the house, swinging gently from side to side whenever someone walked by.

Nessa had transformed her house into something of a winter wonderland at the last minute. She had been spurred on by the unexpected and rather grand additions Will had made, the wants and needs of her daughter, and the prospect of her little sister coming home for the holidays. Up until then, she hadn't known that she still had those kind of feelings left in her after Jake's death, that desire to fill a house with colour and warmth, which to some was 'nice' but not necessary. It was quite an emotional process and Nessa had found herself in tears while writing out the Christmas cards, signing them simply 'Nessa and Poppy'.

It had been, in some ways, a positive distraction. After work, and during the weekend, she'd poured all her feelings of loss and distress into making things as perfect as she possibly could.

Will had come over to celebrate Christmas Eve at Nessa's house, and Kat was back from Leeds. The wine was flowing and Poppy was even allowed a couple of small glasses. Though, bizarrely, she liked to mix them with lemonade, a habit that Nessa found a criminal act against the grassy, fresh flavours of a decent Sauvignon Blanc.

'She dumped me,' Will said dramatically, out of the blue, pulling a face of resignation. He looked a little petulant and teenage.

'Oh, I'm sorry . . .' Nessa said, looking at him sadly, tilting her head to one side.

'Yeah, the last straw was the golf. She could fuck off if she thought I was going to pack that in. She was just sick of trying to change me I suppose – realised it wouldn't work!' he said, laughing to himself before shaking his head a couple of times and taking a swig of his wine, as if replaying some angry conversation in his head for the hundredth time.

'Didn't she like the Alex Monroe jewellery? You can always give it to me if she doesn't?' Nessa said, with a sly wink. Will looked lost for a moment, before smiling vaguely, as if he didn't even have the energy to address the matter.

'Well, on that note, as strange as this might seem, I'd like to propose a toast,' Nessa said softly, holding her glass in the air. Will looked up in surprise, before glancing around the room and raising his glass in the air sheepishly, to join the others.

'This year has been a very difficult year, for all of us. There's really no doubt about that,' Nessa said, feeling tears start to come to her eyes. She glanced at Will as she said this, and gave him a gentle nod to acknowledge his bad news too. The lights on the tree started to blur until she blinked a couple of times.

'We've all faced some challenges, I should say . . . I can't believe that we are facing our first Christmas without Jake. I want us to raise a glass in his memory, for how brave he was, for all the lives he saved, and how much he loved us. To Jake . . .' Nessa said, already starting to feel a little drunk. She was on her third glass of wine, and they'd been drinking for three or four hours already, having enjoyed a boozy lunch courtesy of Will's culinary skills.

'To Jake,' they chimed, raising their glasses in the air.

'I hope he has a great Christmas in heaven,' Poppy said wistfully, picking up a handful of nuts and sorting through them for the ones she liked the most: salted cashews.

'Me too,' Nessa said, struggling to hold back her tears and having to clear her throat and look up to the ceiling to prevent herself from melting down.

'Hey, it's great to have you back, Kat,' Will said after a few moments of quiet. 'How have you been? Is uni going well?'

'Thank you. Yeah it's all going well thanks, I'm getting

some decent grades, so hopefully if I keep going how I am, I will be able to continue with the rest of the master plan.'

'PhD, brain surgeon husband, two Tibetan mastiffs, fridge with ice dispenser and a six-bedroom house in Surrey?' Will asked, matter-of-factly.

'Ha, yes, that sounds about right,' Kat said, laughing a little and throwing her head back as she did so. Nessa noticed that Poppy was watching her in admiration, smiling with her as she smiled, and following her every movement. Her legs were crossed in exactly the same way, with the right leg over the other. Social mimicry was alive and well.

'You're looking pretty tired though, Kat, if you don't mind me, erm, pointing out. God I shouldn't say things like that, should I?' Will said, putting his hand to his mouth and smiling cheekily. 'Sorry, always putting my foot in it . . . What I mean is, it looks like you're working hard,' he finished, correcting himself.

'Oh no, it's fine. I've not been sleeping very well lately actually. That's why I'm tired, I've just got myself into funny habits I guess,' Kat said, looking down at her glass, her face turning a little solemn.

'I would ask you if it's down to too much partying, but I'm guessing it's too many late nights hunched over a text-book?' Nessa asked, shoving her hand into a huge packet of crisps.

Poppy started glugging away at her wine, almost finishing her glass in seconds.

'Stop that, Pops, you're supposed to drink it slowly, savour it a bit,' Nessa said, reaching over to her daughter and taking the glass away. Poppy sighed loudly and reached for the box of chocolates on the table.

'It's dinner time soon,' Nessa added.

'Can't I do anything? You are literally ruining my life,' Poppy cried dramatically.

'Sorry . . . you were saying?' Nessa said, passing the chocolates back to her daughter out of guilt. You had to pick your battles, and she didn't have the energy for this one.

'Well, er, no not exactly . . .' Kat started, uncomfortably.

Will and Nessa looked at her with interest. She seemed troubled all of a sudden.

'I'm still thinking a lot about Tom and Sue, Ness . . . That's why I've not been sleeping,' Kat said, looking a little ashamed. Nessa felt a sudden burst of nerves explode in her stomach.

'Tom and Sue?' Poppy asked, looking momentarily confused.

'Our first foster parents,' Kat said, as calmly as she possibly could. Poppy nodded in disinterest, still picking through the chocolates.

Will's face suddenly changed. He looked at Nessa straight away, a flash of concern in his eyes, a secret message between them.

'Are you still thinking about that? Did it not help, you know, our discussion in the cafe a few weeks ago?' Nessa asked. She felt instantly sweaty and panicky. What if Will thought she'd told Kat the truth, and what if he just blurted it out? Luckily Poppy didn't know anything, so there was no risk there . . . This was awful . . . She was hoping Kat would just move on from it, but it seemed to be turning into 'a thing'.

'I feel bad, you know, for not finding Tom, and saying how grateful we are that he took care of us with Sue . . . We just disappeared, and I know we went because he couldn't cope with us, but still . . . he might feel differently now, and we've never said thanks . . . I mean, what's become of him? It feels rather cruel that we've just moved on with our lives. It just feels like unfinished business,' Kat said, gazing out of the window. Nessa knew exactly what had become of him.

'And you say you're losing sleep over this?' Will said, giving Nessa a look. He knew that she hadn't told her yet. Still.

'Yeah, weirdly enough I am. I feel guilty, I just can't seem to settle my mind,' Kat said.

'Anyone hungry? I've made a lovely meatloaf,' Nessa said chirpily, desperate to change the subject, before getting up and heading to the kitchen.

'Back in a mo. I'm going to help your mother,' Will whispered, addressing Poppy, before scuttling out of the room and shutting the door behind him.

'I cannot believe that she still doesn't know,' Will whispered venomously, standing next to Nessa as she started slicing the meatloaf. It smelt delicious.

'Will, just leave it, please. I'm going through enough right now. I don't know why you're so bloody adamant,' Nessa said quietly, feeling riled. Will had been making things more and more difficult for her recently. Sometimes she wished he would back off a bit.

'I'm adamant because she has the right to know. Secrets like this always come out, Nessa, and it will come out one day, and she'll never trust you again. This could damage your relationship and I know how important that is to you,' Will said, glaring at his friend.

'OK, I really want you to keep your nose out of this, Will, seriously. I'm going to get very annoyed. It's totally up to me how I handle this, and this is what I want. You have no right to do this to me, Will, no right,' Nessa said angrily, slamming a glass container down on the kitchen surface. Will flinched a little.

'But your sister can't sleep, Nessa. For god's sake,' Will said, trying to soften his tone, so he came across less angry. 'She's an adult; she can handle it now,' he added, taking a gulp of his wine.

'No she can't. No one can handle that stuff. I can't handle it. I will never be able to handle it, OK? Never. I have flashbacks and nightmares, and when I think about it I feel like I could be sick. It's changed the landscape of my life, and it will never be the same again. It damaged me, Will,' Nessa said, losing control of her feelings and staring at Will. Tears started to spill down her cheeks, and her whole body began to tremble with the stress of it all.

'But Nessa . . . I know it's—'

'I'm haunted by it, every fucking day. It's the most disturbing thing I've ever gone through and if she doesn't need to go through it then I'm bloody well not putting her through it, OK?' Nessa said, in a kind of shouty whisper. The tears were running fast down her face now. She felt angry at Will for pushing her on it. Why did he care so much?

'I'm sorry, Nessa, I'm sorry . . .' Will said regretfully, pulling Nessa into his chest as she cried. She felt weak. She let Will support her body weight as he wrapped his arms around her.

'I just can't . . . As time goes on, it just gets harder and harder to deal with,' Nessa sobbed.

'God, I'm sorry,' Will said, pushing his nose against her hair. Pressed against her forehead, his lips felt warm and soft. Nessa had almost forgotten what it felt like to have someone else's flesh against her own. She felt a twinge at the bottom of her stomach, and pulled herself away from his embrace.

'More wine?' she asked, in the breeziest voice she could muster. She wondered how she was going to pour it; she was shaking so much.

'Oh, yes please. God, it's terribly hot in here,' he said, running a hand across his forehead, somehow squeaking on the word 'here'.

Nessa poured the wine, her wrist noticeably trembling. She handed him a glass, feeling a little self-conscious.

'Honestly, Will . . . I'm so thankful to you for all the beautiful things you did to the house for Christmas. You've really livened things up. I know it means a lot to Poppy. I had no idea how important it turned out to be for her you know, to try and have a "normal" Christmas after losing her dad . . . If it was left to me we would have been stuck in here alone, doing nothing . . .'

Will smiled and then stared at the floor uncomfortably.

'I don't know how you managed to get those lights up outside too. It must have been very awkward. You could have really hurt yourself. Although I assume you used a ladder . . . And how did you know we had a plug socket near the shed? It's amazing,' Nessa said, blurting out her words before drinking more wine.

'Nessa, I told you this before. I didn't do the lights,' Will said seriously, his face clouding over with concern.

'Oh don't be silly, stop fucking around, Will,' Nessa said, picking up the meatloaf and starting to turn towards the kitchen door.

'Hmm . . . I'm not fucking ar—' Will grumbled.

'Look, if you're embarrassed that you did it, we can play along, like yadda yadda yadda, you didn't put the lights up, Santa's elves did, and the magic of Christmas has come and saved us all from our shitty, sad lives and blah blah blah,' Nessa said, smiling cheekily as she stepped out into the hallway to serve up dinner.

'Nessa seriously,' Will said, walking behind her at speed and holding a huge bowl of vegetables.

'Pah, whatever Will. I will just keep playing your little game if it makes you happy! Dinner's ready ladies,' Nessa said, placing the plate down on the mat and smiling proudly to herself.

It was Christmas Day. Nessa could smell the gravy and the chicken coming from the kitchen. It shouldn't be long now, she thought. She sat on the carpet in the living room, rolling a toy across the floor for Kat, who was sat on her bottom in a romper suit, her hair pulled into a little fountain pony tail at the very top of her head.

All of a sudden, she heard the front door open.

'Aaaand the bells were riiiinging ouuut, on Chrissstmaas daaaayyy!'

Her father staggered through the hallway, slamming the door behind him and singing songs to himself.

'Laaa la laaa laaa la laaa.'

He went straight past the kitchen and stood in the doorway, rocking backwards and forwards and swaying unsteadily on his feet. He tried to focus on Nessa, but his eyes were rolling around in his head, and he eventually gave up, blinking hard and looking annoyed. The mere sight of him was irritating. He stank. Nessa instantly felt sick; she'd not seen him this drunk for a long time, but then again, he had been at the social club for six hours . . . Nessa turned away from her father, picked up her little sister and took her to the sofa. Then she started searching for a video for her to watch. She had to keep things happy and breezy around her. Children picked up on this stuff, even when they were too little to understand what was happening. Nessa had heard it mentioned by a lady from Barnardo's who came to talk in assembly, and from then on, she'd do whatever she could to keep things light, even when all hell broke loose.

'What are you up to? You don't need to stop what you're doing like that and take her away do you?' he shouted, before spinning round on his heel and almost falling over. He grabbed hold of a shelf for support, knocking over an ornament. Nessa could hear it smashing on the floor.

'Stupid fucking thing. Sue! Where are you? Where the fuck are ya? I've just smashed that ugly elephant thing we were given at our wedding. 'Orrible fucking thing it was anyway, good riddance . . . I did the world a favour,' he yelled, opening the kitchen door violently.

Nessa shuddered. Please no, please no . . .

'Get me a beer. Is it ready yet? I'm starving,' he'd yelled. Nessa could hear her mother's hushed tones, telling him that it wouldn't be long now and that he'd had enough beer, and could he please be quiet because of the children.

'Enough beer? Who the fuck do you think you are? I work my bollocks off all fucking week, all fucking year to keep a roof over your miserable fucking heads, and Christmas Day comes around and you think you have the right to tell me I've had enough . . .' her father had boomed, the rage almost rattling in his chest.

Nessa listened as she slotted an old VHS copy of Bambi *in the video player. Her body had already gone into fight or flight mode. She heard a glass smash. Kat had already started to cry quietly to herself.*

'Shh Kat,' Nessa whispered protectively. She sat on the

sofa and pulled her tiny sister onto her lap, smelling her familiar scent of soap and talcum powder. Her hair was so soft and wispy. 'I'll take care of you. Everything's going to be OK,' she said, stroking her forehead and clutching her tiny body to her chest.

Whack.

'No, no please . . .' Nessa whispered, flinching at the sound. She wrapped her hands over Kat's right ear, pushing the other tighter to her chest so she couldn't hear it.

Thump.

'Not my beautiful mum. No . . . no . . .'

'STOP IT. PLEASE STOP!' Nessa shouted, sitting up in bed suddenly. Her heart was pounding and her whole body was drenched in sweat.

'Mum . . . Oh my god, are you OK?' Poppy cried, half laughing to herself. She was standing in the doorway of her mother's bedroom, holding a gift in her left hand. Kat materialised behind her, a look of concern on her sleepy face. Her hair was all over the place, and the remnants of last night's makeup were blotted around her eyes.

Nessa sat up straight, breathless and still a little confused.

'What's going on?' Kat asked, putting her hand on Poppy's shoulder.

'Mum, are you alright?' Poppy walked softly into the bedroom now and climbed onto her bed.

'Sorry Pops, I was having a nightmare . . . I don't know what happened there. It was very strange,' she said, trying to laugh it off.

'Happy Christmas, Mum,' Poppy said, flinging her arms around her neck. 'Ergh you're all wet!' Poppy cried, pulling her arms away suddenly and looking at her mother in horror.

'Yes alright, Pops, I just had a night sweat OK?' Nessa said defensively, wrapping herself up in the duvet.

'Well, Happy Christmas,' Kat said cheerily, bending down and kissing her on the cheek tenderly.

'I'll be down in a bit girls,' Nessa said, smiling now and ushering them out of the room.

Twenty

'So, I think a thank you text is in order for Will, you know?'

After her shower, Nessa finally came downstairs. She had shaken the terror of her nightmares and was feeling calmer. Poppy had the music channels on. Mariah Carey was playing in the snow in a red onesie, frolicking with a red-caped hound.

'Good morning, big sister, I've made breakfast!' Kat said, ushering her into the living room. The table was covered in food: bowls of scrambled eggs with flecks of smoked salmon, a fresh fruit salad and a pile of croissants greeted her temptingly. The smell of freshly ground coffee tickled at her nose.

'Oh Kat, this is lovely . . . how did you? Sorry I shouldn't ask, but how did you afford all this?' Nessa said, smiling, but slightly concerned.

'No worries, it's my pleasure. Little bar work here and there never goes amiss, it's all good. Thank you for having me,' Kat said, sitting down to eat.

'Have you opened your presents yet? Or is that a silly question?' Nessa asked, looking at Poppy, who was frantically doing her makeup in a little mirror.

'Yeah, so cool Mum, Aunty Kat got me some Mac makeup. I literally can't believe it. Famous people wear Mac,' Poppy said, urgently painting her lips in a soft shade of fuchsia.

'This one's called "pink novvel",' Poppy said proudly, pronouncing the second word with a very poorly executed French accent. She pressed her lips together, making a popping sound as she did so.

'Nouveau,' Kat said, correcting her and smiling to herself as if holding back some laughter.

'Ah that's nice,' Nessa said, suddenly feeling a little distant. She stared at an empty chair opposite. Jake would have sat in that one, had he been around. She pictured him in his old pyjama 'bums', a pair of grey tracksuit bottoms that made his arse look unbearably sexy, and some soft cotton t-shirt in olive-green or red, that would just show off the layers of rippling muscle beneath.

Oh god, she thought, an ache filling her stomach. She could almost see him now, shovelling eggs into his mouth before looking up at her and smiling as he chewed energetically, that sparkle in his deep, brown eyes. Adventure. Excitement. Jake brought the magic into everything. He had been the essence of her life. The thing that made it all OK . . .

'So, I think a thank you text is in order for Will, you know?' Kat said gently, shaking Nessa from her thoughts.

'What do you mean?' Nessa asked, glancing up at her sister, who was pouring out three glasses of orange juice.

'I went out this morning to take out the rubbish and look what I found sitting on the doorstep,' she said, turning around and pulling two small packages from the dresser counter. They were wrapped, scruffily, in old-school Christmas paper that looked as if it had been kept for years in a drawer and recycled. They were both tied with a small, silver bow.

'Where are the labels?' Nessa asked.

'There weren't any,' Kat said, shrugging, 'but they obviously weren't necessary because we all know who they are from.'

'But that's bizarre. Will was with us last night. He could have just given these to us,' Nessa said, picking up one of the gifts and turning it around in her hand.

'Well you know what he's like. Will's like that, he always has been. He loves surprising people. I mean it's kind of how he likes to do things, clearly, and that's just another classic Will move,' Kat responded, looking a little cynical.

Nessa suddenly started to open one of the gifts, tearing away at the paper irritably. She didn't know why, but she felt angry all of a sudden. Her emotions were all over the place, she thought. People had warned her this might happen at Christmastime.

'Are you OK, Nessa?' Kat asked, reaching over and putting a warm hand on her sister's arm. Nessa didn't say anything.

The remaining paper soon fell off the package, which was surrounded in layers of newspaper and then bubble wrap. Nessa tore away at the wrapping and gasped when she saw what was inside, capturing Kat and Poppy's attention as they stopped dead and stared at her.

It was an old, vintage copy of *The Tailor of Gloucester* by Beatrix Potter, battered at the edges, worn and loved but impossibly beautiful. The kind of precious thing you could just gaze at forever, and it would only become more wonderful as time went on. Nessa took a deep breath out, feeling emotion sweep inside her. Flickering memories played in her mind, as if from a projector. Nessa and Jake lying in bed. Poppy wedged between them in her soft cotton pyjamas, propped up against a pillow, twisting her hair as they read it to her. Poppy's favourite book: she'd probably heard it spoken softly into her ears hundreds if not thousands of times by everyone close to her. Will had read it to her several times. Once when he was trying to calm Poppy down as she had a hissy fit in the living room, Nessa, overwhelmed, desperately trying to stop a leak in the kitchen. Kat had read it too, many times, and so had Teigen. It was Poppy's book, and it always would be; a part of her identity, like the rippling lines of a fingerprint.

'What is it, Mum?' Poppy asked, standing up and walking over to the table. She had discarded her makeup and was now standing at the table, staring at her mother's trembling hands.

'It's a really old copy of . . . of *The Tailor of Gloucester*. This must be for you,' Nessa said, looking up at Poppy who instantly welled up with tears, her hands rising to her mouth.

'Oh sweetheart,' Nessa said, wrapping a loving arm around her daughter's bony frame.

'Kat was this you . . .?' Nessa asked, smiling at her sister with her eyes narrowed, 'I mean what a beautiful present. So thoughtful.'

'No seriously, they aren't from me . . . Poppy's already opened my gift Nessa, the makeup, and yours is waiting for you over there,' she said, pointing towards a small, red package, sitting beneath the tree.

'Oh yes, of course,' Nessa said, blushing.

Nessa opened the other box, while Poppy continued to wipe tears from her eyes.

It was a silver necklace, a long, delicate chain, with a small silver heart at the end.

'Jesus . . . that's so beautiful . . . so classy,' Kat said breathily, as if she were lusting over it herself.

'Wow,' Nessa said to herself, holding the necklace before her face and watching it turn around in the air. It was modest. Not expensive looking or overly fancy, but very lovely.

'You'd better be careful about Will, Ness. That's all I'm saying. It's the ultimate cliché isn't it? Guy dies after fighting in Afghanistan, widow is heartbroken, cue the "family friend" to come and swoop in and just take things where the other one left off . . . People will start talking. Not great,' Kat said, rolling her eyes cynically and poking at her omelette with a fork.

Twenty-One

'My darling, could you pass the salt please?'

Boxing Day 2012

Nessa couldn't shake the words her little sister had said on Christmas morning. They rattled around her head, like tiny marbles, begging to be picked up and turned over. *People will start talking* . . . she had said, her painted eyebrows arranging themselves into an expression somewhere between concern and suspicion.

Nessa had tried to convince herself that she didn't care, that she could brush off her sibling's words. But she couldn't stop hearing them, or analysing them over and over again. She wondered if Kat even realised how much she'd been affected by that throwaway statement. She pictured her, back at her house now, watching reality TV and eating a giant bag of M&M's, oblivious to the storm she'd started in Nessa's mind.

She couldn't believe that Will was trying this sort of thing, at this time too? Anger started to rise within her chest just thinking about it. She pictured him at some expensive jeweller in Kensington, holding necklaces up to the falsified, commercial lighting and imagining her wearing it. It was a bit creepy . . . And the book? Another image: Will, in a long woollen overcoat and expensive shoes, scouring Notting Hill antique shops for something as special, and personal, as this . . .

Why on earth would he think it was appropriate or welcome? Surely he knew how vulnerable she was and how painfully she missed Jake? He'd seen Nessa trash her own home for god's sake; he'd seen her at her ugliest, and lowest. He'd seen her at times when she was so vulnerable and unhappy she was almost monstrous. The memories of those times still made her shudder as if they'd happened just yesterday. She could picture herself now, obliterating her own home, trembling like a wild animal. He probably thought she was a completely broken human being, deep down. A mess. Now was not the time to complicate things. Now was not the time to try and rekindle some ageing teenage love story that had never really begun . . .

'My darling, could you pass the salt please?' Betsy asked timidly, waking Nessa from her thought process. Nessa smiled and passed the saltcellar, a little porcelain Santa Claus whose nose had broken off during the Christmas of 1998, when Mick had accidentally knocked it off the table. Poppy was eating her meal, thank goodness, Nessa thought, watching her daughter chase some peas around the plate with a silver fork. Betsy had got out the 'best' cutlery. She always did that on Christmas Day and Boxing Day, giving them their annual showcase before they spent the rest of the year in a dark drawer somewhere, collecting dust and nicotine.

She understood where Kat was coming from . . . Even though Will was clearly doing all these things to cheer them up, to make her happy, people probably were starting to wonder. But what should she care what other people thought? She should talk to him perhaps, tell him about her worries, she was sure he'd understand . . . Maybe Will was having a bit of a crisis too. They'd always been able to be honest with each other; it shouldn't be any different now.

'How's Will?' Betsy asked softly as she shook a dense shower of salt onto her roast potatoes and vegetables. It was the second time she'd coated her meal, having eaten away the top layer. Mick sat quietly at the top of the table. He'd finished his lunch and was staring into the void beyond the living room and hallway, his face expressionless.

'Oh yeah, he's OK, thanks Bets. You know, he's just standard Will, bouncing around, trying to set up new businesses and stuff,' Nessa said with a smile. There was an awkward quiet around the table.

'We've not seen him for a while,' Betsy said darkly. 'Lovely man too . . . He used to pop round every now and again, even when Jake was on tour. True gent. It's a little disappointing really,' she continued. Mick muttered Jake's name to himself, and a couple of nonsensical sentences about ice cream and a teddy bear.

'Here Grandad,' Poppy said kindly, serving him some more potatoes. Mick had always adored roast potatoes. He used to put a couple of forks in two potatoes and walk them around the table so they looked like legs, which always made his granddaughter laugh wildly, as if she were being tickled. Mick glanced at them sadly, before turning his nose away from them and staring at nothing again. Nessa wanted to cuddle him, to wish him a happy Christmas, but he would probably get confused. She hoped he really truly knew how much they loved him.

'Oh, I'm sorry to hear he's not visited for a while . . . I will speak to him soon, find out if he's OK,' Nessa said, realising what a strange response this was. She knew he was OK; she saw him all the time, she knew practically everything there was to know about him. At least, she thought she did.

On reflection, she wondered how valid that statement was now. Will was probably struggling to cope with Jake's death, just like everyone else. Perhaps this was his way of dealing with it. Following the loss of her husband, she'd found that some people brought themselves closer – often those who surprised you – and others peeled away quietly, like thieves in the night, never to be seen or heard from again. The fallout from a loss this huge was significant for everyone, Nessa thought to herself.

'Do you still see him a lot?' Betsy asked, putting her fork on her plate and taking a sip of her annual glass of wine. Tesco Pinot Grigio, at £3.99 a bottle. Nessa felt hot around her neck, a tide of panic was rising up her body. Why did she feel like this?

'Erm, yeah kind of, he helps us out doesn't he, Pop? You know, when the car broke down he paid for the repairs, and he helped when Poppy needed to be picked up and stuff . . . He's very nice, isn't he?' Nessa asked her daughter, who nodded moodily.

When lunch was over, Nessa, Betsy, Mick and Poppy padded into the sitting room. It was boiling hot in there, Ness noticed. She pulled her jumper over her head and sat on it. Mick settled into his usual chair, which must have had the perfect imprint of his bony anatomy by now. He was almost becoming a part of that chair. Poppy sat on the carpet and looked up at the TV like she had done as a child. Betsy was perched next to Nessa, cradling a cup of tea in her thin hands and clearing her throat occasionally.

Nessa couldn't wait any longer; she was feeling increasingly anxious. She pulled her phone out of her bag and composed a text message for Will:

> Will, there's something I need to say . . . I want to thank you, for all the lovely, kind things you've done for us recently, the decorations, the lights, the presents and everything else. Honestly, it means so much and I don't know what we would have done without you. I'm just concerned about something and I think we need to talk it through . . . I'm embarrassed to even send you this message, but I just need to get it off my chest . . . Can we talk please? I can make more sense, if we could just talk . . . Nessa x

Seconds later a message arrived on her phone. It was from Will.

> Hey Ness. Erm, I'm kind of busy right now . . . hope everything OK? Nothing too urgent? W

Nessa felt infuriated by this. She couldn't wait. She padded out of the room and went to the upstairs bathroom, shutting the door gently behind her. It was tiled in pale green, a style of decoration popular in the seventies that was long overdue for an update – much like the rest of the house. An old white soap sat in a dish on the sink, great crack-lines running through it like an Arctic tundra. It looked as if it was fused to the ceramic surface it had been there so long.

Nessa picked up her phone and called him. She felt nervous butterflies explode in her chest.

'Hello?'

'Hi, Will, it's me . . .'

'Erm, yeah OK . . . What's up?' he said, sounding a little put out.

Nessa sat on the edge of the bath, feeling hot embarrassment swamp her body. She ran her free hand over the towels to help her stay calm, feeling the soft threads at the tips of her fingers. *We can get through this*, she thought to herself. *Our friendship means more than this.*

'OK . . .' Nessa said softly, trying to be as receptive and open as possible. She tried to remember advice she'd been given by her old boss about how to best handle conflict. Avoiding accusations and aggression, being open and approachable. What you did made me feel like X, Y and Z, how can we address this? How do you feel about it? How can we make it better? Don't use accusatory language. Be fair.

'I'm wondering how to say this without sounding like a complete lunatic,' Nessa said, giggling to herself down the line, trying to lighten the atmosphere that was thick between them, despite the distance.

'Just go ahead . . . It's OK,' Will said, softly.

'Well, you've done some really beautiful stuff for us – the tree, the decorations, the lights, and those presents on the doorstep . . .'

'What presents?' Will asked, suddenly and defensively. Nessa instantly picked up on that tone. The classic kind, embedded in the voice of people who were getting called out for doing something they shouldn't be doing.

'The book and the necklace: you know full well what I'm talking about,' Nessa said, sternly, already forgetting how to have a calm, non-aggressive conversation.

There was a pause, and some chatter in the background. Will seemed preoccupied, or perhaps he was just trying to think about what lie he could spin next.

'Look, sorry, Nessa. Like I said, I'm busy. This isn't a good time. I've gotta go,' Will said in exasperation, before hanging up.

'Hah! Typical!' Nessa whispered to herself, before flinging the phone angrily to the ground and sinking down onto the floor, her hands shaking with adrenalin. *I know what you're up to . . .*

Mick had slept in his chair for an hour, only waking when the adverts came on after *The Snowman* animation. Poppy had cried as she watched it, great sloppy tears gleaming in her huge, dish-like eyes. Nessa guessed she was almost certainly thinking about her father. Missing him. Feeling the huge gap that had now materialised in their lives. The adverts always seemed louder than the programme they followed, promises of sales blaring out already. Mick had jumped, before gazing around the room, his eyes like dinner plates as he tried to work out where he was.

Betsy turned on the main lights in the sitting room, yawning as she did so. 'I'll go and make us all some coffee,' she offered, looking sleepy.

'So how's everything at the day centre Mick?' Nessa

had asked, looking at him and wondering if he would remember. Mick pouted, his great, bushy white eyebrows rippling in concern.

'You know . . . Milton House? The blue building,' Nessa said softly, hoping the name and the colour would trigger some memories.

'Oh yes,' Mick said, his eyes suddenly lighting up with recognition and happiness.

Betsy appeared with a tray of hot drinks, she put them on the table softly.

'Tell them about your new support worker, Ian,' Betsy said loudly, as if Mick were deaf. The china clattered loudly.

'Who?' Mick asked, bafflement on his face.

'You know, the guy who took you to the seaside the other day. Brighton? Remember?' she said.

'Oh yes . . .' Mick said, with a wide smile, 'He's Jake, he is . . . not Ian . . .'

Nessa felt her stomach drop.

'What did you say?' Nessa whispered, sitting up straight in her seat. Poppy sighed loudly, as if she was sick and tired of Mick getting confused all the time.

'Jake came to see me, he took me out . . . he's a good lad my boy,' Mick repeated, as if it were nothing. Betsy crinkled her brow and put down her cup of coffee. She suddenly looked overcome by emotion, as if she'd forgotten that her son had died just a few months ago.

'Mick, it's not Jake darling. Jake has died . . . You and Jake did go to the seaside, many years ago, but it's Ian who took you to the beach recently and he's your support worker at Milton House,' she said calmly. 'Sorry, Ness, he's just getting confused . . . He's always talking about Jake, you know,' Betsy said, looking at her daughter-in-law and shrugging in acceptance, tears filling her eyes.

'Right, yes, of course,' Nessa said, feeling something sink inside her. 'Of course,' she said again, softly.

Twenty-Two

'I think you're doing far more than just managing, Nessa'

January 25th, 2013

'Oh Nessa, it's been such a long time since I've seen you. I think the last time was at the memorial, wasn't it? Time just flies, but I'm so glad to see you,' Teigen said regretfully, pulling Nessa into her arms and subjecting her to a robust embrace. Teigen smelt of jasmine and her wispy hair tickled Nessa's nose and lips.

'I'm so glad to see you too. Thanks so much for taking the time to see me this evening, I know how busy you are with work and stuff at home,' Nessa garbled, extracting herself from Teigen's embrace. 'Oh, and thanks for bringing me here; it's stunning,' she said, gesturing in the direction of the long, wooden table in the Southbank Centre Members Bar.

Teigen peeled off her long designer coat and flung it over the back of her chair. She was wearing a grey pinstripe suit – a blazer that nipped in at the waist, and a tight tulip skirt that lovingly hugged her ample hips and bottom. She wore a pair of modest heels in black suede.

Nessa looked at her old friend from across the table once they were seated. The lanky, slightly greasy teen she had grown up with had turned into a warm, rounded woman, who wore shiny silver jewellery that glinted in the candlelight and expensive perfume. She was blonde now, no longer 'ginger', and a lawyer. She had three children (two boys and a girl) and a husband, and a dog called Marbles who was prone to getting lost in the countryside while chasing foxes. Her eyes twinkled with the same sense of mischief and self-assuredness she had possessed as a kid.

It was nice to be around her again, properly, Nessa thought, feeling slightly guilty that she had pushed her away in the months after Jake's death, unable to cope with long conversations and the general demands of socialising with someone as vibrant as Teigen.

The bar was only half full. Some of the carefully polished tables were still awaiting visitors, while others were populated by students born of wealthy families, tapping frantically into the latest MacBook Air and bobbing their Nike Air Max to the tune of whatever pretentious music they were listening to. Arty academics, bedecked with strange jewellery and reading from obscure, tatty novels, were scattered about, breaking up the odd business meeting that had spilled over from the working day into another buzzing Friday evening. They could see Big Ben and the London Eye from where they sat, sharp lines and spikes set against a dull grey sky. It was bitterly cold outside and a relief to be indoors, away from the harsh snap of the January wind.

'What do you want to drink?' Teigen asked, excitedly.

'Erm, a coffee? Orange juice perhaps?' Nessa responded, looking around her for a menu.

'Pah! No, it's Friday night darling, this calls for champagne,' Teigen said, grabbing her handbag and marching towards the bar, leaving Nessa basking in a cloud of drifting fragrance and infectious enthusiasm.

Jesus, Nessa thought, how was she going to afford tonight? She was skint . . . Nessa was that post-Christmas-poor she'd experienced every year of her adult life, but it was much worse this time without a steady salary coming in from Jake's work. She was probably going to have to move into a smaller home eventually, and god knows how her daughter would take that. Another big change, more dramas, she thought to herself. She watched Teigen jostling around near the bar, talking to a stranger and laughing enthusiastically at their muffled jokes. She flicked her hair flirtily over her shoulder as she spoke, drawing the attention of several businessmen nearby who glanced over with hungry eyes and whispered amongst themselves.

Within a few minutes, Teigen was on her way back, great energy in her walk as she charged across the room. She was clutching an ice bucket with a bottle of champagne bobbling around helplessly in the freezing water. Two delicate flute glasses, weaved between her long slender fingers, made clinking noises as she sat down.

'So, how are you?' Nessa asked sheepishly, as her friend poured two fizzing glasses of champagne.

'Oh sod me. It's just the usual: work, work, work and more bloody work; taking the brats to rugby, and ballet and bloody recorder lessons. Recorders by the way, *fucking recorders*. What's the point? Horrible things they are. Oh that and constantly batting off the advances of my sexually frustrated husband who is literally like a walking erection these days. It's all rather dull.

'I want to talk about you though, Nessa, not me. You've had an incredibly tough time lately . . . How are you feeling?' she asked, setting down the bottle, putting a warm, slightly sweaty hand on her friend's forearm and squeezing gently.

Nessa tried to process everything her friend had just said: she was like a hurricane. She felt a little lump appear in her throat and looked out of the window. It was starting to get dark. She hoped Poppy was OK . . .

'Erm, you know, we are OK. We are just managing, you know?' Nessa said, taking a sip of her drink. It tasted good.

'Just managing? I think you're doing far more than just managing, Nessa. You know, Mum used to always say this lovely thing, and I don't know if you remember it,' Teigen exclaimed nostalgically. 'I think it's a sentiment that would serve you well now, with everything you're going through, because I don't think you give yourself anywhere near enough credit for how well you're handling everything.'

'What was it?' Nessa asked, smiling now at the thought of Jan and her raggedy hippy clothing, the constant smell of incense and some unidentified vegetable soup bubbling away on the stove.

'Above all, be the heroine of your life, not the victim,' Teigen said, and Nessa chimed in on the last three words in unison with her friend. Teigen nodded her head softly, proudly even.

'Ah yes, Nora Ephron, right?' Nessa said, recalling Jan

in the kitchen, saying these words, in between lectures on the dangers of sniffing glue and why men could only be trusted for 15 per cent of the time.

'Correct. You are the heroine of your life, Nessa, I'm so very proud of you and I know Mum would be too. She really loved you, Nessa. In fact she wanted to adopt you and Kat after what happened . . . but she was too ill sadly; her cancer was spreading fast,' Teigen said, melancholy clouding her usual bright eyes.

'Yeah, she was amazing,' Nessa said, smiling to herself and staring at the bubbles rising to the top of her glass. At that very second it hit her just how many people she'd lost: her foster mother; Jan, another mother figure; and now her husband. They had all left such huge holes in her heart that felt as if they'd never heal.

'What do you think she'd say to you now? If she was around, Ness?'

'Goodness . . . that's quite a question, isn't it?' Nessa said, running a hand along the smooth wooden table and looking back towards the throbbing bar where a group of suited businessmen were laughing amongst themselves. 'I think she'd tell me that everything is going to be OK. I think she'd say . . . yes, she'd say that there was happiness waiting in my future even though right now it might feel like that's impossible, and that everything is so dark and frightening. She'd say that I need to just hold on and have faith in what will be.'

'Yep, and I agree. I'm so sorry for what happened to you, Nessa. I realise I never really got to know Jake very well, but he was such a great man. He loved you so, so, so much,' Teigen said, pouring more champagne into the glasses.

Nessa took a deep breath in, and then blew it out slowly between her lips, feeling the emotion swell towards the tips of her toes, like the ocean.

'Hey, I'll tell you who else loves you – although I really shouldn't say this,' Teigen said, smiling cheekily and leaning towards her friend as if she were about to share a secret.

'Who?'

'Will!' Teigen said, rolling her eyes as if it were the most obvious thing in the world. She clapped her hands together with glee, bobbing up and down in her chair a little.

'Jesus, Teigen,' Nessa growled, looking around her as if she was concerned someone she knew might overhear.

'Oh come on, Nessa, get real. Are you paranoid or something?' Teigen said, winking and reaching towards a bowl of peanuts sat between them.

'No, it's just . . . It's inappropriate, Teigs. I don't feel comfortable,' Nessa whispered, suddenly feeling as if she could burst into tears. *What was Teigen thinking?*

'I mean seriously, though, I get what you're saying,' Teigen insisted, throwing a handful of snacks into her mouth, little crumbs and particles of salt sticking to her red lipstick. She seemed oblivious to the offence she was causing. 'But he's rich – really fucking filthy rich – and he's bloody good looking. I mean there's a guy who has aged well; I mean *I'd* sit on his face alright! He's funny, and he's been besotted with you since he was 17 or something? I mean, surely you can see how great he is?'

'Fucking hell, T. What the hell do you think you're doing?' Nessa exclaimed, slamming a fist on the table. Teigen sat up straight, and looked shocked. A few people sitting nearby glanced over, and a couple grimaced at each other. The atmosphere had turned electric.

'Ness . . . now come on . . . I didn't mean—' her friend said, quietly this time, reaching out a hand and softly holding her forearm in a bid to appease her.

'Yeah, I obviously get that he has a lot going for him, and there have been times when, well, you know, I've wondered what might have happened if we had got together. But no. He and I missed our boat years ago. I fell in love with Jake, and that was it, you know? I don't have eyes for anyone else. I'm not sure I ever will. How can you even dream of talking about this?'

'I understand that, I really do, and I'm sorry, Nessa. It came out wrong. I just, I saw his face the day you married Jake. He was happy for you, of course he was, but I could see that his heart was breaking into a million pieces as you said your vows. You've always been the love of his life, I'm just not sure you realise it,' she said softly, glancing at Nessa, nervously now. Nessa shook her head resolutely, crossing her arms over her chest.

'I'm saying this all wrong. I think what I mean is, and while there's no rush of course, one day you'll have to move on my darling and it will be absolutely OK for you to do that. You're a living, breathing human being with wants, needs and desires, and that can't be ignored forever,' Teigen said powerfully, taking another gulp of her drink.

Nessa glared out of the window and thought to herself. She bit her lip, reflecting on the strange things that had happened lately. Who was the real Will? She wasn't sure she knew anymore.

'I mean Nessa you're stunning, just *look* at you. You're beautiful and young and – let's face it – neither of us will have these perky tits and asses for much longer; you want to make the most of those bad boys before they are tickling your ankles. So don't hide yourself away in the shadows, that's all I'm saying.' Teigen smiled warmly at her friend and winked mischievously. Nessa felt the urge to flee the bar, but she didn't have the energy. However idiotic her friend's comments seemed to be right now, she still really needed her . . .

'Thanks Teigen,' she said, half-heartedly, before taking another sip of her drink.

Will, I need to see you. Tonight . . . Can you come round, please?

Nessa had texted Will on her way home, woozy on the train from all the champagne and wine she had drunk with Teigen. Her friend's characteristically blunt words rattled around in her mind. They remained stuck there, in spite of the din of theatre-goers and late-night diners who had packed themselves onto the train, chatting amongst themselves about the shows they had seen and the delicacies tasted. *Wasn't the singing incredible? And the lead lady – what was her name again – Katalina? No, Karina. She was stunning, looked just like my grandmother when she was in the Russian National Ballet all those years ago. The prawns were lovely, and the pâté too. I think we'll go there again.*

Nessa had never intended to get so drunk, but the conversation had been flowing as readily as the wine, and the hours just slid by after the initial awkwardness of Teigen's attempt at advice. Now she found herself on the last train, aka the 'vomit comet', suddenly desperate to smooth things out with Will. She couldn't stand it anymore, this horrible pregnant pause in their friendship. The awkwardness, the texts unsent, those stilted, edited words, waiting hopelessly in the drafts folder. It was nothing that a little courage couldn't overcome. She knew it.

Her heart thumped hard in her chest as she sat in the darkness of her living room. She supposed Poppy was fast asleep upstairs. How long would he be? He said he wouldn't be long, but it felt like she had been waiting forever. She checked the time – five minutes had passed. She hurriedly applied some more lipstick in a mirror she kept in her handbag, her fingers trembling as she did so. It was hard to trace the soft Cupid's bow of her lips when she was so nervous. Wobbling lines, frantically corrected and daubed with a nearby tissue. She felt slightly nauseous – a cocktail of alcohol and nerves – and decided to grab a bottle of wine from the kitchen to share with Will, so the conversation might be less awkward, less frightening somehow.

He turned up ten minutes later, complaining of the cold and rubbing his hands together as he came through the door.

'Shh! Poppy's asleep!' Nessa said, grabbing Will's cold hand and leading him into the living room. She struggled to walk in a straight line, and upon realising this tried desperately to appear as sober as possible.

'Oh I can't drink, Nessa, I drove . . . but thanks anyway,' Will said a little coldly, as soon as he spotted the bottle of wine and the two sparkling glasses on the coffee table.

'Come on Will! Just get a taxi. We need to talk. It'll be just like the old days!' Nessa gushed, as if this justified the late-night binge drinking. She felt so different around him tonight, unable to really be herself.

'Oh well . . . erm, I suppose so. Jesus, you know it

doesn't take much persuasion with me,' Will said, slightly stiffly. She could tell he was uncomfortable. Perhaps he was nervous too? She just wanted to get everything out in the open, she thought, as she poured out two large glasses of wine and handed one to Will.

'So this is kind of a late-night meet-up,' Will said quietly, his eyebrows raised in surprise as he spoke. He smelt good, Nessa noticed, although he always did.

'Yeah well, I figured we needed to talk. Things have been a bit weird between us lately,' she said, watching Will grimace. He looked down at the floor, saying nothing, scratched the back of his head and then rested his hand uncomfortably on his leg, his posture radiating unease.

'Will, listen,' Nessa started, putting a hand on his leg. She wasn't sure why she did that, but it seemed like the right thing. She was trying to sound as warm and as understanding as possible. 'I know how you feel, OK? I know it's you, doing all this lovely stuff. Everyone knows it . . . It's just very bloody obvious what's going on, OK?' Nessa whispered kindly, almost trying to squeeze a confession from him with the sweet tones of her voice.

Will continued to stay silent, still unable to make eye contact. His eyebrows were now furrowed, as if he was deep in thought.

'The thing is, I know you're just looking out for me, and Pops, of course, and I know you care.'

'Of course I care,' Will said, with slight hostility, before trying to speak, only to be interrupted.

'And the thing is, I know it makes sense – you and me, me and you – Will and Nessa circa 1990-something. I mean we go back, don't we? It makes total sense. There's me here, struggling without my husband, and Poppy having a tough time without a father. There's you over there, in that sprawling house of yours with all those quiet corridors and empty bedrooms. And we've known each other for so many years. There's friendship there, there's the foundation for so much.'

'Ness—' Will said urgently, looking shocked and surprised. But Nessa, irreparably tipsy and unaware of herself, cut in again.

'Listen, I know you love me, OK, Will? And it might not be a bad thing that you care . . . thinking about it now, I know life would be a lot less lonely with you in it. It might be easier, easier than trying to do all of this alone,' she said, before doing something she never expected to do. He just looked so unbearably handsome there in the half-light: his lovely expressions, the kindness that just ebbed from him. Teigen's words had returned. Maybe she was right? Maybe they had irritated Nessa as much as they did, because she knew they were true?

Nessa lurched forward, holding Will's face with one hand. She pressed her soft lips against his and felt sparks simmer and fly as their skin touched. The sensual smell of his aftershave, the warm, familiar scent of him, made butterflies explode in her stomach. But in moments, the room started to spin. It wasn't right. *This wasn't right.* Nessa was so drunk, it was unbearable to close her eyes for this kiss and enjoy it. She felt sick, as if she were a reckless teen, snogging an 'unsuitable' on a fairground waltzer, the regret sinking in before the hangover.

And before she knew it, Will had pushed her away, prising her from his face with a strong right hand against her shoulder, their bodies now distant, cold air and shock swirling between them.

'Listen,' Will said breathlessly, a look of horror on his

face. Nessa looked up at him shamefully with tears in her eyes. She noticed how stiff his whole body was, as if locked in horror.

'You don't . . . You just, you don't love me like that, OK?' Will said, angrily, before getting up and storming out of the house.

Twenty-Three
'What's going on, Mrs Bruce?'

March 16th 2013

'Asil, I need your help now, please,' Nessa gasped down the phone, pacing up and down the kitchen floor. Poppy stood in the doorway, her arms crossed and her forehead wrinkled with concern. Her mother repeatedly pulled back the curtains and peeked out at the road, but it was the same view she'd seen just seconds before. Her car sat innocently beside a lamppost that cold Saturday morning. An old man wearing a flat cap and a pair of leather gloves was walking his dog painfully slowly, a kind of stilted shuffle in the direction of the recreation ground.

'Sure, Ness. What's up? You sound really upset . . .' Asil responded down the line, his familiar voice a little distant. She could picture him now, rolling his eyes at a colleague, mouthing her name as he put his hand over the mouthpiece. She didn't want to be known at the station as the local nutter, constantly getting in touch about stupid things.

'I need to . . . I think I need to take out a restraining order against someone. I can't believe I'm even saying this,' Nessa said, a sick feeling swamping her tummy. As she spoke she turned to face her daughter who was nibbling her thumb, looking concerned and confused at the same time.

'What's going on, Mrs Bruce?'

'It's my friend, well an old friend of mine, William Turnbull. You've met him already actually: he was helping out with the search for Jake. He's doing some things that I feel uncomfortable about, and I really need some help,' she said, between great gasps of panicked breath.

'Nessa, please try to remain calm, OK. Just do your best to tell me what's happened,' Asil said, his voice just audible for Poppy, although slightly tinny, and high pitched, like the squeak of a mouse.

'OK, this morning, I left the house and went straight to my car because I need to do some food shopping, and the car's been . . . been . . .'

'Broken into . . .? Mrs Bruce?'

'Been . . . no, no, the opposite of that. It's been fixed up. As in, it's been cleaned and polished within an inch of its life; it has brand new windscreen wipers, four new tyres, stuff like that . . . I didn't even notice it straight away, I just knew that it looked different, and that was when I realised,' Nessa said, feeling a shiver down her spine.

'Sorry, what? You're telling me that your car has basically been serviced. Without your knowledge?' Asil asked incredulously.

'Yes, that's exactly what I'm saying. And I'm saying that this has happened overnight while my daughter and I were asleep, which is quite frankly terrifying. But that's not the only thing, there's been stuff going on for months: gifts left on my doorstep, Christmas lights put up outside my house . . . The list goes on.'

Nessa heard a sigh down the phone from Asil, and some shuffling, as if he were doing something else at the same time as talking to her. Nessa thought back to that night with Will, when she seemed to have totally lost her mind and tried to kiss him. What had she been thinking? But now it was all happening again, like some kind of sick nightmare that wouldn't end. And the worst thing was that she had probably encouraged it somehow, or at least that's how the police would see it. If she told them that part . . .

'Are you listening to me? It's Will. There's no doubt about it, and I'm not OK with it anymore. It's making me feel really uncomfortable, and quite frightened actually,' Nessa said, switching on the kettle, wondering when would be the right moment to mention, and explain, the kissing thing, because she should probably let them know about that. But she felt so ashamed of what she had done that she felt like throwing up every time the memory flashed in her mind.

'OK, Nessa, please stay calm. I'm trying to get my head around this. How could Will have accessed your car?' he asked. Nessa instantly picked up on a tone in his voice, as if he was humouring her.

'I don't know. He's helped out our family for years; he's pretty much a part of it. He definitely has keys for the house so he could have let himself in to get the car keys, I guess. I don't know,' Nessa stated.

'Do you not think perhaps he's just trying to support you?' Asil asked, flatly.

Nessa cried in exasperation. 'All I know is that I'm sick and tired of it, and the way he is going about it is making me feel extremely uncomfortable. Doing all this stuff slyly like this. I mean surely if it makes me feel this way, and he knows it does, then it must amount to harassment!'

'OK, hang tight Mrs Bruce, I'm on my way round. I'm going to be bringing a police counsellor though, OK? See you shortly,' Asil said, hanging up the phone abruptly before she could answer.

Ness was back at work and preparing for a local book week. The tiny library was humming with activity for the first time in a long while. Children of different ages from local schools were due to come into the library for talks and activities aimed at inspiring them to read. She would be speaking to a group of secondary school kids later that afternoon, and she was dreading it.

Secondary school kids were the scariest, she found – more frightening than really young children who didn't understand the dangers of hot drinks and plug sockets, and certainly scarier than the inquisitive nine-year-olds who would randomly ask basic questions about times tables and life, prompting a cold sweat as she tried to remember what nine times seven was, and why the sky was blue, in front of large groups of people.

Teenagers were just mean miniature adults without filters. They had not yet developed the subtle art of saving face. Judgements and loathing just kind of seeped out of them. Poppy had been in one of the classes due to visit the library, but had resolutely refused to experience the ordeal of listening to her own mother talk to her classmates so had decided to take the day off sick. Nessa kind of understood this, she thought, as she organised some poorly photocopied worksheets for the afternoon's session on the staffroom table.

'There's a call for you Nessa. It's your mother-in-law, Betty?'

Kristy, the library secretary, was standing at the entrance to the room, holding a cordless phone, pursing her lips and raising an eyebrow. She was wearing a tight, purple dress that only just seemed to hold her together. Her buxom breasts looked as if the tight polyester was suffocating them, and poorly stitched seams seemed to scream out from the effort of holding everything together. Her outrageously long nails tapped against the plastic casing impatiently.

'Betsy . . . Right OK, thanks. I'll be down in a sec,' Nessa said, taking the phone from her hands and shutting the door gently behind her.

'Hi Bets, are you OK?' Nessa asked nervously. Betsy never called her at work. She had a sudden feeling of concern for Mick. Had something happened to him? She always worried about this: a fall; an illness, perhaps. The phone call she dreaded.

'Hi darling. Listen, I'm sorry to ring you at the library like this . . . I just had to get in touch straight away, and you know I'm no good at the texting. I just want to thank you so much,' she said, gushing down the line.

Nessa could faintly hear the sound of Mick singing Sinatra in the background, and felt relief slide down her body. At least he was OK.

'Thanks for what?' Nessa asked, tucking a great swathe of hair behind her ear and sitting down.

'The garden, silly! That was such a kind thing to do. Who did you get to do it? I know you obviously wanted to surprise us this time, but can you let us know who it was so I can speak to them about doing it in the future? I'm blown away,' she said quickly, almost tripping over her words. There was a huge smile in her voice as she spoke. The sound of Mick humming 'High Hopes' started to get louder.

'Come on darling, dance with me!' Nessa heard him say playfully, in the background.

'Sorry, Nessa. You still there? Yes, it was just a wonderful thing to come outside and find the garden so beautiful. We've been indoors for most of the day, so we didn't notice at all. Your plot worked! I guess we should really open the curtains a bit more; it is springtime after all!' Betsy said, excitably.

'What has happened to your garden?' Nessa asked.

'Well there are new beds, and some beautiful flowers, all planted in and ready for the better weather. The hedges have been trimmed, and everything is just looking generally lovely. There was a pile of rubble that neither of us could clear away and that's gone too. It's just remarkable!' Betsy said, breathless with happiness.

'Are you sure you didn't arrange it yourself? We've all had so much to think about, perhaps it slipped your mind?' Nessa asked, narrowing her eyes and looking at the floor.

'Oh come off it Nessa. I'm not that senile, thank you very much!' Betsy cried, 'So you didn't arrange it? I'm sorry love, I just assumed it was you,' she said, embarrassment in her voice. There were a few moments of uncomfortable silence. Nessa picked up something in Betsy's tone, as if she was perhaps disappointed that Ness wasn't behind it. God this was uncomfortable. They had clearly made a mistake – got mixed up.

Nessa had heard about this kind of things from friends: elderly parents getting more and more confused. Missed appointments, and others that were never booked, all springing from nowhere. How sad it all was . . .

Kristy appeared in the doorway suddenly, as Nessa tried to gather her thoughts.

'Nessa,' she whispered, apologetically, 'area manager, downstairs. Now,' she added, frantically.

'Betsy, I'm sorry. I have to go. Things are really hectic here,' Nessa said. 'I love you. I'll ring you later,' she said before hanging up the phone and running downstairs.

Twenty-Four
Is that her at the door?

April 10th 2013

The house was eerily empty. Nessa shuffled about on the sofa, trying to get more comfortable. A cushion shaped like an owl slowly rolled away from her and landed on the carpet with a torpid bounce. She didn't have the energy to pick it up. She hadn't felt this tired for a long time.

Kat had been in touch an hour before, calling her from her chilly, small university hall bedroom. She had told Nessa that she wanted to track down Tom. She wanted to see him face to face. She had finally decided that she wanted to thank him for looking after her all those years ago, to be able to put her mind at rest.

Nessa was speechless, her chest flooding with panic. The moment she'd been terrified of was here. But she still couldn't say it. She still couldn't tell her what had happened.

The TV was on with the sound muted. Nessa had been struggling to read a book to take her mind off things, finding the silent buzz of activity on the screen beyond her eye line strangely comforting. But it was impossible to focus. How would she stop Kat trying to find Tom? She didn't even know where to start. Those sharp concerns were swirling around with melancholic thoughts of Jake, and Will, and all that had happened over the past year or so.

She had decided against taking any kind of action against Will – not that she had much in the way of options, it had transpired when she spoke to Asil. She had hated the way he'd looked at her with a kind of half-sympathetic smirk, as if to say, 'well the *real* issue here is that you're going a bit crazy'. She'd despised the way he asked if she'd consider seeking treatment for anxiety and depression. His manner was a little patronising: thinly veiled distrust screaming out from behind his eyes. Anyhow, even if she had been able to do something, anything along those lines seemed ridiculous now that she had calmed down.

It had been a knee-jerk reaction, perhaps, a little embarrassing. She didn't have a leg to stand on, given 'the kiss' – *that kiss*, that awful thing she did. And how embarrassing it was. No explaining would get her out of that one. No one would understand how the pressures of her life had built up and exploded, making her do something she would never normally do. Nessa had simply told herself that she had to keep as much distance as possible from Will Turnbull.

But she couldn't stop thinking about him on this companionless Friday night. She wondered where he was and what he was doing. She imagined people asking him why he didn't see her anymore. They would open their mouths in shock. They would gasp and sigh in sympathy. They would believe him, of course, and think that she was being weird. Then, they would probably nod sadly and say that she had gone through such a hard time losing her husband, and perhaps she would 'come round soon', or some other, similarly wishy-washy sentiment . . .

Her thoughts shifted to her daughter who should probably be back soon, she thought, looking at the time on her phone. Nessa sent her a text, to ask how she was getting on. She tried to lose herself in her book once again, but it was impossible. Intrusive thoughts about Jake appeared like shadows in the darkness. She imagined him alive, walking around in the midnight rain, trying to find his way home. She pictured him, unshaven and hungry, shivering beneath the clouds. She started to cry quietly to herself, tears dripping from her eyes and flowing down her cheeks. *Everything was such a mess.*

She sat on the sofa, totally consumed by her thoughts for what felt like 15 minutes. But when the doorbell went, she noticed it was 1.30 a.m. *Shit*, she panicked, *where the hell is Poppy? Is that her at the door? Is it the police?*

Her heart raced as she got up to answer it.

Twenty-Five

'What on earth has happened to you?'

Nessa ran towards the door through the darkness of her hallway and opened it as quickly as she could.

She saw a small figure, crumpled in a dark heap on her doorstep. 'What on earth?' she said out loud, feeling immediately frightened. She kneeled down nervously to take a closer look. It was difficult to see in the darkness, but when Nessa pulled back the soggy hood of a jacket she didn't recognise she could make out the side of her daughter's pale face in the moonlight. A great clump of hair flapped over her eyes and hung down to the ground.

'Fuck,' Nessa whispered to herself, starting to panic.

She frantically started pawing at her daughter's limp body, putting her hand beneath her head, which flapped lifelessly from her neck, in order to see her face. Poppy's eyes were closed. Her face was expressionless, her mouth slightly open. Her skin was frighteningly white and her lips were tinged blue. She looked desperately ill.

Thankfully her skin was warm. Nessa pushed her face urgently towards Poppy's mouth. She could feel her daughter's soft, shallow breath against her nose and lips as the night air blew towards them and rattled in the doorway. *Thank god,* she thought to herself, her whole body trembling with fear and adrenaline. Poppy stank of alcohol and vomit, Nessa noticed, wrinkling her nose. She was momentarily distracted by the sound of something moving in the bushes a few yards away from the door: a fox perhaps. She looked up quickly, but there was nothing to be seen.

Shaking, she picked up her daughter, willing every muscle in her body to be strong enough to carry her in from the cold. Poppy's body was completely limp and, because of this, remarkably heavy. Nessa struggled through the hallway, her heart thumping hard in her chest.

A million thoughts ran through her mind as she carried her daughter into the living room. She sat in the darkness with Poppy, the TV still flickering away quietly. A man dressed as Count Dracula was laughing on the screen, his great pale face lit up in a brilliant white light. Had Poppy been attacked, or drugged? How had she made it home? What on earth had happened to her?

She was so surprised that she'd just drifted off like that. It was unlike her. She couldn't believe that she had been sitting fixed to the spot for hours, lost in thought, as time slipped away and her daughter was in danger all the while. *Now I'm a terrible mother too*, she thought to herself, becoming breathless with panic.

She called an ambulance and waited tearfully, stroking her daughter's forehead and saying silent prayers to herself.

'What on earth has happened to you?' she said quietly, as she collapsed in tears, holding her daughter close to her chest and rocking her gently like she used to when she was tiny.

'She's going to be OK,' the nurse said, smiling sympathetically and handing Nessa a glass of cold water. She gestured towards a plastic chair in the small consultation room, set away from the general A&E waiting area and the busy wards that throbbed with emotion. Stripped down and simple, the room reminded Nessa of the police meeting rooms she'd spent so much time in in last year. It brought back painful memories and feelings; a kind of heaviness spread through her limbs.

She sank down into the chair, feeling completely shell-shocked. It was 5.45 a.m. The nurse was a Chinese lady in her late forties, grey streaks running through her black hair, which was pulled into a bun. She looked tired, but there was kindness and understanding in her face too. Her voice was gentle and soft.

'We had to pump Poppy's stomach,' she said, consulting a piece of paper on a clipboard and tucking a few flyaway strands of hair behind her right ear. 'Your daughter has quite serious alcohol poisoning, so she will need to stay here until we feel she is well enough to go home. It could be a day or two. She is on an IV line so we can make sure she is hydrated. She has a catheter,' the woman said, nodding her head as she spoke. Her cheeks glowed.

Nessa felt herself breaking down with relief and sadness. She was glad that her daughter was safe, but terrified that it had come to this – that her daughter was lying in a hospital bed just feet away, with alcohol poisoning, having had her stomach pumped. It was the stuff of nightmares. It was far too extreme. How had it come to this? *Anything could have happened.*

'Do you know what happened to your daughter last night?' the woman asked.

'I don't, no. She went bowling with some friends. She was supposed to be at home at 10.30 p.m. I didn't hear from her and then that was it. I heard a knock at my door, hours later, and there she was, lying on the doorstep,' Nessa said, wiping tears from her eyes. She felt so guilty. How could she have been so selfish to be sitting there, daydreaming, while her daughter was clearly going through some kind of ordeal?

'Has your daughter experienced anything particularly stressful recently? Any problems at school? Does she have a boyfriend?' the woman asked in quick fire, starting to make her own notes with a blue biro.

'No. No, she doesn't have a boyfriend as far as I am aware, but, of course, you never know. But the biggest thing is that her father died recently. He was a solider,' Nessa said, softly.

'How recently?' the woman asked, willing Nessa to speak on.

'We don't know exactly. It was last year; he committed suicide. But we, we don't know exactly when or how . . . It's quite a messed-up situation unfortunately. He was never found.'

'Right,' the woman said, solemnly. She looked sadly at Nessa for a few moments, before starting to write again. Her pen made little scratching sounds against the paper.

'Are you getting the support you need?' she questioned, passing Nessa a box of tissues. Nessa nodded in thanks, and blew her nose loudly.

'I guess so, yeah . . . It's never easy. It just feels like a nightmare, you know? Since it happened, a continual nightmare,' Nessa said, feeling a headache coming on. The nurse nodded understandingly.

'I think you and Poppy may need some more help. I am going to refer you both to psychiatric services for assessment at a later date, if that's OK with you? It's pretty clear from where I'm standing that Poppy was trying to dilute her feelings with alcohol. It's quite common,' the woman said, unblinkingly.

'Yes, I understand, but before we speak about that. I'm really worried. Do you think there's any chance she was . . . attacked tonight? It's all I can think about. I don't know where she's been or how she got to the house. That's the thing that's troubling me so much. It's pretty terrifying,' Nessa said quickly, almost ashamed to put her thoughts into words.

'I sincerely hope not. There's no obvious sign of that at the moment and she has been examined, but when she comes round properly we will be able to talk to her. Unfortunately she may remember very little of the night due to the amount of alcohol she had. There was a great deal of it in her blood, but no trace of drugs, which may be, some relief to you,' the woman said, nodding seriously as she spoke.

'OK. Thank you, so much . . . for looking after my little girl,' Nessa said, reaching out and squeezing the nurse's forearm.

'Oh, it's OK. It's my job. You stay here for a while if you like and come through to Poppy's room whenever you're ready. She's still asleep though. She is going to be very tired tomorrow too, she may struggle with some kinds of food, might be best to start with toast,' she said, before stepping up and walking back towards Poppy's room, shutting the door behind her.

Once again Nessa was alone. The brilliant white walls and the tube lights on the ceiling coupled with the sudden tiredness that hit her like a speeding train. Now she knew her daughter was safe, she felt as if she could sink onto the floor and fall asleep. And right now, she couldn't think of anyone she wanted around her more than Jake.

If only he was here . . .

Twenty-Six

'You can call me Steve'

April 12th 2013

'Hello, Dr Jutting?' Nessa asked as she opened the door timidly. She angled herself into the office, not quite committing to coming in yet.

The young doctor looked up from his paper work and nodded, not saying a word, still clearly lost in thought.

'It's great to meet you,' Nessa said, walking into the small room now and shaking his hand. She studied his thick ginger beard as he finally welcomed her, noticing an air of social awkwardness about him. He possessed a set of pale blue eyes that seemed to penetrate her gaze so intensely she could barely look at them. His fingers were remarkably long and thin, she noticed, and his skin was cold.

'You can call me Steve,' he said, cracking a difficult smile and picking up his notepad.

There was a long pause as Dr Jutting rifled through his notes. Nessa felt an urgency overwhelm her. What was going on?

'Steve, is everything OK with my daughter?' she blurted out, unable to hold herself back. 'Sorry, I'm just quite worried,' she said, cracking the knuckles on both hands to try and relieve some of the tension she could feel building up within herself.

'The reason I called you in this afternoon is because of something your daughter told me during our session this morning that I felt you should be aware of . . .'

Nessa could feel her heartbeat thud in her ears.

'Poppy was talking to me about the night she got drunk, and had to be hospitalised . . .'

'Right, OK, well that's good, right?'

Dr Jutting nodded, gently.

'She told me that she finally remembered how she got home. Because of course that's very much been a question mark ever since,' he said, calmly.

'Yes, of course . . .' Nessa said.

'She says her father carried her home,' he said, matter-of-factly.

'Pardon?' Nessa responded, feeling the blood drain from her face.

'Yes. She said she started having dreams about it, but also daytime experiences, similar to flashbacks, while she was awake too. She was very reluctant to tell me, and says she hasn't told anyone because she thinks she may be going crazy, and that in her own words, she might be "locked away". She was very concerned about my telling you, but I assured her we could be trusted to do the right thing, and of course there is no question of her being "locked away",' he uttered, pausing to compose himself before continuing.

'I believe she might be suffering from what we call false delusions, potentially linked with psychosis, Nessa,' he said, softly. There was a sadness in his eyes. He tilted his head to one side when he finished speaking. *Ergh, that look of sympathy again.*

'OK. What did she say about it? These "flashbacks", what were they?' Nessa asked frantically, feeling as if she were flying out of the room on her chair, being pulled backwards by a force she couldn't identify.

'Not too much. She said she remembers him scooping her up and taking her home. She said she could tell it was him from the shape of his nose and his face, and the way his arm felt under her back. It's a clear delusion, obviously, we don't need to go into why that is. It's quite common in children and young people who lose a loved one and have experienced this kind of trauma. It's incredible what the mind can do. To reassure you, it's certainly not the first time I have heard this kind of thing from my patients,' he added, almost in admiration of the capabilities of the human mind. He didn't seem at all surprised or fazed by the revelation.

The doctor leafed through another few pages of his notebook, his beady eyes scanning the carefully penned letters. Nessa could hear a high-pitched humming sound in the distance. Against the backdrop of the magnolia wallpaper and the low light seeping from the broken lamp, Dr Jutting's head seemed to melt from one into three, all dancing there before her.

'Can you hear an alarm?' Nessa asked, sitting up and looking around from left to right and then once more, just to check. Her hair whipped around her head as she moved, a little frantically, she realised, feeling the gentle crack of a bone at the top of her spine.

'Er no, I don't believe I can Mrs Bruce,' he said. His voice echoed in ways it hadn't done before, while the humming sound grew louder, more pronounced. It seemed to run through the core of her brain, in a perfect line from ear to ear.

'Anyway, as I mentioned before, Poppy was very concerned about me telling you this. She said she hadn't told you yet because she didn't want to upset or scare you. Of course everything that she tells me is in the strictest confidence, but I did ask that, given what she was saying, I might have her permission to talk to you today. She was, eventually, OK with that, once I had explained that her treatment might have to be altered.'

Nessa didn't know what to say.

'Mrs Bruce, you look a little pale. I can understand that this must be very upsetting for you,' Dr Jutting said, leaning forwards in his chair.

'What, what do you propose we do? And psychosis? That sounds terrible,' Nessa said, trying yet failing to pull herself together. She blinked several times, but nothing helped. She just wanted to close her eyes and listen. Everything suddenly seemed so very bright, so overwhelming.

'I firstly propose that you don't panic. What Poppy is experiencing is by no means unusual. There are brilliant treatments available now for psychosis. Medications can hugely improve the quality of life for so many of our patients, and she may never suffer from it again. Sometimes these things are a one-off, sometimes not, but I feel we have to look into it as it's too early to know at this stage,' he said.

Psychosis. Medication. Patients. Nessa felt the world start to buzz and throb, like an old TV with a broken signal. She blinked again, hard.

She could hear a sob. It took her a moment or two to realise that the sound was coming from her. Dr Jutting shuffled in his chair uncomfortably and thrust the tissues in Nessa's direction again, muttering something about how everything was going to be OK.

'Nessa, I would recommend that Poppy has a new assessment, given these possible delusions. This would replace the assessment that led her to be treated for anxiety with me. And then, then we can see where we go from there? I can make sure the appointment happens quickly. It usually does where it concerns children, and these kinds of symptoms,' he said, soothingly.

'Right, sure. Whatever you say,' Nessa muttered, feeling sick to her stomach.

Twenty-Seven

'Just a lemonade then please'

May 18th 2013

Nessa couldn't believe she was doing this, but she had to find closure. It was all part of the process, to cope with the loss of Jake.

Nobody knew where she was going. Not Poppy, Betsy, Mick, Will or Teigen. Teigen had popped round for dinner just a few nights ago. Nessa had resisted the temptation to tell her what she was about to do, despite the amount of wine they drank. There were moments when she had wanted to tell her, and get some kind of support from her best friend. It was alluring, the idea of her plan being validated by someone who loved her. But she needed to think straight and listen to what she wanted, and no one else.

Nessa had mentioned something to Poppy about visiting a sick relative called Mabel who lived 100 miles away. She had said she would stay in a hotel that night, and she'd be back by 11 a.m. on Sunday. Poppy was to stay at a friend's house.

Guilt filled her stomach as she navigated the tree-lined roads of Beckenham, away from her small, troubled home and heading towards Kent. It was drab and rainy, the kind of day she would have quite liked to ignore by hiding beneath a duvet with a good book. She felt guilt for lying about what she was doing. She just had to do this for herself. For some peace.

It took two painful hours to get there. It should have only been an hour and a half, but she'd got stuck behind an infuriatingly slow tractor on the way, that couldn't handle any kind of upward gradient. It kept spitting chunks of horse shit and hay all over her windscreen. When it had finally pulled down a winding country road, Nessa had tried to make up the time, pushing her foot down on the accelerator a little harder than normal. She hated being late.

All she could think about was how they might react to her, how they might look at her. Would their eyes betray any anger? Would they resent her? They had all seemed fine on the phone when she had plucked up the courage to call them. Nessa's fingers had trembled so much that she had struggled to tap the right buttons on the screen of her phone. And when they answered, all the twitch fibres in the muscles of her hands and arms seemed to beg her to hang up. But something kept her on the phone . . .

Nessa finally pulled into the pub car park. She could hear the gravel crunching beneath the tyres of her 17-year-old VW Polo. When she got out, she could hear the distant sound of the motorway, carried a mile or so across the fields by the breeze. It was strangely comforting.

Feeling sick with fear, she stood up tall, leant back

against her car and took two long deep breaths: in and out, in and out. She tried to calm down, but her heart seemed to be thudding faster and faster, out of control. *I can turn away now,* she thought. *I don't have to go through with this. I could get back in the car right now and drive off, and that would be the end of it. I would never have to see them again.* This option seemed tempting. Nessa looked at her car keys, which sat glistening in the palm of her hand. But that would be the easy way out . . .

'Right. Come on. You can do this,' she said to herself, firmly.

As soon as she made it inside, she was greeted by a fierce heat, radiating from a roaring fireplace. Her cheeks flushed all of a sudden. Even her ears felt like they were on fire.

Nessa went to get a drink to buy herself some time. Perhaps if she did that, she could stop the fear that seemed to be building in her ribcage. She was late anyway. They were probably already there, waiting for her, with their own glasses of watered-down orange juice and flat cola.

'What do you want?' a sullen, joy-bereft barmaid asked her, with one hand on her hip. Her hair was tied into a ponytail at the very top of her head. Her makeup made her look a little dirty.

'Just a cranberry juice, please,' Nessa replied politely. The men in the bar stared at her as if she'd asked for some incredibly rare beverage only available from some fountain in the desert that had to be reached by camel.

'Oi Mark!' the woman screamed. She turned around in the direction of some stairs at the back of the bar that presumably lead down to a basement full of barrels and regret. Her ponytail whipped in the air as she moved.

'Do we 'ave caneberry juice?'

'You wha?' came a bellowing voice, presumably 'Mark's'.

Nessa could hear the sound of clattering metal, followed by some expletives.

'It's cranberry,' Nessa corrected her, blushing. A few titters came from the men, clutching their pint glasses and staring into the distance.

'Oh, sorry love – CRANberry,' the barmaid repeated, with a sarcastic inflection on the opening syllable.

'Nah,' said the man.

'Nah,' the barmaid said, turning back to Nessa and shrugging her shoulders.

'Just a lemonade then please,' Nessa said, wishing this moment would end as soon as possible.

The barmaid poured out the drink reluctantly and handed it to Nessa, who was shaking so much with nerve, by this stage, it was hard to dig the change out of her purse. She looked around and approached the stairs, her stomach plunging with each step. One. Two. Three. Four.

She turned the corner, the floorboards creaking beneath her feet. And there they were, sitting around a table in silence, looking at her.

Twenty-Eight

'So, how are you all doing?'

'Hi guys,' Nessa said softly. Two of the faces broke into gentle smiles, the others looked nervous. Perhaps they were as nervous as she was, she thought, although right now she didn't imagine that was possible. One of the group, a tearful lady with a shiny, chestnut bob, approached her, enveloping her in a tender hug. Nessa felt detached, like she had fled her own body and was simply watching from above.

When they were all sat down, Nessa took a moment to study the faces around her. Elaine Wyatt, Rick Martin, Kerry Blatt and Lisa Reynolds were only just illuminated by a few candles and a dull lamp in the corner; the drab afternoon light seeping through small, set-back windows did very little to brighten the corner table. But despite the gloom, Nessa recognised in these faces something she'd seen staring back at her from her own bathroom mirror. A bluish grey, pallid tone was evident on their skin. And the tiredness – it was there in the bags beneath their eyes and the premature wrinkles.

It was a look that came from loss, and she could see it mirrored back at her in the four faces of the people who loved Thomas, Michael, Liam and Gabriel. They had loved their men and still did, of course, just as much as she loved Jake Bruce. The thought sent a wave of emotion trickling down her body.

'So, how are you all doing?' she asked, a little lamely. She could feel tears building. She wrinkled her nose, trying to stop them in their tracks before they overwhelmed her.

'Well, you know . . . it's been difficult,' Elaine said, softly. Rick nodded in understanding. The others just looked down at the table, their eyes flickering over the surface.

'I understand,' Nessa said, 'and I'm so grateful to you for coming to meet me. It must have been very hard,' she said. A few of her nerves began to disperse. She was eventually strong enough to be able to pick up her glass, and take a sip of her sugary, fizzy drink without visibly trembling in front of everyone.

'Well, I think it was a good idea,' Kerry said in a Liverpudlian accent, tugging at a long ginger curl that hung over her shoulder. Her fingers were decorated with lots of tiny rings. 'I've been thinking about you a lot since Liam passed away. I was going to contact you myself, actually, when the time was right, you know? I was struggling to pluck up the courage.' A few of the others nodded in agreement, as if they might have been about to do the same thing.

'Guys. I have to just get this out in the open, to clear the air. I'm so, so sorry about what happened. I know that Jake took total, personal responsibility for the loss of your loved ones; as you'll probably know, he never recovered from it . . . never forgave himself,' Nessa blundered on, her words coming out so quickly it was as if they had control over her, as opposed to the other way around.

Gabriel's partner, Lisa, was the one who had given her a hug when she arrived. She had one of those kind faces that instantly put others at ease, and she was the first to speak. 'Nessa we are so sorry to hear about what happened to Jake. We aren't angry at him, or you, or anyone . . . We were just talking about it before you came. Our men went into the army knowing that they were working together, and there was risk involved in that. They knew what they were opening themselves up to. Jake was a brilliant leader and we all had so much respect for him,' she said, softly running her fingers over the bridge of her nose with her left hand.

A huge tear ran down Nessa's cheek. She pictured Jake in the photograph he had sent her, lying on a dust sheet, that beautiful twinkle in his eye. *He was beautiful*. He had been the most beautiful thing she'd ever known.

'Thank you,' she said, suddenly glad that she had done this, proud that she followed her heart. 'I would have seen you all earlier. I just didn't know how you would react.' She looked up at the four unblinking faces before her, a couple of them tearful too. The pub was painfully quiet. She could only hear the crackling of wood burning in the fire, and the distant chatter of the old men by the bar.

'I know this sounds a bit cliché and all that, but I think Jake died the same day your loved ones did, you know, in a way. Does that make sense? I think it was intolerable for him to live with that knowledge, that he hadn't protected them. That was the end for him,' Nessa said. She saw the people before her crumble a little, with sadness and disappointment, their body language a collective sigh.

'I'm so sorry, Nessa, about what happened to Jake. It was terrible news, I couldn't believe it when you told me on the phone,' Rick said.

'I actually brought something with me,' he added after a few moments of quiet reflection. He pulled a piece of crumpled paper from the pocket of his black jeans. 'I was going through some old stuff the other day, and I found a letter that Michael had sent me when he was out on tour with your husband.'

The group paused, anticipation buzzing between them. Rick coughed a couple of times and cleared his throat before continuing.

'There was something he wrote in that letter, that I thought might interest you,' he said, opening up the paper. It made a gentle rustling sound.

'There was a line in this letter, which was sent to me about a year ago. Here we are: "Jake's great to work with. I swear to god if it wasn't for Jake, there would be so many more tragedies round here, so many more lives lost. One day, I'd like to be as great an officer as Jake . . .",' he said, trailing off to a profound silence.

'It's just something small, but I thought you might like to know,' he added, smiling warmly. Nessa felt overwhelmed with emotion. She nodded and smiled to thank him, reaching over and squeezing his hand, unable to see clearly through her tears.

Two hours seemed to pass by in what felt like ten minutes. They spoke about the funerals they had held for Thomas, Michael, Liam and Gabriel, and about Jake's memorial. They talked about how their kids were doing, the need to start downsizing houses, of perhaps moving away and starting again. They discussed memories and sadness and what it felt like to try and move on.

'How's life generally?' Nessa had asked. 'Apart from, you know, what we've been talking about?'

There were some blank, searching looks, as the four people gathered with her rattled their brains for positive things to say. Nice things. Nessa knew how that felt, how life had become totally consumed by her loss and everything else just paled into nothingness.

'It was my daughter Kara's eleventh birthday the other day,' Elaine said, smiling to herself. 'That was nice. We had a little party for her, with cake and balloons and stuff.' Nessa nodded and smiled warmly.

'It was weird though. Someone gave her a bike. Not a new one; it looked like it had been all fixed up, though, and it was just left outside the house with a little bow on it. We still haven't worked out who it's from. It's very funny! She'd wanted one of these mountain bikes for a couple of years, but we'd never been able to afford it . . . Oh well, we'll get to the bottom of it soon I'm sure,' she said, smiling to herself in amusement.

'I finally finished my degree with the Open University, after like six years or something. That felt pretty good, although it would be have been nice to have had Mike at my graduation ceremony,' Rick said, sadly.

'Yeah, it's so weird how life sort of just goes on isn't it?' Kerry said. 'Birthdays, exams, stuff the kids are doing at school. You know the world will still turn, but you don't really expect it to at first,' she added, draining the last droplets of coffee from her mug.

As everyone started to leave, Nessa felt a deep disappointment start to engulf her. She wasn't ready for this to end yet, but she didn't know why. There was a lump in her throat. She almost wanted to beg everyone to stay, but they had places to go, things to do. Their lives had to go on, even if it felt like hers hadn't.

They shared hugs and kisses on the cheek and promises to stay in touch. But she doubted those promises would be honoured, in reality. Realistically, this might be the last time she ever saw these people.

She walked out to the car park with Elaine, feeling just as lost as she had before. Perhaps, she thought, this wasn't the magic step she had to take to start accepting it all.

Fear filled her tummy. It had finally stopped raining, but it was dark now. A long strip of lights from the motorway could be seen in the distance. It was starting to get foggy. The cheap hotel she was staying at was just a couple of miles away. She felt exhausted and couldn't wait to sink into whatever strange starchy bed would be hers for the evening. And then perhaps, just as she'd hoped, she'd wake up in the morning a new person.

Twenty-Nine

There's nothing to be scared of

Later that day . . .

It had seemed like such a nice idea at the time, to book herself a night away and have some alone time after such a big day. Money was so tight that she'd put it on a credit card, opting for a cheap hotel that looked relatively nice inside. She'd imagined herself having dinner alone, like one of those classy people in the films, flicking between a glass of wine and a highbrow novel in a nearby restaurant or a cosy country pub, before going back and soaking in a huge, luxurious bath. She'd hoped to sleep peacefully for hours. Then in the morning, she'd feel refreshed, and ready to go home. Ready to face her life again. But the reality was so much less pleasant than she'd pictured.

The bed was stiff and uncomfortable. When she rolled over, she could hear springs crunching. The wallpaper looked old, faded pink and white stripes seemed to merge into one another. There wasn't even a bath, only a narrow unwelcoming shower with magnolia tiles and god knows which life forms being successfully cultivated in the cracks between them.

Nessa felt worse than she had before she'd had the meeting, and it had hit her suddenly, like a cold wave of sheer panic. Her grief was so complicated, so all consuming. She kept doing strange things like she had done that day. They were like rituals, in the hope that one of them just might be the missing experience she needed to have, to be able to start feeling a little better . . . somehow normal again . . . At that very moment, Nessa felt so uncomfortable that she couldn't even be within her own skin. If she could, she would have fled herself, run away and come back later perhaps, when things weren't so . . . unbearable.

She sat up in bed and looked around her at the cold, uninviting room, resting her copy of F. Scott Fitzgerald's *Tender Is the Night* on her lap. She realised that she would rather sleep anywhere but here. She'd never missed Jake more than she did right now. And all she wanted was to talk to Sue . . . She wondered over and over what kind of relationship they'd share if she were still alive, because she'd sure loved her when she was around. Nessa recalled walking around Sue's bedroom as a child of about eight or nine. She had run her fingers carefully across the spines of the novels she'd read, wondering that if she too absorbed those beautifully constructed sentences she might be, somehow, a little bit more like her . . . She had smelt the neckline of her jumper, and taken in the magical scent of her. She had touched the things Sue touched, glass bottles of perfume, glistening silver jewellery, a feather brooch, just to try and comprehend her magnificence . . . Nessa knew that if her first foster mother were still around today, she'd be kind to her, tell her something that might bring some hope to this waking nightmare her life had become.

Nessa got out of bed, tearfully got dressed and hurriedly packed her bag with the few possessions she'd brought with her: the book, some creased cotton pyjamas, underwear and a battered toothbrush. There was somewhere she had to go. Only one place where she could, in some strange way, be close to him . . .

Nessa would normally have been frightened to be in this situation. If someone had told her what she was about to do. If they were sitting across from her in a coffee shop and detachedly describing the actions of someone else, she would have shuddered at the account of it. She would have thought they were crazy, or a bit thick, like the victims in horror films who stupidly go down to the basement armed with a slipper and a bent fork, after hearing something go bump in the night . . . But she had to do it. She had to . . .

It took her about 45 minutes to drive from her hotel room to leafy Sevenoaks. The roads were blissfully quiet. She arrived just before nine. The rain had started again, but only softly; little droplets had been splattering the windscreen as she travelled from the outskirts of Maidstone to this small, suburban town with its gleaming gem, Knole Park and Knole House, a National Trust property steeped in history, with an incredible literary background. Virginia Woolf's novel *Orlando* had fascinated Nessa, and she felt the place was still infused with the tender admiration of the writer.

Knole Park was Jake's place. It was why they had lived where they did. Why they spent weekend after weekend exploring its rolling, curving grounds, rebelliously feeding forbidden carrots to the deer and rolling down hills.

Nessa drove up a steep slanted road that led to a golf club. She knew there was a way into the park if she walked past the club, a few small farmhouses and a boggy field. They'd gone that way before, to avoid the buzz of the main Knole Park car park, which was usually heaving with posh parents and their screaming children on a Saturday afternoon. She wouldn't be able to get in the other way now anyhow. The big gold and black gilded gates would be locked firmly shut.

She pulled into a spot near the back of the car park, before digging around in the boot of her car, and finding a thick, woolly blanket she'd kept there in case she ever broke down and needed to keep warm. She'd never had to use it until now. Nessa knew what she was doing was crazy, but *she simply had to*.

A wedding reception was in full swing in the golf club. Eighties music thumped into the night and rotating disco lights flashed through the windows. A couple enthusiastically stumbled out of the front of the building as if they'd been pushed. The woman was giggling wickedly, some feathers attached to her skirt quivering in the night air. The man sniggered, and lit a cigarette, clouds of smoke spiralling away from his fingertips. Nessa walked past them, her head down. They probably wouldn't notice her, she thought.

Walking down the narrow pathway towards the houses, she could still hear the woman laughing and the occasional clatter of her thin, towering heels. There were no streetlights anymore. It was pitch black. The road surface was irregular and occasionally she plunged her foot into a deep puddle. She felt cold water seep through the holes in her trainers, but didn't care.

She was in a trance of sorts. The kind of grief she was

feeling, it absolved all reason and sense. It deleted her shame, or the kind of embarrassment she might feel should anyone find out what she was doing. She just didn't care anymore.

She walked past the cottages. There were four in total and they glowed from the inside, a warm and inviting light seeping from the windows. Two of them had the curtains drawn. In one of the cottages she could see a few adults gathered round a table, laughing and drinking from huge glasses of wine. One upstairs bedroom was illuminated. It was a child's room; the wallpaper was patterned with rockets and stars. *They are families. They are together*, she thought, enviously.

Soon Nessa was at the edge of the field. She stopped for a moment and took a deep breath. She could see the forest in the near distance. It resembled a blot of oil and she estimated it to be about a quarter of a mile away. It was night-time, but the sky was a bewitching light navy. The branches of ebony trees at the edge of the forest stood out against this inky backdrop like splinters of black lightning. It was a clear night and hundreds of stars twinkled in the sky. It was getting cold now. Nessa could see her breath billowing ahead of her. The park suddenly felt foreboding, as if she had been drunk and was slowly sobering up.

She still had to do this.

There's nothing to be scared of, she told herself, clutching the blanket as close to her chest as she could and starting to walk towards the forest once more. Her shoes sunk into the springy ground. She could hear wet, squelching sounds as she walked. This was just nature, she thought. What was there to fear in the night? The only difference was that the sun wasn't shining; everything else was exactly the same.

Why should trees and soil and leaves be frightening when shrouded in darkness?

Within five minutes Nessa was at the edge of the forest. She looked behind her one last time before she physically committed to what she was about to do.

She stepped into the forest and soon found herself enveloped in leafy blackness. She fought through some bracken, wet twigs and leaves scratching her face and running through her hair like cold, thin fingers. A sense of panic washed over her and her chest tightened. She reminded herself that she was safe here and nothing would hurt her, but it still didn't help when she was tangled in trees, unsure of the best direction to follow. Thick roots caught her legs as she walked, as if they were spindly, cold hands, trying to hold her back. It seemed as if she might never emerge.

Eventually, after what felt like forever, and a lot of struggling, she found herself spat out on the other side of the bracken. She was in a clearing, which was lit up surprisingly brightly by the platinum full moon. She suddenly recalled that night in 1999, when the same moon had hung over her and Will as he dramatically declared his love for her. It still made her chuckle. *But look how things are now . . . How sad.*

Nessa stood still, trying to catch her breath, her chest rising up and down. She took a few steps forwards and looked down, trying to take everything in. She was at the top of a hill that overlooked the whole park, which sprawled out beyond her like an open map. The silvery light had illuminated the curves of the hills, making the dull matt pathways glitter. She could see the large stone walls of Knole House, just visible, and miles of natural beauty. It was breathtaking.

Her heart started to slow down and she felt safe again.

She looked out at the darkness of a place that used to be so familiar to her. She remembered her and Jake walking a winding pathway to the right, when she was pregnant. Her legs had ached and he'd held her hand and told her how excited he was for the future. By the eighteenth hole of the golf course was a tree that had been his favourite climbing frame to enjoy with Poppy, while Nessa sat patiently at the bottom reading or eating sandwiches, the sunshine warming her feet. There was a little pond just beyond the house that Jake had taken his daughter to when she was little, carrying bottle green nets to dip for newts and frogspawn.

Nessa wrapped the blanket around her back and shoulders, closed her eyes and tried to feel his presence. She focused hard on it. Was he in the wind that blew softly against her cheeks? Was he in the moonlight that coated everything in glistening magic? Either way, being here helped. This was his favourite place and it lived and breathed right now, just as he had.

She was sure that dozens of little eyes were probably watching her right this very minute. Rats, voles, birds and foxes, little faces poking out from the undergrowth and between damp, mossy branches. *There is nothing to be sacred of*, she thought to herself. This place was teeming with life and it was the closest she could get to the man she had loved and who was no more.

She closed her eyes and tried to drink it all in. But suddenly, she felt a hand clamp down on her shoulder.

Thirty

'Yeah, yeah, alright, that wasn't the smartest idea'

'Fuck!' Nessa yelled, gasping sharply inwards. Her blanket tumbled to the ground. The hand was strong and cold, like a robot's hand. It almost hurt the bones of her slender shoulder. She felt sick and breathless. Her blood accelerated around her body, rushing through her veins and making her feel dizzy.

Ideas flashed through her mind as she span around, about how she might be able to protect herself. All the snippets of advice she'd been given by various people as she'd been growing up came back to her now. In split seconds she recalled messages about scratching your attacker above the neck so they couldn't get away with what they'd done, or dropping to the floor so you became a dead weight, impossible to move or carry away. There was stuff about kicking shins and bollocks, and punching throats.

All her senses were sharpened, like a wild animal. She

turned around quickly, ready to attack. She felt as if she could smell every droplet of rainwater on every blade of grass, and the heaving, breathing ground that squirmed with life beneath her feet. She prepared to attack and launched herself at the person before her.

'Whoa, whoa, whoa! What the 'ell are you doing?!' cried a man with a cockney accent, who was shielding his face with his arms as Nessa started clawing at him frantically, her arms swinging around like a blade-clad windmill. He sounded quite old. His frame was slight, his skin wrinkled and his long hair streaked with bright silver strands. In one of his hands was a small torch with an intense beam of light that illuminated a tiny section of the woodland, its pinpointed spotlight wobbled around as he struggled against his attacker.

Nessa stopped quickly and stood, breathless, staring at the figure before her, until he eventually straightened up, no longer defending himself.

'You *absolute* fucking idiot,' Nessa said, gasping. Her legs were trembling so much that it was difficult to stand up. She felt giddy.

'Sorry love, sorry, I'm so sorry . . . My name's Derek. I'm jus' a park warden. Live in a little cottage over there,' he said, pointing into the darkness. Nessa blinked, unable to see anything of note. She had been almost blinded by fear. It felt as if her eyeballs were quivering in her skull like little balls displaying the week's lottery numbers. 'I was gettin' some wood for the fire and I saw you standin' there.'

'And thought it would be a great idea to slam your hand down on my shoulder, while standing behind me, to announce your presence?' Nessa yelled frantically. The man nodded weakly and flinched. 'You could have just cleared your throat or something. I nearly shat myself,' she said, furiously.

'Yeah yeah, alright, that wasn't the smartest idea, like. I'm sorry I scared ya, but to be honest, I never see people 'ere at night. You could have been anyone,' he said, apologetically. 'I had to protect myself too.'

Nessa tried to calm her breathing. Still feeling unsteady on her feet, she walked over to a fallen tree just a couple of metres away and sat down heavily in frustration. She felt the cold dampness of the wood seep through her jeans, hoping she hadn't squashed a slug or any other innocent creature of the forest with her cold, wet buttocks. She hardly cared anymore. The weekend had been an absolute bloody disaster.

'If you don't mind me askin', what the bloody hell are you doin' here?' the man said animatedly, while sitting down next to her.

'I just wanted to be here,' Nessa said, tearfully, shivering to herself, all her anger melting away. She felt silly now, very silly. Was she going mad?

'Why? Why at night?' the man asked, starting to roll a cigarette in the moonlight. 'I don't know anyone who'd come out 'ere in the dark like this, especially a—'

'A woman?' Nessa asked, defensively.

'Well, yeah . . . sorry,' he said, curtly.

'I just came here to be . . . close to someone,' she confessed, shamefully, her head bowed down towards her damp feet. All of a sudden she felt overwhelmingly cold.

'You lost someone? Today? No one tol' me. I always get contacted if someone is lost in the park,' he said, holding up the stuffed cigarette paper and rolling it, expertly into a thin, tight tube.

'No, no no. I've lost someone, but not like that,' she

said, sadly. 'My husband died, and he loved it here. It all happened quite some time ago . . .'

'Jesus Christ . . . You're not who I think you are, are ya?' he asked, dropping his hands down to his lap and turning to look at Nessa. His mouth hung wide open in shock and wonder, as if she was a celebrity or an apparition.

'Are you . . . Are you Nessa Bruce?' he asked, sounding concerned.

'Yes I am, how do you know?' she asked, looking up at him. The craggy features of his face looked like chalky cliffs, set dramatically against pitch-black crevices.

'How could I not?! When Jake, I mean your 'usband, sorry . . . When he first went missing the police were crawlin' over this park like ants, literally searchin' every inch of it. Because he loved this place, like you say. Of course it was the first port of call, like. I was interviewed a few times and tol' to look out for anything suspicious meself. It kinda took over my mind ever since . . . An' when I see a figure standing in the park in the middle of the night, it's probably somethin' I'm going to look into, innit?' he said, sympathy in his glittering eyes.

Nessa nodded softly, starting to feel bad for being so aggressive towards him. It must have been hard for him, having this circus envelop his home. To never quite know what he might find . . .

'So you're sayin', in all honesty, that that's why you came 'ere? Because he liked this place?' he probed again, as Nessa put her blanket around her shoulders again.

'I just wanted to feel like I was with him, in some way. I just miss him, so much,' she said. 'I know you probably think I'm crazy. I wonder sometimes too . . .'

'Nah, naaah, not at all. I get it, and it's a beautiful place, much better than saaaf London, where I used ta live. But you can't stay out 'ere all night. You'll make yourself ill. It may be springtime but it's due to get cold tonight. That cold, it'll get into ya lungs and ya bones,' said Derek wistfully. His attention had turned back to his cigarette. He lit it with a large metal lighter. It had a heavy lid that flicked back with a simple movement of his thumb, making a satisfying crunching sound.

Nessa nodded in agreement. Her feet felt like blocks of ice.

'Hey, listen, come with me . . . The wife and I were goin' to go to catch the end of some fiftieth birthday party down the social with some ol' friends, but to honest, I can't stand 'em anymore. I'd rather poke my eyes out with a cocktail stick. It's a great reason to stay 'ome . . . Like I say, I was 'bout to light the fire, we've roast chicken and a spare room. If you want to be close to the place your 'usband loved but also not freeze to death, you can stay at ours?' the man asked kindly.

Nessa thought about his offer. She'd put herself in so much danger tonight, it almost seemed farcical to become precious about where she was headed now. He seemed trustworthy and nice, and she was in no fit state to drive, her nerves frayed.

'Come on, love. It's the leas' I can do,' he said warmly, his cigarette dangling between his lips as he spoke.

'Yeah, OK. That would be lovely, thank you,' Nessa said, standing up and walking with him towards the cottage, the night breeze tickling her face.

Thirty-One

'Where's the label?'

The following day

'How was it, Mum?' enquired Poppy. She was sitting on the sofa, already wearing her slippers and pyjamas. She had wrapped herself up in her duvet and seemed very comfortable, despite having only been home for half an hour. Cartoons flickered on the TV, lighting up her dewy, youthful complexion in hues of electric blue and canary yellow.

The Tesco delivery man had arrived just a few minutes earlier, and every free surface in the kitchen and living room seemed to be covered in groceries. Will stood in the hallway throwing a courgette up in the air over and over again, making it spin with a flick of his wrist that seemed to satisfy his boyish mood immensely. He had turned up out of the blue, acting as if nothing at all had happened. His timing was uncanny, given what Nessa had experienced the night before. If she needed anything right now, it was a friend. It was as if he'd somehow known this.

Nessa had awoken in the groundskeeper's cottage at eight that morning, staring out at the sun-drenched park through windows coated in a film of condensation. It was the calm after the storm, she'd thought, as she studied the deer picking their way through the bracken. She'd felt so horrendous the night before, but the first thing she thought of that morning was Will. A page had been turned, just like she'd wanted. And now she realised that she missed her friend, and courted an overwhelming desire to just move on and forget about whatever had been going on between them.

Ordinarily, Will would have been the person she sought out to talk to about things like this, and so when she pulled up outside her house and found him hanging around there, she'd felt a huge sense of relief.

She hoped Poppy wouldn't ask any more questions about where she had apparently been. She hated lying, but there was no way she could tell her daughter what had happened that night. She couldn't talk about her meeting with the partners of the men who had died so tragically under Jake's watch; of the cold, stiff hotel room she had deserted before the bed had even warmed to the soft sinews of her body; or about the strange night in the woods before she'd gone back to Derek's house, met his rotund rosy-cheeked wife and gorged hungrily on delicious food and hot tea. She remembered studying the burst blood vessels on his nose in the candlelight and being calmed by the creaking of his rocking chair as he read the paper. She hadn't said much – she'd not had to. They had just let her be. *How kind they were.*

She didn't want Poppy to know how cripplingly lost she felt; how she wasn't sure, each morning when she awoke, how she'd make it through the day; and how that trance of grief had led to her wandering into Jake's favourite place in the middle of night just hoping to feel something, to perhaps remember a particular laugh of his that had slipped from her mind, or a facial expression she could no longer recall. As time went on, she felt she was losing him bit-by-bit, memory by memory; her ability to command the exact sound of his voice, or the image of him, was fading. Did he lift his right eyebrow when he laughed, or his left? Was the small scar he'd got in childhood at the top of his forehead, or lower down? Nessa had to be the strong one, she told herself.

'Yeah it was fine, thanks Poppy. Have you had lunch? Do you want a yoghurt or a banana or something?' Nessa asked, surveying the chaos around her.

'No thanks,' Poppy said. 'There were some flowers left for you Mum, by the way,' she added. She gestured towards a bunch of bright and beautiful flowers that had been hurriedly stuffed into a vase, with their paper wrapping still on. Typical Poppy, Nessa thought. She walked over to them, and held a luscious, red rose in the palm of her hand. She traced her left index finger over its velvety petals thoughtfully.

'Who from?' she asked, turning around and glaring at her daughter.

'No idea. The label just had the letter N written on it. It was a bit cheap if you ask me,' she said, raising an eyebrow suspiciously.

'Where's the label?' Nessa had asked, casually. She wondered if she might be able to recognise the handwriting.

'I put it in the bin. It was all wet and horrible,' Poppy responded, casually.

Nessa released her grip on the flower, and walked away, trying to focus on other things. The house looked as if it had been hit by a bomb. Will threw the courgette into the air again, with so much focus his tongue hung out of his mouth. 'Yusss, four spins!' he cried, pumping the fist of his left hand with satisfaction, before getting an evil look from Nessa which prompted him to put it down guiltily.

'How was Aunty Mabel?' Poppy asked.

'Aunty Mabel?' Nessa asked, confused.

'You know . . . Aunty Mabel, who is ill? Aunty Mabel who you literally just saw? Duh,' Poppy said, giving her mother one of her cutting 'you're-an-idiot' expressions.

Shit, Nessa thought. *How amateur.* 'She's getting better now, thanks,' she responded, as calmly as possible. 'She was glad to see me and sent her love to you, asked how your exams were and stuff.' Nessa had to stop her daughter asking questions. She was exhausted and not very good at thinking fast.

'Do you need some help?' Will asked from the hallway, picking up the courgette again and wiggling it in the air, like it was a magic wand.

'Yes please, Will, can you just help me carry some of this stuff into the kitchen?' Nessa asked, scooping a bag of frozen fish fingers and an extra-large cauliflower in her arms and walking through the hallway. Will followed suit.

'So I've not heard about Aunty Mabel for a long time now, Nessa,' Will said quietly, as he opened a kitchen cupboard and started filling it with tins of chopped tomatoes.

'Yeah, well, you know . . .' Nessa said, nervously.

'I thought she went to a nursing home a couple of years ago?' Will probed, shutting the cupboard door and bending down to start emptying a paper bag full of fresh vegetables.

'Yeah, yeah she did,' Nessa said, starting to feel hot with panic.

'Didn't she move quite close by in the end?' Will questioned. 'Like half an hour or so?'

Nessa said nothing and continued packing. After a

minute of quiet, broken only by the rustling of plastic packaging and paper bags, she tried to change the subject.

'How's little Fran, by the way? She's a sweetheart isn't she, and so studious! Bet she'll be a scientist when she grows up. What a lovely, *lovely* girl,' she said cheerfully.

'Ness, if Aunty Mabel lives half an hour away now, why did you say you had to drive really far away and stay in a hotel?' Will asked, stopping his packing now and standing dead still. Nessa couldn't believe he could remember this. She hadn't mentioned her aunt to Will in over a year, and even then it had only been in passing. She wasn't even sure if he had been listening. She felt confident that Poppy didn't know where Mabel lived now; she seldom listened.

'Shh . . .' Nessa said, raising her index finger to her soft pink lips before pointing frantically in the direction of the living room, where her scowling, sweet-munching daughter was sitting just a few metres away. She had another therapy session coming up the next day, she was always particularly aggressive the evening before because she was nervous.

'*Where were you last night?*' Will asked, narrowing his eyes. He had her cornered.

Nessa put both hands on her hips in frustration and looked down at the floor.

'Have you met someone?' Will asked, his features collapsing into an expression that made the bottom of her stomach roll over. He turned pale. Nessa looked up at him noncommittally, the cogs turning in her brain. She said nothing.

'That's it, isn't it? You've met a guy and that's where you were last night. That explains the flowers perhaps,' he said.

Nessa couldn't tell him the truth. Quite literally anything

was better than the truth, even this. She was just going to have to roll with it.

'Yes Will, I have, but please, don't tell a soul. I'm not ready for everyone to be gossiping about it,' she said softly, surprised by how easily this untruth was slipping out. It was the only way she could wriggle out of the situation.

Will looked momentarily as if he'd been winded, like the air had been sucked from his sails. Nessa studied him, shocked and fascinated in equal measure by the sight of her friend, clearly struggling to hide his outwardly visible upset. It looked as if he was in pain. Actual pain.

'Sorry, is there a problem with this?' she asked, having gone too far to reverse now, her right hand in the air, 'Are you, are *you* judging me, Will?'

'No, no, of course not. You're *perfectly* entitled to move on,' he said, deliberately trying to suppress his obvious horror from just a minute ago by rearranging his facial features into a painful-to-see expression of faux 'coolness'. He put his right hand in his thick, swirling hair and awkwardly fiddled with a tuft that stood on end from time to time, and had done ever since he was 14.

'It makes total sense. You're a beautiful woman, you, you must get plenty of interest and, erm, I dunno. It's just . . . I don't . . .' he continued, stroking his strong jaw now and bumbling over his own words. 'It's just a bit of shock,' he said softly.

'I need to spend more time with him. To be sure,' she said gently, turning back around and rearranging some things in the second shelf of the fridge. 'I hope you understand.' She was cringing all over by this stage.

When she turned around again, she saw Will standing there with tears in his eyes. He looked away sharply, so she wouldn't see, but it was too late. It took her breath away.

'Will?' she asked, feeling guilty now, and stepping towards him.

'Sorry, Nessa. I've got to go. I'm sorry. I'll see you soon,' he said self-consciously, grabbing his keys and rushing out of the door before she could say another word.

As soon as the front door had shut behind him, Nessa closed the kitchen door and opened up the bin. She dug around reluctantly, screwing up her face in disgust as her fingers moved egg shells and plastic wrappers, until she found it. The label.

She picked it up and held it under the light attached to the extractor fan. The letter 'N' was running and faded, having got wet. She didn't recognise the writing. It was written on a bit of brown paper, like a paper bag . . . She turned it around, and there were a few words, scarcely readable: 'Whych's Cross Farm Shop'.

Thirty-Two

'Well, I hope you didn't come a long way'

June 22nd 2013

Whych's Cross was a tiny village in the Midlands with a small stream running through the centre of it. Nessa knew this because she had been there before, several years ago, as part of a family holiday.

The paper bag label on her flowers had reminded her of the place and how beautiful it was. A strange magnetism had made her want to go and see it again, to perhaps rekindle some memories and get away from suburban London for the day. She was curious too about where the flowers had come from. She didn't know anyone who lived in the area. She had no connections to the village anymore, at least as far as she knew. She thought the paper bag had probably been kept in a drawer for years and recycled, passed on from shop to individual, reused and passed on again. It meant very little really, she thought, no more than coincidence. But, it was a beautiful summer's day and she was glad to be prompted to visit again.

Nessa had asked Poppy if she wanted to join her on the trip, but her daughter had grunted something from the depths of her bedroom about going out with her friends. So Nessa had decided to go alone and enjoy some time for reflection.

The village dated back to the sixteenth century and boasted some of its original buildings: beautifully preserved half-timber cottages that attracted great interest from architects keen to replicate the features of the time. It had been locally famous for its buzzing market trade, but in recent years the ageing independent retailers and humble artisans had mostly died off. The short, cobbled high street consisted of a small branch of Tesco, two newsagents, a charity shop that seemed to be closed most of the time, and a couple of takeaway joints. The rest of the shop fronts were boarded up or covered in 'To Let' signs. Sadly, the place seemed to be dying on its feet . . .

The sun was still shining when Nessa rolled into the village, parking her car near a tiny cottage at the edge of the high street. An elderly lady, peeking through her curtains, shook her head angrily at the sight. The slack skin of her cheeks flapped around her face like the jowls of a dog, as she furiously and silently berated this 'new person' from behind the glass. Getting out of the car, Nessa tried her best to ignore it, as if she hadn't noticed the woman at all.

She had decided to visit the farm shop, which was around two-and-a-half miles 'out of town' nestled between an elderly, crumbling church and acres of sprawling, rolling countryside, but she wanted to see the village itself once more, and grab something to eat.

She popped into one of the two newsagents and greeted the shopkeeper, an old man dressed in a dark green and black flannel check shirt, his back hunched in a right angle, giving the impression that he was always gazing at the floor wherever he went. He was reading a home furnishings magazine and looked up animatedly as she came in, contorting his body to be able to see her. He had been notified of her presence by an over-zealous bell on the other side of the door, clattering loudly as she opened and closed it. He pushed his glasses up his nose with a knobbly, wrinkled finger in order to better study her.

'Is that Robbins' girl?' he cried dramatically, squinting. His voice was remarkably loud, making Nessa's ears wince a little.

'Hiya. No . . . I'm not, I'm Nessa. I'm not from round here. How are you?' she asked sheepishly, forgetting that in other places – places that weren't London – people often liked to talk to each other, using actual words and gestures, perhaps even eye contact.

'Nessaaa,' he said, in fascination, repeating the word a couple more times to himself for practice. He stood up briskly, although it made virtually no difference to his modest height.

'I'm so, so. So, so, so can't complain,' he said laughing to himself with glee, as if he was more than used to entertaining himself to get through the long, quiet hours. 'What can I do you for?'

'Erm, just a . . . erm . . .' Nessa said, scanning a dusty shelf for something to eat. The shop had a slightly odd selection and the 'merchandising' was interesting, to say the least. The four shelves in front of her hosted a tantalising mix of old faded packets of rubber bands a basket with a couple of marrows and two onions in it, a box full of ballpoint pens, and a few dusty chocolate and cereal bars. Nothing seemed to be in any kind of order. Still, he was running a promotion on fishing magazines. Two for £5. *How could one resist*? Nessa thought to herself, sarcastically. She grabbed a cereal bar, put it down on the counter and pushed it towards her new friend.

'Certainly love. That'll be 70 of your finest pences please,' he said gleefully, pressing a button on his till that prompted a metal tray to shoot out and knock a cup of tea all over his crotch. He stood upright, waving his hands in the air, either side of his head, a look of total shock on his face.

'Oh, goodness me, are you OK?' Nessa asked, as the man stared at his trousers, which were covered in presumably rather hot, milky liquid.

'Oh, sod it,' he said, furiously. 'I do that all the time. You'd think I'd learn, wouldn't you?' He grabbed a small towel from behind him and started to clean up the mess. Nessa put the change on the counter and started to turn to leave. She wasn't sure she could deal with all this weirdness right now. It was all too much.

'Say, what are you doing here? We don't get many passers-by these days,' he asked, looking up again and squinting through the thick, dirty lenses of his glasses.

'Oh, I'm just here to visit the farm shop. You know, it's about two miles away?' she said, pointing outside the shop as if she knew which direction it was in, when really it could have been anywhere.

'Ohhh, that place . . . Well, I hope you didn't come a long way,' he said gloomily, scratching the top of his head. A few tiny flakes of dandruff floated through the air and landed on his shoulders.

'I did, yeah; I came from London. Why?' Nessa asked, feeling her heart sink.

'They had to close it love, just a few weeks ago. People kept ordering online, didn't they, and having stuff delivered to their homes, the lazy bastards! I heard that some of them, right, they ask the delivery men to put the food in their fridges and cupboards and stuff, because they can't even be bothered to unpack the bags! It'll be the death of this town, it will!' he cried apocalyptically, holding his fist up in the air and shaking it about as he spoke. He was terribly dramatic.

Nessa thanked him and left the shop hurriedly, as he continued to chatter away to no one in particular.

Thirty-Three

'Can I ask what you're doing here please?'

Later that morning . . .

The farm shop building was deserted. The old man was right. Even though it had only been closed for a matter of weeks, it looked as if it had been shut for much longer. Long grass was starting to envelop the building, giving it a rough border to frame its neglect. Nessa walked around the property quietly, as if she were intruding, stopping occasionally to look in the windows. It was hard to make out the shop's interior, given the darkness inside and the brilliant sunlight that clashed against the glass.

She pressed her face right up against the window and cupped her hands around her eyes so she could block out the sunshine. Once her eyes had adjusted, she saw that it was dark and dingy inside. Wooden trays that had once been packed with fresh fruit and vegetables had been emptied, but the shelves still held jars of homemade jams, pickles and marinades. A pair of rubber gloves had been carelessly abandoned on the cash desk, all fingers and thumbs. Nessa's gaze flickered over the empty shelves and boxes, a set of pricing cards, a black marker and some flyers for a local summer fete. She remembered looking around with Jake and Poppy all those years ago. Poppy had begged them to buy her a weird aubergine key ring with googly eyes. Jake had commented on how 'beautiful' the vegetables were, holding up a marrow and admiring it as if it were a painting, saying how he only wished they could *always* shop in places like this.

Eventually Nessa saw a solitary paper bag, on the ground near where she stood. *Whych's Cross Farm Shop*. Disappointment and sadness washed over her.

Walking to the back of the building, she looked through another, smaller, dirtier window to what must have been the staff kitchen. The signs of a once-buzzing workspace were all there: coffee grindings around the sink, a half-empty bottle of washing-up liquid, and a pile of stale gossip magazines were piled up on a small wooden table in the centre of the room. Nessa sighed, feeling a sadness not only for herself, because she wouldn't be able to take the trip down memory lane she'd pined for, but because of the loss of this place, which looked as if it had been evacuated suddenly, one melancholy day, by people who didn't really want to go.

It was wonderful once, she reflected, looking beyond the building and seeing the start of acres of countryside and woodland, illuminated a hopeful gold by the summer sunshine.

Nessa slumped down on a step around the back of the shop, and sighed loudly, unsure of what to do next. She listened to the summer breeze, as it snaked its way through the sycamores, jostling with the slender and pale green leaves.

'Erm, excuse me?' came the voice of a woman to Nessa's left, just a few metres away.

Nessa nearly jumped out of her skin. She felt suddenly ashamed, sitting at the back of a building that someone had once owned (or perhaps still did), having studied the detail inside so gratuitously, as guilty as if she was caught peeking in someone's diary.

'I'm so sorry,' she said, standing up quickly. She looked at the woman, who was standing at the edge of the building, peeping around it with one hand on the brickwork. She had thick, blonde hair that looked as if it were regularly cut and coloured at an expensive salon. She wore designer horse gear by the likes of Jump, a brand that Nessa had seen before at a country show where padded coats were sold for £250, and you couldn't get a pair of wellies under £75.

The woman had sharp, drawn features, and an intimidating look about her that came naturally, as if she had once been a headmistress, or a city worker.

'Can I ask what you're doing here please?' the woman asked, slightly bitchily, jangling a large set of keys. Nessa nodded to herself, stood up and started to walk from the back of the building towards the front. The woman followed her.

'I'm sorry. I came here to visit the shop for the day. I just arrived and found it was closed, that's all. I'm a little tired, so I had a sit down. I'm sorry, that's all it was,' Nessa said, a little embarrassed.

The woman put one hand on her hip, and glared at Nessa a little. She spun the keys around in her free hand, making them clatter and jangle rhythmically.

'Honestly . . . I wasn't going to break in or anything!' Nessa said, starting to feel a little riled, yet trying to reassure her.

'Sure, sorry. I shouldn't be so rude . . . I'm just a little stressed – overtired,' the woman said, breaking character and suddenly morphing into someone quite different. She ran a hand down the bronzed skin of her face, in a kind of exhausted defeat.

'Pah! Join the club,' Nessa said, smiling to herself and looking down at the mixture of straw and thick grass she was standing on.

'This was my shop. I've just come here to clear out some more stuff,' the woman said wistfully. Nessa looked up at the perfectly executed thatched roof of the building, and then around her, at the car park – empty apart from Nessa's car – the golden countryside before them rolling out into a huge, lush green forest in the distance.

'Oh, I'm sorry to hear that . . . That must be very hard,' Nessa said sympathetically.

'Yeah, it is. We're going to have to move back to London. My husband's keen to go back into his old job – at least it earned some decent money. So long to the country-living dream, eh?' the woman said sadly.

'I'm from London,' Nessa responded chirpily, as if that might help. There was an uncomfortable quiet. Nessa felt herself turn red.

The woman started speaking again, but Nessa couldn't digest a word she was saying. Something about not having the help of her mother nearby and how expensive urban nurseries were. Did she know of anyone she could recommend? Where was good for going out nowadays? She was looking for quiet, gastro-pub kind of venues, not bars anymore. She hated bars. Were the main museums still free? And had the London Underground gone 24/7 yet? It was about time, that was for sure.

Nessa stared beyond her, daydreaming, as the words

tumbled out of the woman's mouth, floated through the air, and swirled around her head in a meaningless halo.

That was when she spotted it. The small, dark outline of a figure, a man. Someone was running across the top of one of the fields, in the direction of the forest. And there was something about the stance that caught Nessa's attention: the bounce in that run, the set of his shoulders. Something she recognised . . .

Nessa's ears started to ring. She walked towards the woman, unable to speak and still looking slightly beyond her, not taking her eyes off the blot in the distance that was becoming increasingly familiar to her. Nessa squeezed the woman's shoulders in some bizarre attempt to convey, 'I'm sorry. You'll be OK, everything will work out. It always does' through the tips of her fingers, as her legs melted to jelly.

And then she fled. Running. In the direction of the figure, which had just disappeared into the depths of the forest.

Thirty-Four

Is this madness? Is this how it feels?

The ground seemed to speed up beneath Nessa's feet. Grass, straw and soil rushed beneath her, faster and faster . . . She looked up occasionally, terrified she might turn her ankle on a molehill, or a clod of mud. She wasn't sure if she'd feel it even if she did hurt herself. Adrenaline's natural painkilling qualities coursed through her limbs.

Nessa had never run this fast in her life. She hadn't even known she was capable of it. Her breathing had regulated, so she was able to propel her legs forwards, launching herself over obstacles. She bounded forwards, her calves and thighs working like pistons. *Faster, faster.* She wasn't sure she'd be able to stop now, even if she tried.

Is this madness? Is this how it feels?

The field looked as if it might go on forever. The forest was seemingly moving backwards in the distance rather than getting closer, as if it were a cut-out paper prop controlled by a child, gleefully moving the goalposts.

Nessa came to a low gate. She didn't have time to fiddle with it to get it open and then close it behind her again, so she put one hand down on the rough warm wood and launched her legs over it. She landed, surprisingly hard, on some damp soil on the other side. The shock from the landing reverberated up her body so that her teeth smacked against each other, catching the tip of her tongue. It hurt so much it brought tears to her eyes. She could taste the metallic, iron flavour of blood in her mouth, but she didn't care. She had to keep going. A small group of cows in a nearby field watched on casually, chewing slowly and moving their mass from hoof to hoof, the occasional shake of a tail to bat the flies away.

Eventually, Nessa reached the opening of the forest. She kept running; her feet landed on dried-out twigs and branches that crackled and crunched beneath her feet. The sunshine pierced through the canopy of trees that provided a roof of broken shelter over the forest. The light glittered, shimmering on the ground. She didn't really know where she was going anymore. She just had to keep going. Where had the tiny figure disappeared to?

'Jake!' she yelled, the word booming from her chest. She imagined each letter of his precious name growing wings, rising up and getting tangled in the trees, each singing their own desperate song of a woman who had, quite literally, lost a man.

'Jake!' she cried again, louder this time, her eyes still watering with the pain in her mouth. More blood.

'Jake!' she cried, as if her life depended on it.

'JAKE!!' she yelled again, furiously this time. She hoped that if he might somehow be able to hear her, he would know how livid she was with him.

The forest seemed to reduce itself towards a small, dark

Pleasant Ridge Library
Phone: 905-653-READ

Check out receipt

Date: 12/24/2019 11:50 AM

---

1. **Midnight in the Pacific : Guadalcanal : the World War II battle that turned the tide of war**
   Barcode 33288901392979
   Due by 1/14/2020

2. **The waiting game**
   Barcode 33288501022372
   Due by 1/14/2020

Total 2 article(s)

Total number of items checked-out: 4

To renew: 905-709-0672
www.vaughanpl.info
Please complete the customer satisfaction survey
https://www.surveymonkey.com/r/DZGKFRP

archway created by a particularly thick group of trees that bent towards each other at an angle. There were two other pathways, to the right and left of this rabbit hole, but she decided to take the central route. She slowed down, but kept running, stooping as low as she could to get into the tunnel. The sunshine barely penetrated this place, and she was plunged into near darkness.

Nessa slowed down, suddenly feeling exhausted, slinking into a fast walk, her breath rattling in her chest. The running and adrenaline had caught up with her. She felt more tired than she ever had.

And then suddenly, as if from nowhere, someone grabbed her from behind, their arms clamped so tightly around her waist, it felt as if they might break her lower ribs. Her feet were swept off the ground, effortlessly.

Whoever it was had firmly pressed a finger to her lips, to stop her making a sound. She could feel hot, fast breath against the soft skin of her cheeks. Nessa would have normally screamed, or started to fight, but this time she didn't. This time, she let herself be swept away in the person's arms. Her head began to spin. She started to black out. The finger still pushed hard against her lips.

Seconds later, the oxygen started to rush around Nessa's body again, as if she'd been splashed with cold water. The sensations came back to her legs and arms, muscles and nerves. She was standing upright – only just – pulled backwards into a bush by the person behind her. He was still holding her tightly, his rough index finger still planted tightly against her face. She wondered how long she'd been there for. She breathed hard and stared ahead, through the branches and bushes, into a clearing in the forest, only just lit up by some shards of sunlight.

It was quiet now. Nessa could hear the soft trill of birds singing. Her heart rate started to slow down and her vision was starting to focus again. She felt that if she wasn't being held in the way she was now, she would collapse, and sleep for days.

She wasn't frightened. She didn't know why. She felt the calmest she had felt in a long, long time. Whoever had grabbed hold of her, pushed his face towards Nessa's cheek and let his lips rest against her soft skin. He breathed in deeply through his nose and then out again, his warm breath curling around her face. The feeling was so familiar, it was as if she was being shown a part of herself reflected back at her, a long-lost sensation. The scent coming from him, a recognisable sweetness that she'd not experienced in such a long time.

It was Jake . . .

It was Jake.

Nessa turned her head towards the warm, soft and stubbly face that was pressed against hers. She saw the depths of those dark brown eyes as they met hers. Her eyes flickered over the edges of his plump, soft lips, the perfect, beautiful contours of his face. He looked straight into her eyes and she felt tears overwhelm her – tears of relief, and anger, and everything in between.

'Jake . . .' Nessa said, her gaze still glued to his. 'You fucking arsehole,' she cried, freeing herself from his grip and spinning herself round. Rage flew through her body and she started to push him, falling almost instantly into his arms, exhausted from it all.

She curled her hands up into fists and started banging them against his chest, as hard as she possibly could. Jake stood still, tall and strong, biting his bottom lip as he struggled to contain her. To add to her frustration, she didn't seem to be making any kind of significant impact at all; it was like having a fight with a tree.

'How could you . . . How could you do it?!' she screamed, crying now. She couldn't believe the rage that remained. She felt like he had betrayed her, cheated on her somehow.

There he stood, the person she'd yearned for and thought about, night and day. The ghost of her dreams.

It all fell into place. Why his body had never been found. The Christmas lights, the gifts, Betsy's and Mick's garden, the bike at Elaine's house, the flowers . . . the torn-out section of a paper bag that had led her here . . .

Jake was a lot thinner than he used to be. The skin on his face looked tanned and a little dirty too. There was something so different about the look in his eyes, like something marked had altered within him, never to go back to how it was before. He looked pained at the sight of her so engulfed in fury.

'Nessa, stop . . .' he said calmly, softly even.

But she couldn't. She wanted to destroy him, this mirage of a man she'd loved more than anybody else, who had run away from her when she needed him the most. How could he play her life like she was just a puppet on a string he was operating from a distance? *How could he?*

'You sick, sick fuck!!' Nessa screamed, hearing her voice reverberating around the forest.

'Nessa, stop this. Right now,' Jake said firmly, grabbing both of her wrists with a remarkable strength and managing to prevent her from thrashing around within a matter of seconds. Nessa's lungs heaved in and out; she felt a layer of cold sweat covering her skin.

'Come with me,' he said firmly, releasing her wrists and leading her by the hand into the clearing.

Nessa stood and stared at the space with her mouth

open. It was remarkable. He had created some kind of shelter, presumably building upon a structure that was already there, or using pieces of wood he had found and hammered together. A few of his clothes had clearly been washed in a nearby stream and were hanging to dry from a piece of twine, strung between two gnarled trees that bent towards each other. He had a few dented pots and pans, and it looked like he had one set place for a fire, dug out in the earth and surrounded with large grey stones. An old, raggedy sleeping bag was bunched up in the corner of the shelter, on top of pieces of presumably stolen tarpaulin. He had one of the farm shop wooden trays, with a couple of apples inside and a few ageing vegetables that no longer looked fit for consumption. A pile of old, paperback novels was stacked up in the corner, the pages rippling from the damp that must have seeped into them in the early hours of those cold, wet mornings.

Despite the primitive nature of his handmade living space, deep in the heart of the forest, everything was remarkably clean looking and tidy. Jake, while thin, looked good.

'Do you want to sit down? I can make you a tea?' Jake asked, casually. Nessa stared at him and nodded feebly, sinking to her feet and keeping her gaze on him the whole time. She still wanted to launch herself at him, but she was exhausted.

She watched in fascination as Jake lit a fire. His brows were furrowed in concentration and there was a soft, subtle smile upon his lips, as if he knew she would find him eventually. He was, well he always had been, the most beautiful creature she'd ever seen – breathtakingly wonderful. But she despised him for what he had done.

He lifted a small steel kettle from behind him, which

already had water in it, and placed it on a metal rack he'd made so the kettle could sit neatly above the flames. In his rucksack were a few teabags and some powdered milk. The birds were still singing in such a carefree way, as if nothing remarkable was happening. But it was.

She'd finally found Jake.

Thirty-Five

'Yes . . . that was me'

Later that night . . .

The darkness enveloped them beyond the trees like a thick, impenetrable blanket. A small glow was emitted by the fire, which was now burning down to its embers. Nessa lay reluctantly in Jake's arms inside the sleeping bag, beneath the roof of his makeshift shelter. He held her close, but her body language was cold.

'Do you have any idea how angry I am with you Jake, how hurt I am?' Nessa whispered, burrowing herself further down in the sleeping bag to stop the cooler evening breeze making her neck cold and ruining the toasty environs they'd created.

Jake said nothing, his gentle breathing the only sound coming from him.

'Poppy and I . . . we basically held a funeral for you. Do you even realise that? We had to cope with losing the person we love more than anything in the world. Do you not get that?' Nessa cried.

'Of course I do,' Jake said, softly.

'We had to try and adapt to life without you. And your mum, your poor mum . . . It's been horrendous Jake, losing you. I simply can't believe you put us through it,' she cried, starting to weep as she spoke. Nessa considered scrabbling out of the sleeping bag and getting away from him, but something was keeping her there.

'I'm so sorry . . . I've been thinking about you all the time, seriously, every second of my day. I knew it would be tough, of course I did, but it was all I could do. I had no other choice,' Jake said, resolutely, stroking Nessa's hair with his free hand, his touch warming her body.

'No other choice? Are you fucking insane?' Nessa asked, half-sitting up now and staring at him.

'And all this good deed bullshit you've been doing. What the fuck were you thinking?' Nessa asked, pausing and scanning her surroundings, gathering her thoughts so that she could work out what to say next.

Jake flinched as she spoke, as if experiencing pain with each word that tumbled from her lips.

'Oh my god . . . Hold on a minute,' Nessa said, thinking aloud. 'Poppy, that night she got drunk . . . Was it? Was it *you* that carried her home that night?' Nessa asked, a look of horror upon her face.

Jake nodded, shame etched across his face.

'Brilliant. Absolutely bloody brilliant. So we've all been telling her that she's having psychotic delusions for no reason at all! Well that's just fucking *fantastic*,' Nessa spat, trembling with rage.

'Yes . . . that was me,' Jake whispered. 'I was in the area doing some things for you guys, stuff to help you out, and I actually saw her by pure chance, staggering around outside the bowling alley and then collapsing on the floor. She was ridiculously drunk and all her friends had just pissed off.

What else was I supposed to do? Leave her there? She's my little girl for god's sake!' Jake cried.

'Yes, she certainly is your little girl, so why the hell did you leave her alone in the first place?' Nessa yelled, leaning her head against Jake's chest and closing her eyes for a moment.

There were a few moments of silence, tension rippling through the air.

'Listen, I'm glad you looked after her that night, of course I am. Like you, the thought of her that drunk and vulnerable fills me with horror, but I just don't think you have a clue the trouble you're causing . . .'

Jake looked down towards his chest, unable to maintain eye contact with his wife.

'Can you please explain what on earth is going through your mind, making a choice like this? You, acting like a stupid child, running off to live in the woods like some fucking fairy to escape the reality of your life, leaving me at home, fighting the fight of my life alone, because right now I just don't understand,' Nessa said sharply, looking up at her husband with more tears in her eyes.

Jake sighed loudly, as if reluctant to speak.

'This is hard to say . . .' he started, raising his free hand towards his chin, and stroking the stubble that had grown greyer than Nessa recalled it before.

'I decided, Nessa, that I didn't want to live anymore. Because of what happened with my men. I made the choice, that I effectively wanted to . . . to die,' he said, matter-of-factly, coldly, as if he were a judge or a policeman, discussing a case. Just the facts. Nessa watched his jaw move as she lay on his chest. She softened a little and traced her fingers over his warm skin.

'I was due to come back to the UK and I couldn't stand

the thought of it all, living with the knowledge that I didn't prevent their deaths. I was depressed. The lowest I have ever been. They no longer had their families anymore, so I certainly didn't deserve mine. I knew I wanted to end my life,' he said, a flicker of emotion in his voice.

'I'm not sure you'll ever understand, Ness, how it feels to be me after that accident. And I don't blame you. *How could you understand?* It became unbearable to even exist, to wake up in the morning and be able to breathe and walk but wish more than anything that I was dead . . . I could hear their cries, all the time. When I closed my eyes the images would flicker in my mind. Blood, horror, every grotesque second of it, in full colour – a film of those events playing over and over, installed in my mind forever. An eternal punishment,' he whispered, tears coming to his eyes as he spoke.

'But we could have—' Nessa piped up.

'No we couldn't, Nessa. We couldn't have made it better. We couldn't have got through it together. We couldn't have made pizzas, and played board games pranced off for weekend trips to the Cineplex and saved me,' Jake said, bitterly.

Nessa gulped, swallowing her words, remembering the heated exchange in the car with her daughter the day they went to meet him.

It's actually an insult to Dad. You just don't get it . . .

'But we would have, Jake. I know you don't believe me, but we would have got through it. I understand more than you know, OK? What about what happened to me, when I was a kid?' Nessa said, starting to cry.

Jake nodded sympathetically. 'We aren't as free as we think, Nessa,' he continued, 'and no one is free after experiencing what I have. I couldn't face being in the pub on a Saturday night and listening to people's mundane bullshit, after what I've been through . . . what I've seen. The idea of it all was just intolerable to me. Unbearable. Sometimes, Nessa, you just can't go back,' he said, drawing to a halt suddenly, seeming to collect his thoughts.

Nessa felt a terrible dragging feeling tear through her, as if she was losing her husband all over again. He was so resigned to it, so done. She didn't know what she could do or say to make him realise that *they could get through it*.

'I could have just ended it all. I was so close to doing that, but the only thing stopping me was you and Poppy. I had to make sure that I could still take care of you, and some other people too. I had to watch over you,' he said, smiling tearfully to himself as he spoke. Nessa started to weep, unable to control the racking sobs that were tearing through her body.

'I realised that this was the only way I could watch over you guys and provide for you, you know; to disappear, quietly, to die, in a way, and simply dedicate the rest of my days to watching over you, to doing whatever I could in my own small way,' he said, kissing Nessa's forehead.

'I know you think I'm probably nuts, living out here in the forest, but I like it here, Ness. You know I've always loved the great outdoors, right? I don't need big TVs, takeaways, baths – all that shit. This is me, this is what I like. I love the peace, the quiet, the simplicity; just surviving.'

'Jake, I understand what you are saying, but if you'd come home we would have taken care of you. I know you feel to blame for the death of your friends, and that must be worse than anything, but we are supposed to be in this life together, aren't we? You're only human. You just made a mistake. What you're experiencing – the flashbacks, all that stuff – it's an illness. It can be treated,' Nessa said, softly.

Jake gave no response and just stared ahead. His jaw hardened, as if he were holding back some words.

'I know you might think that you are helping us in your own little way, but that's nothing, Jake, I'm sorry to say it. It's nothing compared to what you could do if you came home,' Nessa said, as softly as possible.

'The most helpful, courageous thing you could do right now, Jake, would be to come home and be there for us. Be my husband, be Poppy's father. Lie next to me in the night and hold me in your arms. Be a husband and a father, not just a mirage that flickers in the shadows. Jake, no matter how you feel now, you do deserve to live, and you do deserve a future . . . We need you,' Nessa said, tears tumbling from her eyes.

Jake shook his head, holding back his tears. He squeezed Nessa closer to his naked chest, his fingertips gripping her skin tightly as if she might be taken from him.

'Jake . . . another thing, while I think of it now. Have you been seeing your dad?' Nessa asked.

'Yes,' he said, a mere whisper.

'No way . . .' Nessa said, smiling to herself.

'Yeah. The security at that day centre of his is a fucking joke. No questions asked. I've been taking him on days out, to the seaside and stuff like that. Not very often – only three times – but it's lovely to spend time with him again, Nessa, it really is.'

'God, as angry as I am for all this, that's . . . well, it's beautiful,' Nessa said, managing a tearful smile. Then feeling suddenly frantic, she cried out, 'Jake, I love you. I need you to come home. This can't carry on. Surely you know that this can't go on? That you can't keep living like this?'

'Nessa, please don't tell anyone I'm here,' Jake implored, anxiety taking hold.

'Why? Why not?' Nessa pleaded.

'I'm not ready OK? I'm just, please . . . I'm not ready. I'm begging you, please,' he said, in a panicked voice.

Nessa couldn't bear another moment waiting for him to be the person she needed him to be. She needed to take control of the situation; to make things happen the way she wanted them to happen.

The passion she felt at that moment seemed to light her from within. Her cheeks flushed with heat and her heart raced. She needed Jake, more than anything right now. She held his face and kissed his lips, feeling as if she were melting into his skin and becoming a part of him. Everything about him turned her on: his hot, sweet breath, the way his muscles felt as he moved, rippling beneath his soft, warm skin. The hard bristles on his cheeks dug into her fingertips as she traced them over his face. He kissed her softly and then harder. He held her bottom lip between his teeth gently, before kissing her neck. With one strong hand he swept her hair behind her neck, gathered it in his fist and pulled gently. Nessa felt like a million sparks of electricity were running through her body, parts of her starting to melt.

He pulled her vest top over her head, ran his fingers down her naked back and squeezed her tightly in his arms; and, breathless with desire, she rolled on top of him and ran her fingers over his body, over the contours of his frame, those familiar parts of him that she had always adored: every wrinkle, every dimple, every freckle of him. He smelt incredible. It wasn't aftershave or shower gel, or anything synthetic; it was just the smell of him, perfect to her. He was the most desirable thing she'd ever known. After months of feeling numb, feeling dead inside, those feelings had all come back. Now she was alive.

Nessa and Jake made love under the stars, wrapped close together in his sleeping bag. Afterwards, they fell asleep, peacefully entwined with one another. The final embers of the fire went out, leaving them in darkness, the stars shining brightly above them.

Thirty-Six

'We've got a guest by the way'

The following day . . .

Nessa pulled into the driveway and parked her car. She sat in the front seat for a moment, drinking in her last moments of peace before walking through her front door and into the usual chaos. The passenger seat was empty. She couldn't believe what had happened over the past 24 hours.

Jake had by no means made a decision to come home, but Nessa was sure that she could make it happen. It would take time and understanding, and it would have to happen step by tiny, little step. Jake had begged her not to tell anyone, and something in the tone of his voice made Nessa genuinely frightened of the consequences if she handled the situation badly or clumsily. If she did that, she really might lose him forever. *But she wasn't going to give up . . .*

Turning off the engine and semi-reluctantly getting out

of the car, she noticed the light was on in Poppy's bedroom. As she closed the front door behind her, she could hear Poppy trilling away to herself in her bedroom, trying to perform some bizarre vocal acrobatics and sadly failing.

'Hey Pops!' Nessa shouted to announce her presence, hanging on to a banister at the bottom of the stairs. The singing stopped abruptly. Still shaky from her bizarre experience, Nessa found herself barely able to focus on anything amid her thoughts of how she would get her husband home.

'Oh hi, Mum. I'll be down in a bit. We've got a guest by the way,' Poppy said, uncharacteristically cheerily, before starting to sing again. Nessa grimaced a little. This was the last thing she needed. She just wanted to run a hot bath and think. She wanted to be alone.

Walking into the kitchen, Nessa was surprised to see Kat sitting at the breakfast bar and drinking a cup of tea. Her hands were trembling, her face looked swollen and blotchy, and she had black eye makeup smeared down her face.

'Hey Kat. What are you doing here?' Nessa asked, feeling instantly stressed at the sight of her sister so upset. For a moment, all her preoccupations seemed to slide away as she walked towards Kat and wrapped her arms around her small, bony frame. As she did so, her sister melted into a flood of tears, her body trembling in Nessa's arms.

'Oh sweetheart! What's wrong? What on earth has happened?' Nessa asked, concerned but secretly wishing she could just have a break from it all . . .

'I've left uni. I don't think I should have. I think I've made a big mistake, but it's probably too late,' Kat said, taking great gulps of air into her lungs as she cried.

'What? Why?' Nessa asked, as she took off her jacket and hung it on the back of a nearby chair. She sat down opposite her sister and held both of her hands in her own.

'Because I'm so stressed, I just can't cope with everything. It's all too much! There's just so much pressure!' Kat cried, talking at a million miles per hour and running a hand through her bright red hair.

'Whoa, whoa, whoa . . . Just please try to stay calm. Tell me, what's happened?' Nessa asked.

'I want to do so well in life . . . We came from such a difficult background you know, two sets of foster parents, all the moving around, the instability. I just want to do well, so I can have a good life, you know? But I'm exhausted, burnt out. I just can't take it anymore. I worked so hard for this paper – like *so fucking hard* – stayed up night after night studying, and I got a shit mark! And now, right, I'm probably not going to get a first, and that means I won't get into the uni I wanted for postgrad because the competition is insane and, and, I'm in credit card debt I can't pay off and I think I might lose my job at the bar, and just this whole thing with our foster parents, Ness . . . It's driving me crazy. It's all too much!'

Nessa was slightly taken aback, listening to this stream of worry flow from her sister's mouth.

'We have no roots, Nessa! I want roots in my life; I want to feel like somewhere or someone is home. If I have a family, I don't want them to go through what we had to put up with, and so I just feel this never ending pressure. Plus, I'm trying to find Tom, but I'm just not getting anywhere. He's not on the electoral roll, no one seems to know anything about him. The council won't tell me anything because they've lost some records or something, and it's just terrible. I can't focus on my uni work. I can't sleep or eat properly. I think I'm depressed! Or I'm having a nervous breakdown, or something!!' she exclaimed, throwing her hands into the air and starting to cry.

Nessa felt sick to see her little sister like this, and guilty that just a few moments earlier she had felt like her presence was an intrusion. She had been so wrapped up in her own life, she'd had no idea things were *this* bad . . . Should she tell her now? Was this the right time in the many legions of times she could have told her, but never did? Guilt enveloped her whole being.

'And you've been so distant lately, Nessa, only half listening to me, when I need you!' Kat cried, more tears rolling down her cheeks.

Nessa looked down at the worktop, which had sprinkles of hot chocolate granules scattered over it.

'I'm sorry,' she said guiltily, thinking of Jake and his strange existence in the woods. If only she could tell Kat then it would make sense. *It would all make sense . . .*

'God, I'm sorry, Nessa. I can't believe I just said that, after all you've been through lately . . . *Shit*,' Kat said in shock, as if she'd only just heard the words that had come out of her mouth, and now deeply regretted them.

'No. No, Kat, you're right. God, I'm sorry. I've not listened to you properly . . . I didn't take you seriously enough when you spoke about Tom and Sue. To be honest, I just thought . . . well, I hoped you'd just forget about it,' Nessa said, before taking a deep breath in and breathing out slowly, as if trying to compose herself. She felt decidedly sick.

Nessa suddenly heard her mobile ringing in her handbag.

'You should get that,' Kat said, taking another sip of her hot drink, her fingers trembling.

'No. No, it's fine,' Nessa said, reaching down into her bag and flicking it to silent, without looking at the screen. The phone started to ring again, this time just vibrating, urgently, within the depths of her bag.

'Listen Kat . . .' Nessa said, desperately trying to ignore her phone, wondering how she would say all this. She felt coldness swamp her; all the hairs on her arms stood on end. It was time. It was now or never. She couldn't escape this any more. The truth was coming out, whether she wanted it to or not.

She got up and shut the kitchen door before sitting back down again slowly. Keeping the volume of her voice as low as possible – she didn't want Poppy to hear a word of this conversation – she started talking: 'Sometimes Kat, terrible things happen that are irreversible. We can't turn back time and we can't pick up the pieces and we have to, somehow, just keep going, knowing these things happened . . . And you know when you love someone so much, you will do literally anything to protect them, yes?'

Kat nodded at this, confusion etched across her features.

'It can be hard to cope, knowing certain things. You can't unknow them, if you get what I mean,' Nessa said, in further hushed tones.

'I'm confused,' Kat said, slowly moving her hands away from her cup, and placing them palm down on the table, as if bracing herself.

'I know something about our first foster parents that I have deliberately protected you from,' explained Nessa, 'quite simply because I never wanted you to suffer. OK?'

Kat nodded softly. Nessa could tell she was holding her breath.

'So we have a choice here,' Nessa said gently, feeling nervous butterflies overwhelm her.

'I want to know. Please just tell me – what the fuck is going on?' Kat pleaded.

Thirty-Seven

'Come on, just say it . . .'

Nessa stood up and walked over to the kitchen sink, pulling up the blinds and opening a small window. A lukewarm breeze curled through the small gap, tickling the soft skin of her face. She placed her hands on the sink and slumped forwards over the washing-up bowl, taking a deep gulp of air before she spoke.

'Nessa?' Kat cried, 'Come on, just say it . . .'

'Tom was a violent man . . . He used to beat our mum and fight with her night after night, while you were a baby, lying in your cot, fast asleep, totally unaware of what was going on,' Nessa said, before turning around and leaning back against the edge of the sink.

'One night he beat her, particularly hard,' she said, feeling a lump form in her throat. Kat's mouth was gaping open now, tears forming in her eyes again.

'He pushed her, well shoved her, really rough, you know? She fell backwards. And her head . . . it hit the edge of our coffee table, a very sharp corner, and that was it,' Nessa said, feeling a strange numbness spread through her body as she spoke. 'Tom killed her, Kat . . .'

Kat's hands soared through the air towards her mouth.

'He's in prison. It was never covered by the press because there were all sorts of child protection concerns surrounding us at the time; so his name, and mum's and our names, stayed out of the papers, to ensure we wouldn't be identified. The press could barely touch it at all, and of course they lost interest after a while. It became just another of those tragic domestic violence incidents, another death behind closed doors . . . That's why you haven't found anything online about it . . . Tom has been locked away, where he belongs, for a long time.'

The kitchen was enveloped in silence for a minute or two.

'That's why we left so suddenly Kat. That's why we don't stay in touch with him. I'm sorry,' Nessa said.

Your voicemail has one new message, left by unknown, at 4.30 p.m. on Sunday, June 23:

'Hi Nessa. It's only me, Jake, just calling from a phone box, so you can't call me back unfortunately. I've been thinking . . . about the things you said . . . I've been so selfish. I'm sorry. You're right. I need to face my life and not run away from my problems. I'm going to come home to you and Poppy, really soon. I've got a few things to sort out first, but trust me. I will be home soon . . . I love you, so much baby, and I'm sorry . . .'

Thirty-Eight

'Nessa, I'm sorry to just turn up like this'

June 24th 2013

Kat had been shocked into a kind of fog of angry exhaustion at the news Nessa had told her. The news she'd wanted to hide from her, forever. Kat had crawled her way upstairs after their chat and thrown herself into Nessa's bed, saying that she just wanted to be alone for a while. Nessa had tried to sleep on the sofa, but had spent a restless eight hours tossing and turning amid the cushions, juggling her overwhelming joy at finding Jake, and that voicemail, with the guilt and confusion over the bombshell she'd dropped on her sister that evening.

Jake is coming home . . . Thank god. It was almost too wonderful to believe. She didn't want him to let her down again, and she knew how unpredictable he was, so she was still putting up a barrier, like a tiny fence around her heart. She wouldn't tell anyone yet, despite the voicemail. The situation was too delicate, like a feather in the breeze.

Nessa was glad Kat was still asleep at 1 p.m. the following

day, getting some much-needed rest. But she was worried about how she was going to repair the damage to the relationship she had with her sister, who was obviously angry with her for keeping this secret.

Poppy was at school and Nessa had called in sick to work. She needed to try and put things right with Kat. She had also made contact with her university to try and reverse her sister's sudden decision. She sent frantic emails to deans and admissions staff, attempting to explain the circumstances, saying that Kat had just had a bit of a breakdown. It looked as if she was making some headway.

As Nessa typed up an email to the contact for Kat's halls, she heard a knock at the door. She got up and opened it slowly, not sure what or who she might discover. She'd had more than her fair share of unexpected moments in the last 24 hours.

It was Will. He was a little breathless.

'Nessa, I'm sorry to just turn up like this,' he said nervously. 'I didn't think you'd be here and I was going to come and see you at work, but then I saw your car in the drive. Can I come in please?' he asked. She could tell from his body language, and those expressive blue eyes of his, that the matter was urgent.

'Erm sure, yes, come on through,' she said, suddenly feeling apprehensive. They walked through to the living room. Nessa sank down onto the sofa but Will looked distinctly uncomfortable and was pacing the floor of her living room.

'Will, you look a bit stressed out. Is everything OK?' Nessa asked gently, suddenly worrying about what he might be about to tell her. Was he ill? Had something terrible happened? *Does he know?*

'Nessa, I have to say something to you,' Will exclaimed, staring at his indigo blue jeans, before looking up and directly into her eyes. Nessa suddenly got a flashback of Will, all those years ago, his face lit up by the moon before he blurted out those confessions that they would both laugh at, but never forget.

'OK. What's up?' she asked, putting her hand on the sofa to encourage Will to sit down, because he was starting to make her feel unsettled. Reluctantly, he obliged.

'Nessa, I love you,' he said, looking tearful. As he said those words, the most beautiful smile spread across his face, like he was proud that he'd finally done it.

'I can't go on acting like I'm just this family friend, who is OK with what happens to you when things go wrong . . . I want to be there for you properly,' he said urgently.

'I've always, always loved you. And when Jake died, it was of course never the right time to tell you. I wouldn't have dreamt of it. But I know you're seeing someone now, and there's something about it that just seems so unfair . . . I can't bear to see you struggling, and I want to support you and Poppy and give you the life you both deserve. I want you to excel and flourish in the way you deserve to. You could become a midwife. You could train – you'd be wonderful, I know you would. You're a star. You deserve nothing but the very best, Nessa,' he said softly, running his hand through his thick, dark hair.

Nessa was speechless, she realised she was holding her breath.

'Nessa, you are the most beautiful woman I've ever known, both inside and out. You're funny, you're hard working and you inspire me all the time. I don't know of anyone who makes me laugh like you do, or listens in the way that you do. There just aren't many people in this world like you. It hit me recently, as much as I have been in denial about this, that I have loved you ever since I was a teenage boy; I really have. Nothing has changed ever since that night when we sat on that park bench and I made a fool of myself by telling you the same thing then. And you know what? I might be doing the same thing all over again right now, but I just can't keep it in anymore . . .'

Nessa nodded quietly as he spoke, surveying this handsome, lovely man, saying such beautiful things.

'I've dated other women and none of them have worked out. And it's because they aren't you, Nessa, and they never will be. I've tried, so hard, but no one makes me feel even close to how I feel about you. You are the missing piece . . . I've realised that the reason I feel so lost in my life is because I love you, still, and haven't been able to say it . . .' At this he paused and took a deep breath.

'I know you've lost Jake, and you probably aren't ready to really move on, as much as you might think you are . . . I know you're probably scared about people talking round here, or judging you. I don't even know if you feel *anything* for me, not really. This all might be such a big mistake. But I can't stand back anymore and keep falling more and more in love with you from a distance without saying anything . . . I'm sorry, I just can't. It's too painful . . . I'm sorry, Nessa,' he said, putting his hands together, staring down at the carpet and biting his bottom lip anxiously.

Thirty-Nine

'Do you think everything's going to be OK, Nessa?'

A week later . . .
Jake still hadn't come home.

Hours thickened like treacle. Days melted into years again. *Make it stop. Please. I can't bear another second . . .*

Nessa hadn't gone back to work. She couldn't face it. The tension of waiting for Jake, the worry about her sister, it was all too much. Her doctor had signed her off for a week or so. It was as if some newfound exhaustion had swept over her and all she could do was lie in bed with Kat and sleep the days away until she felt ready to face the world again.

Kat had eventually said that she understood why Nessa had wanted to protect her from the truth, but things still felt a little frosty.

'Do you think everything's going to be OK, Nessa?' Kat had asked, one sunny afternoon as the summer breeze floated through an open window.

'What do you mean?' Nessa replied, looking at her sibling's profile, lit up in the sunlight.

'Like, I just wonder if I'm ever going to be able to stand on my own two feet, if I'm ever going to be able to take care of myself and someone else, like you do with Poppy. I find life, the future, all of it, absolutely terrifying,' she said.

'Of course it will be OK. It will be more than OK, Kat. You're remarkable, and I believe in you . . . I'm sorry to tell you, though, it never stops being terrifying,' Nessa responded with a half-smile, before picking up a novel from her bedside table and curling up beside her sister.

When was he coming home? How long would she have to wait?

Nessa had awoken in what felt like the middle of the night. She'd been confused when she first stirred, confused and fumbling around in the darkness of her blackout curtains for her phone, her vision blurry with sleep. It was 4 a.m.

She heard three frantic knocks at the front door, the sound having bounced up the stairs. That must have been what woke her up in the first place, she thought . . . As Nessa became more alert, her first thought was of Jake. Was this him? Was he outside, waiting to be let in? Her heart soared at the mere thought of it . . . She knew he wouldn't let her down. Not this time. Not really . . .

She imagined opening the door to find him there, handsome, tired, with a backpack at his feet, ready to live his life again. Would she wake Poppy straight away? And what about Kat? She would probably completely freak out. In fact they both would . . .

Kat started to wake a little at the hammering at the door and squirmed in her half sleep, making squeaking noises as she did so, before burrowing deeper beneath the duvet. Nessa hoped the banging hadn't awoken Poppy. She needed to handle this carefully . . .

Nessa hopped out of bed, and hurriedly made her way down the stairs to the front door. The hopeful, early morning sunrise made her smile.

This was it. He was here, she just knew it . . . Their suffering was finally over.

Nessa opened the door, but was taken aback to see two police officers standing at the doorstep. One of them was Asil, the other a female officer she'd never seen before.

'Erm, hi . . . Sorry, I was asleep, what are you doing here? And at this time, too?' Nessa asked, squinting at the light from beyond them, and fiddling nervously with a strand of her hair.

'Hi Nessa. We are very sorry to call you at this time, but it's very important and it couldn't wait. Can we come in please?' Asil asked, a nervous expression across the soft features of his face.

Nessa was speechless. She nodded, pulled open the door and let them in, leading them through to the living room.

'I'm afraid what I am about to tell you is going to come as quite a shock,' Asil said gravely as he sat, stiffly on the sofa. The female officer sat too, not saying a word. She looked decidedly uncomfortable.

'Huh?' Nessa asked, instantly confused.

'We have found a body. Sadly, we believe that body to belong to your husband, Jake,' Asil said, gently. Nessa was speechless, and started to shake her head in disbelief. A small part of her wanted to burst out laughing. They were a pair of idiots, she thought. *Absolutely bloody useless.*

Jake was fine, Nessa thought to herself with satisfaction. Jake was coming home soon. They must have found someone else, some homeless guy probably, who had died months ago. This was undoubtedly a mix-up. Police did this sometimes, she considered; she'd read novels and watched films where they got this stuff wrong. It happened.

'Sorry, what?' Nessa asked, still disorientated by her tiredness. She ran a hand through her long, tangled hair and sat forwards on the edge of the chair, her feet tickling the carpet.

'Our officers attended the scene of a road traffic accident at approximately 1 a.m. this morning. A driver had got in touch with us, very shaken. She was an elderly woman, who said she had been travelling along a main road, not far from your home . . .'

'Right,' Nessa said, the word getting caught in her throat. Her secret gloating stopped. All the hairs on her arms and the back of her neck stood on end. The room started to spin.

'She struck a man who was walking along the road. He was wearing dark clothing and it was raining. This happened late last night . . . It is possible she may have aquaplaned a little, due to the rain; our forensics officers are looking into it,' Asil said, genuine sadness in his voice.

'Unfortunately, we believe this man, who died at the scene from a head injury, to be your husband, Mr Jacob Bruce,' he said, softly.

'I'm so sorry,' he said.

Nessa stared ahead. The female officer looked down towards her feet, as if she couldn't cope with it any more.

'Mrs Bruce?'

Tears started to fall from Nessa's eyes, slipping down her skin and running down her neck. She tilted her head back and felt the agony as it flowed from her, as if the blood in her veins was running from her, draining her of life, second by second.

Great rasping sobs heaved in her in-breaths; ghastly choking sounds emanated from her throat. It was the most pain she'd ever felt. All she could do was sit there as it ripped her apart, like an explosion. This was something bigger than her – a force of nature, tearing at every shred of her being – the hurricane within. She ran the tips of her fingers through her own tears as they slid down her skin. She let the feelings sweep over her. She let them carry her away.

Nessa felt as if she had floated up the stairs after the police had left. She crawled back into bed, feeling the warmth of her sister's body to one side of her.

'Nessa, Nessa, what's going on?' Kat asked, waking up properly now and sitting up in bed. She put a hand on Nessa's shoulder, rubbing her eyes with a free hand.

'Jake's died . . .' Nessa had said in a wobbling voice as she lay on her back and stared at the ceiling.

'I know,' Kat said, confusion in her voice as she lay down next to Nessa to be closer to her. 'It's hard to take in, even after all this time. I sometimes forget for a moment too and it hits you hard when you realise he has gone and isn't coming back.'

'No, I mean, only just now. He just died. Last night. I've been downstairs, talking to the police,' she whispered, turning on her side and closing her eyes, only to see a million images of him.

'What?'

Kat wrapped her arms around her sister, and stroked her hair as Nessa lay frozen in shock.

'Help me, Kat. Please, please help me,' Nessa sobbed, her body shaking so much it made the bed tremble.

It never stops being terrifying . . .

Forty

'Mum. Piss off, will you? You're staring!'

January 14th 2015 . . .

'Oh my god, I'm so, so nervous,' Kat said, standing opposite her sister in the frozen car park. Her scarf came unravelled from her coat and blew in a rippling curl, jostled by the freezing cold wind.

'Me too. Are we sure that this is the right thing to do?' Nessa had asked, looking back at her car. The air was so cold it was making her eyes water. Poppy sat in the back wrapped in a blanket, reading a book. She looked up and waved at her mother and aunt, smiling at them reassuringly.

Nessa walked back to the car and knocked on the window. The window rolled down.

'Are you sure you're going to be OK in there, honey? I bet there's probably a cafe nearby, where you can go and be warmer? It seems a little daft for you to be sitting in the car like that,' Nessa pleaded, looking at her 17-year-old daughter, who was growing more sophisticated and breathtakingly beautiful every single day. But, naturally, her 17-year-old daughter still wouldn't do what she was told . . . Some things would never change.

'No, Mum. I'm here to support you and Aunty Kat, OK? I'll be fine. You're leaving me with the keys anyway, so I can put the heating on. I've got my book and this blanket. So just go! Just do what you need to do . . .'

Nessa stared at her daughter, slightly speechless. Her rounded childish features had been replaced with a slender, angular face that seemed to hold more wisdom than Nessa felt she possessed even now. She still had her long, Rapunzel-like tumbling hair, but she'd had a sharp, straight fringe cut in, that made her look more grown-up. Somehow she was now a young woman. Somehow, they had got through it all. How had her tiny baby girl grown up to be such a beauty? How did she have such knowing in her eyes, that self-assuredness Nessa had never had herself . . .

'Mum. Piss off, will you? You're staring!' Poppy said, pushing a button and laughing to herself as the window rolled back up to the top, sealing her in the vehicle.

'Come on, Ness. She's fine. Let's go,' Kat pleaded, shuffling around on the spot in a desperate attempt to keep warm. She rubbed her gloved hands together and breathed onto them.

'OK, fine. Let's do this . . .' Nessa said, turning away and walking towards her sister.

'Good Lord, look at you girls,' the man said, starting to cry. He was old now, Nessa thought, her eyes flickering over the wrinkled folds of his skin and his short, grey hair, that had been shaved close to his head. His blue eyes were a watery grey now. The whites of his eyes were a soft shade of pink, the occasional thread-vein tracing a broken line. He still had the scar on his eyebrow that Nessa had completely forgotten about, a diagonal line that cut through the thick, wiry hairs of his brows.

She didn't know what to feel, looking at him. Here was the man who had killed her beloved foster mother, Sue. Had he not done it, Nessa was sure she'd still adore her foster mum now. They would have had a proper, normal, mother and daughter relationship that would have lasted until Sue turned old and grey and she had grandchildren who loved her. Then she would have been ready to leave this world as she slept, one quiet afternoon. That was how Nessa had wished it had gone. That's what Sue had deserved.

Kat didn't say anything. Nessa glanced at her sister and squeezed her hand to reassure her. She could tell how hard she was trying to process all this: she could tell from tiny things, like the movements of the muscles in her face and the way her eyes scanned the man before her. She was trying to work out if she recognised anything about him – perhaps his expressions, or the tone of his voice – but there was probably nothing.

'I can't believe you wanted to come and see me,' he said, gathering himself together and wiping his eyes with the palms of his hands. He pushed his nose against his fingers, his elbows resting on the table, and looked out of the window at the freezing grey day. After a moment or two, he gathered the courage to turn back to Nessa and Kat, guilt in his expression.

'Well, you know. I think we decided it would be the best thing for both of us. To try and move on from what happened, somehow,' Nessa said, taking a sip from her Styrofoam cup of coffee. It had cost 50 pence from the waiting room vending machine and tasted terrible.

Tom would have served his time by now, and would have been released. But it had turned out he had been involved in some fights in prison and his sentence had been lengthened. He clearly still couldn't control his anger.

'I'm sorry I took your mother away,' he said, collapsing into tears, his shoulders rising up and down as he wept. Looking at him now, he was a slip of the brute he had been. He'd always been a coward but he had been strong and now his muscles had wasted away, leaving him still tall and broad, but half the size he had once been to her. He was nothing.

'Can I ask you something?' Kat asked. Tom nodded to himself, trying to meet her eyes but clearly struggling to see through the blur of his grief.

'Why did you do those things to her? Why did you shout at her and hit her? Why did you bully her until she died?' she probed. And as she said each word, he flinched as if they were physically hurting him.

'I've thought about this, over and over again, and I've never worked it out. I seemed to just have all this anger, well to a degree I still do, and because she was the closest to me, I took it out on her. It became habit. I was stressed, under so much pressure. Your mother wanted you both so much, and I think I just couldn't cope with suddenly having two children and this family, that had never been there before . . . I wasn't getting all her attention, I guess. The truth is, for the first time she loved something more than she loved me,' he said.

Nessa didn't know what to say. Did this mean that she and Kat had caused her mother's death? That perhaps, if they hadn't come into their lives, if Sue and Tom hadn't fostered them, things would never have spiralled so far out of control; she would still be alive today?

'Did you resent having us around?' Kat asked, narrowing her eyes.

He took a deep breath and exhaled slowly, his wrinkled lips forming a small 'o' shape while he considered how to answer the question.

'I did . . . I'm sorry. We're all adults now, and I owe you the truth. I know this makes me a terrible person. I'll never forgive myself . . . If I had my time again, I would handle everything in a completely different way. I was a monster. I know where I'm headed,' he said, hanging his head and running the pads of his fingers over the shiny surface of the table.

'One thing you must know, though, girls. I'd never seen your mother happier than the day you came to our home. She adored you both, and she'll always be watching over you. It's amazing to look at you both now. She'd be so proud of you, just completely overwhelmed . . . Like I am,' he said, quietly.

Kat and Nessa glanced at each other. The hum of the room seemed to get louder for a moment. At the table next to theirs, a man hugged his wife as his daughter sat on his lap, giggling to herself and patting his rounded belly. Tom was watching them too, but he had to look away.

'What did you both do with your lives?' he asked, looking first at Kat, with her flame-red hair.

'Erm, not that you have any right to know, but I've just graduated from uni. I got a first. Not sure what's happening next, I'm trying to find a job in marine biology – just a starter lab position to get me going,' Kat said, reluctantly and awkwardly, struggling to hide her contempt for this strange man before her.

'That's incredible. Well done . . . How about you,

Nessa?' he had asked, clearly trying to ignore Kat's sharp comment.

'Oh you know. I have my own daughter now. Poppy, she's 14 and she keeps me busy. I work in a library, as a manager. Nothing too special,' she said, not keen to engage in too much conversation with this man. He wasn't her friend. He had no right to know anything about her life now.

'You wanted to be a midwife, didn't you, Nessa?' Tom asked, as if he was wracking his brain to remember correctly. 'Yes, that was it. What happened there?' he questioned.

'Do you know what, I don't know. Life just got crazy I guess . . . I got pregnant young, with Poppy. My husband, he died six months ago, sadly,' she said, her thoughts drifting to Jake and the park he loved, where his ashes had been scattered by Poppy. She thought about the crazy past few years she'd experienced, and about Will, her long lost friend; she wondered what he was doing that cold January afternoon.

'Well, Poppy sounds like a big girl now. What are you going to do with the rest of your life?' he asked, as cheerily as possible, breaking into a grin.

'I think we should go,' Nessa said, unable to take a moment more of this tense, awkward conversation. She couldn't bear to make niceties with this man. She stood up, her chair scraping loudly against the floor. Kat started to follow suit, gathering her bag and scarf from the floor, concerned for her sister. Tom looked upset. Nessa paused for a moment, staring at this man who she knew she'd never see again. She knew he could no longer have any control over her life either. They'd done the right thing today, but it was time to go.

'Nessa,' Tom called out after them, as they started to

walk away. Kat kept going and gestured towards Nessa that she would be waiting outside the door.

'What?' she said, turning around. As she leaned towards him, he clamped his hand down on hers, desperation in the grip of his fingers. That strength, it was still there. She remembered it now: the shouting, the screaming, the weeping. The sound of hitting.

'I'm so sorry Nessa. I'm so, so sorry for what I did. Do what Sue would have wanted . . . You go, live your life now, and live it for her. Don't wait for anything, or anyone, to follow your dreams. Do you understand me? Go out there and get what you want,' he said, letting go of her hand and sitting back in his chair, turning towards the window once again.

'Oh I will,' she said, before walking away from him for the very last time.

Forty-One

'What are you doing here?'

Later that day . . .

Nessa ran up to his huge front door, trying not to slip over on the frozen driveway, which snaked up to his grand, six-bedroom house. Her heart thumped in her chest. Frost glittered in the darkness, beneath the burnt orange light, bleeding from two nearby streetlamps. Her breath billowed out before her in the bitter air. Tiny clouds.

She placed her hand on the gold knocker, noticing how cold it was to the touch. His door had a sheet of stained glass, through which she could see the gentle glow of light in his hallway. She hit the door with the knocker twice and waited.

Nothing.

'Oh come on Will, please. It's bloody freezing out here,' she whispered to herself, shuffling from one foot to another, as the cold started to bite her skin beneath the layers of her coat. His car was in the driveway and she could smell food wafting from the letterbox. He was definitely in.

She waited for a few more seconds, before knocking again. Still nothing.

'For fuck's sake, Will!'

Nessa knocked again and, eventually, the door opened slowly.

There stood Will, in nothing but a pair of checked, flannel pyjama bottoms, his hair ruffled wildly around his head. He squinted and smiled. *He's gorgeous,* Nessa thought to herself, unable to hold back her grin.

'Nessa. Shit. What are you doing here?' he asked, shuffling awkwardly on his feet before beckoning her in. 'Sorry about the state of me. I er . . . I fell asleep on the sofa after dinner, I'm knackered. Worked like a dog. Something to do with hot air balloons, well worth the investment I think, but anyway come in then; don't just stand there in the cold.'

Nessa felt like her heart was in her mouth. She was so nervous . . . She stepped inside and took off her coat and they walked into the living room.

Will sunk into his sofa and Nessa followed suit. She didn't know how to sit comfortably. Where would she put her hands? Did she cross her legs? And if so, which way round was comfortable, because nothing felt comfortable right now. How should she say this? Will yawned, and grabbed a t-shirt from the floor, pulling it over his head, his hair ruffled and disturbed by the fabric. The large fire in his sitting room crackled gently. He was halfway through a giant glass of red wine.

'Want some wine?' he asked. Nessa shook her head quickly.

'OK . . . What's up?' he asked, one of his arms now slung around the back of the sofa.

'Will. Erm . . . I know I've not seen you for rather a long time,' she said, breaking into a nervous laugh.

'Tell me about it,' he said, smirking sweetly before running a hand down the back of his head.

'I . . . I miss you, Will. A lot.'

'Well I miss you too, hideously. I wrote a song – *a fucking song* – about you. Can you believe that?' he said, laughing to himself.

Nessa felt something snap in her stomach, like a little twig. A song about her, what she had always wanted . . .

'I love you, Will; I really do. I really, really love you,' Nessa said, blurting out the words, her eyes widening.

Will looked down at his thick carpet, a huge, lovely smile overwhelming him. He was absolutely, inexplicably, bloody gorgeous, Nessa thought to herself as she cocked her head to one side to study his face.

'Well, you know how to keep a man waiting don't you. . . .' he whispered.

'Can I hear the song?' Nessa said, breaking into laughter and wiping a tear from her cheek.

'No. Absolutely bloody not. It's terrible,' he said laughing, and pulling her into his arms.

Epilogue

'I understand, son, it's OK'

December 6th 2012

The wintry wind sprinted across the surface of the English Channel, as if carrying urgent messages from the emerald shores of Étretat to the kebab-littered streets of Brighton.

The collective roar of pebbles could be heard as they were jostled by waves. Tension. Water pulled back like bow and arrow, before surging forwards and crashing to the beach. Small frothy explosions of salty water burst into the air. The occasional seagull could be heard, shrieking as it swooped towards the watery chaos.

'Dad, are you sure you're warm enough?' Jake asked, looking at his father's profile. It had weathered slowly over the years and was now cliff-like, so strong and clear against the grey cloudy sky.

'Oh yes, son, quite sure. It's just nice to be outdoors and not stuck in that stuffy day centre anymore,' he had said, chuckling to himself.

'I've not seen you in a long time, son,' he said, looking towards Jake and smiling warmly. As he grinned his large teeth showed, covered in light brown stains from his years of drinking black coffee and smoking cigarettes. They were large and square, like the keys of a broken piano, with dark, gaping holes where a couple were missing.

But that face. The face of his father and the stories it held. *It is wonderful*, Jake thought, trying to photograph it in his mind so he would never forget a wrinkle.

'Yeah, well, you know how it is,' Jake said, looking down at the remnants of his chocolate ice cream, which seemed to be going on forever.

'I understand, son; it's OK. You young people are very busy these days and life's tough, not how it was when I was raising a family. They must be keeping you very busy at that bank, I'm sure. Long hours, is it?' Mick asked simply, staring out towards the ocean again. He took a great, deep breath inwards through his nostrils, which flared as he did so. There was a pink hue illuminating the skin of his wrinkled cheeks.

'Something like that,' Jake said, starting to eat the cone. Great cracking sounds emanated from the waffle at each tentative bite.

Brighton Pier twinkled in the near distance. The sound of hysterical clashing music could be heard, and thousands of little twinkling lights seemed to merge into one warm glow.

'Hey, before I forget, I brought something you might like,' Mick said suddenly, starting to search through the inside pockets of his coat beneath the layers of blanket that Jake had wrapped around his father.

'Oh, bloody hell. I hope I've not forgotten it,' he said, frustration starting to build in his voice. 'I've kept it in here the whole time, just in case I see you – because of course I can never remember what I've got on – and now you're here it's . . . Oh, good, here it is,' he said joyfully, pulling a delicate silver chain from a pocket near his chest.

'What's that?' Jake asked, leaning closer to the beautiful piece of jewellery that dangled from his father's wrinkled, stained fingers, the chain suspended between the nails of his thumb and forefinger.

At the bottom of the necklace was a tiny, silver heart.

'Now, I bought this a while ago and I wanted to give it to my Betsy, but the thing is, I thought you might like it son, to give to your lovely Shelley. It's real silver you know. Solid stuff,' Mick said proudly, thrusting the necklace towards Jake as it was thrown about by the wind.

'Nessa, Dad . . . Shelley was my first girlfriend from years ago, when I was a kid,' Jake said calmly, correcting him.

'Oh . . . OK. Well anyway, I thought, you know, it might be a nice gift for you to give her. I know you're hard-up son and these women they don't half need spoiling! So there you go; it's yours,' he said kindly.

'I can't take that Dad . . . It's too much,' Jake said.

'I won't accept a "no", boy,' Mick said sternly, putting the necklace into Jake's open hand and shutting his fingers over it.

'God . . . thanks Dad. That's so kind of you. She'll love it. I know she will,' Jake said, slipping the necklace carefully into his pocket as his father stiffly patted him on the knee.

'I love you, Dad,' Jake said, quietly, but his father was muttering to himself, lost in his own thoughts again.

Acknowledgements

There are so many people to whom I will be forever thankful for their part in making this book happen.

First, I want to thank my agent Sheila Crowley at Curtis Brown. I admire your positivity and energy so much; and only hope that one day I can achieve a mere smidgen of your grace and exuberance! Thank you also to the lovely Rebecca Ritchie, Sophie Harris, Katie McGowan and all at the agency for everything. It really is a privilege and a blessing to have your support.

Charlotte Hardman, Fiona Rose, Mark Booth and the team at Hodder – thanks for all your hard work and encouragement! I'm so grateful and will never stop wondering if any of this has actually happened to me or if I've been stuck in a daydream for the past few years! *Thank you*.

Incredible kindness was shown by some people whose lives have been affected by dementia. They helped me with some sensitive and challenging subject matter. Without them, I wouldn't have been able to develop Mick's character in the way I would have wanted to. Your stories were moving, heartbreaking and beautiful too. I will never forget them, or you. Thank you for sharing them with me.

Bon. Many thanks for taking the time to advise me on the details I needed to help tie things together. I'm not sure what I would have done without your know-how!

Crouch, Danielle, Jen, Louise, and Jess . . . as always, your support means more than I can say. You're so busy, and yet you always make time for me and my writing. I adore you guys. You are unicorns.

I dedicated this book to my family, including of course my amazing mum and dad – Graham and Bea – who never cease to make me smile with their unique blend of quirky. Also, of course, my brothers and sisters, Angie, Greg, Helen and Richard; my ADORABLE nieces and nephews, Hugo, Carla, Con, Charlie, Ava, Amelia, Sid and 'we need more ice' Annie; Uncle Adrian, Aunt Hilary and Cousin Nick. And not forgetting, of course, Fudge the dog. I love you all so much. *Thank you for your understanding, and your patience.*

Brenda, how lucky I am to know you! Thank you for your help, your eagle eye for errors, your love of 1,000 piece puzzles and reality TV (thanks for recording The Face). You're simply wonderful.

Panda. Thank you for everything you are, and all you do to support me, day in day out. I love you. You're the best.

Thanks to all mentioned above, and everyone else involved who is not named individually here . . . I hope you know how much your support means to me.

And finally, thanks to the amazing readers who take the time to send me emails, Tweets and Facebook posts with feedback on my books. You are the reason why. You make it all worth it. Keep reading, always, and *thank you* . . .